SINCE I FELL

FOR YOU

~ The New York Sullivans ~

Suzanne Sullivan & Roman Huson

Bella Andre

SINCE I FELL FOR YOU

~ The New York Sullivans ~

Suzanne Sullivan & Roman Huson

© 2016 Bella Andre

Sign up for Bella's New Release Newsletter

http://eepurl.com/eXj22

bella@bellaandre.com

www.BellaAndre.com

Bella on Twitter: @bellaandre

Bella on Facebook: facebook.com/bellaandrefans

Suzanne Sullivan doesn't need a bodyguard. After all, she's one of the most successful digital security specialists in the world—so she can most certainly take care of herself, despite the problems she's been running into lately. Unfortunately, her three brothers don't agree. So when Mr. Way-Too-Handsome shows up bound and determined to protect her whether she wants him there or not, sparks definitely start to fly. Because she has absolutely no intention of falling for the bodyguard she never wanted in the first place...

Roman Huson has vowed to do whatever it takes to protect Suzanne Sullivan from harm. And her brothers would kill him for so much as looking at her the wrong way. The only problem is that he's never been hired to work for anyone so beautiful, or brilliant, before. Between trying to keep up with her—and working like hell to keep from kissing her breathless—he's up against the most difficult challenge of his life. Especially when it turns out that the passion and connection between them is hotter than anything he's ever known...

A note from Bella

Since I Fell For You is my fiftieth book (50!), and I was just as excited to write Suzanne and Roman's love story as I was my very first book. Even *more* excited, actually, because I simply cannot get enough of the Sullivan family! I want to say a big, huge THANK YOU to the millions of readers from around the world who have written me such lovely emails and sent me messages via social media to let me know that you, too, can't get enough of the Sullivans. I plan to keep telling their love stories forever!

If this is your first time reading about the Sullivans, you can easily read each book as a stand-alone—and there is a Sullivan family tree available on my website (BellaAndre.com/sullivan-family-tree) so you can see how the books connect together!

For years, I've wanted to write about a bodyguard, but it wasn't until Suzanne Sullivan came along that I knew I had the perfect heroine to match up with a super-sexy, super-protective alpha hero. I had the best time watching the sparks fly between Suzanne and Roman from the first moment they set eyes on each other.

I hope you love watching them fall in love as much as I have.

Happy reading,
Bella Andre

P.S. I can't wait for you to read Alec and Harry's upcoming stories, the third and fourth New York Sullivan books. Please be sure to sign up for my newsletter (BellaAndre.com/Newsletter) so that I can let you know as soon as I have the release dates and titles for their books—and so that I can contact you as soon as the newest Sullivan book comes out.

I also wanted to let you know that two New York Sullivan spin-off books will be released soon! If you have read *Now That I've Found You (New York Sullivans #1)*, you have met Calvin, the Mayor of Summer Lake, and Christie, who runs the Inn at Summer Lake—and you are about to see much more of them in *Since I Fell For You (New York Sullivans #2)*.

Calvin's story will be released in Spring 2017, as he reconnects with a lost love in *The Best Is Yet To Come*. Christie's story will come next in Summer 2017, when she falls in love with the last man she ever thought possible in *Can't Take My Eyes Off Of You*.

ARE YOU READY TO FIND OUT THE SECRET BEHIND...

The Sullivans

WWW.BELLAANDRE.COM/SECRET

CHAPTER ONE

Suzanne Sullivan didn't need a bodyguard.

No one was jumping out at her from dark corners as she headed down West 22nd Street toward D'Oro, the New York City gallery hosting a show tonight for her brother Drake. She hadn't been hit with any calls from untraceable numbers or had her computer servers taken down during the past week either.

Tonight, the air was crisp, the stars were shining brightly in the sky, and she felt *great*. As though anything was possible—and nothing could possibly go wrong. Especially not all the horrible things her brothers were worried about.

Okay, so during the past several months she'd been bombarded with thousands of calls from untraceable numbers, and several attacks had been made on her personal and corporate computer servers. But she wasn't a top digital security software specialist for nothing. She could take care of herself and her business—no matter what her brothers seemed to think.

The fact was that when you were competing in an

industry worth billions of dollars, not every competitor was totally aboveboard. Though she didn't roll that way, she understood better than nearly anyone how to defend herself from cyberattacks. When pressed by her brothers for more information a few weeks ago, she had told them the calls were likely coming from one of her many competitors. Unfortunately, since she'd been too busy working on her new software release to actually pin anything on anyone yet, her brothers now seemed convinced that she was dealing with more than just corporate high jinks.

They worried that someone was after *her*.

Then again, they worried every time she went out on a date too. Which was why she'd stopped telling them about her dates a long time ago.

She didn't blame them for being overprotective, not when the four of them had been looking out for one another since they were little kids. A mother who had taken her own life and a father who had subsequently checked out emotionally for the next twenty-five years had made the Sullivan siblings a unit as tight as they came. But she did wish her brothers would stop pestering her about hiring a bodyguard.

In any case, she was still on a total high from the fabulous Monday she'd had at the office. After six months of sweating over the design of her new digital security software—one so cutting-edge, yet so affordable that technology insiders around the world had said it could never be done—the new code had finally fallen into place. Tomorrow morning she would be giving her investors the good news that Sullivan Security was ready to move into its first round of beta testing for the product she had named MavG1. The five billionaires who made up the Maverick Group might be family friends, but they still demanded the best from the companies they invested in. And she wouldn't dream of giving them anything but the best.

Though she still had half a block to go, Suzanne could see throngs of people out on the sidewalk hoping to get inside the gallery. And no wonder, considering her brother Drake had created a dozen of the most stunning pieces of art Suzanne had ever seen.

He was considered one of the best painters of his generation, and his shows were always very well attended. Tonight, however, it wasn't just the quality of his paintings that had people going crazy for his work, it was also his subject. Rosalind Bouchard was not only an internationally famous reality TV star—make that *ex* reality TV star, now that she'd quit the show. She was also Drake's new girlfriend.

After spending time with Rosa during these past weeks, Suzanne understood precisely why her brother had fallen so hard for her, pretty much at first sight. Rosa was smart, funny, and incredibly brave. Rosa's bright light shone forth from every brushstroke on Drake's canvases. If only Suzanne could find a guy as intelligent, as loyal, and as handsome as Rosa was pretty...

Alas, the only part of Suzanne's life that wasn't coming up roses right now was her dating life. More than once she'd wished that she could tweak the guys she dated the same way she could rewrite lines of code—until all the bugs were gone. But by thirty-one, she knew better: You couldn't change people.

And you definitely couldn't make them love you unless they wanted to.

That was why her brothers were so important to her. They might think they knew how to run her life better than she did sometimes, but she never doubted for one second that Alec, Harry, and Drake loved her for who she was—a brainiac geek who got a rush from staying up all night writing computer code the way other women got a rush from buying shoes.

In any case, the endless hours she'd been spending at her computer working on the new code meant that she hadn't been out for a night on the town in a really long time. She was ready to have some fun tonight. And who knew? Maybe she'd check the final box on her perfect-day checklist by meeting Mr. Right and getting him past her brothers before they sent him running.

"Suz, you're here!" Rosa threw her arms around Suzanne mere seconds after she'd stepped inside the gallery.

Drake was right there beside her, and it wasn't until he let Suzanne out of his own hug that she was able to ask, "How's tonight going so far? Are you both doing okay?"

Suzanne knew how nervous Rosa had been about letting anyone know that Drake was painting her. Rosa had been convinced that she would taint him with the stain not only of her bad-girl reputation from the show, but also from the pictures that had been taken of her naked without her permission and leaked to the press earlier that year.

Drake pulled Rosa against him at the same moment that she tucked herself under his arm. Yet again, it struck Suzanne what a great fit they were. Having to deal with the nude-photo scandal had made Rosa draw deeply from an inner well of strength she hadn't realized had been there all along. But Drake had immediately seen how amazing she was, and he'd been steadfast in his support.

"People can't get enough of Drake and his paintings," Rosa said with pride.

Suzanne knew the last thing in the world her brother cared about was impressing a bunch of art snobs. Love was all that mattered to him now, and seeing him so happy filled her heart with joy.

"Everyone is on their best behavior," he told Suz. His expression was fiercely protective as he drew Rosa even closer. "They'd better be."

Suzanne agreed. No one had better dare say a bad word about Rosa. All of the Sullivans had her back. Especially Suzanne, who was working on software for Rosa's anti-cyberstalking foundation whenever she could find a spare moment.

Candace, Drake's sharklike agent, materialized with air kisses. "Suzanne, you're looking as gorgeous as ever. I'm sure you don't mind if I steal Drake and his muse away to meet with an investor who is considering an *enormous* bid on all twelve paintings."

Drake sent her a silent *sorry* over his shoulder as his agent steered them away. Grabbing a glass of champagne from a passing waiter, Suzanne enjoyed the sweet bubbles dancing on her tongue as she let herself relax for the first time in what felt like forever. She had only just begun to look around the room to see if she knew anyone else when her attention was grabbed by a man walking through the door.

Wow.

Now *that* was a man. Dark hair and eyes. Square jaw. Tanned skin. As a relatively tall woman, she was able to gauge a man's height pretty accurately. Six foot four sounded right, and when you added in his broad shoulders in his dark, impeccably tailored suit, the whole package was seriously yummy.

Her mouth started to water as she watched him move through the crowd with the feral grace of a well-muscled lion. She ran the pad of her thumb over her lower lip to make sure she wasn't actually drooling.

"Roman, over here."

She recognized her older brother Alec's voice. He was standing with her other brother, Harrison. They knew him?

Roman. Even his name was yummy.

As the three men did a half handshake, half hug, she was tempted to dash over to introduce herself. But past experience told her it would be better to gauge the situation first from a slight distance so that she could try to figure out Roman's relationship to her brothers.

She'd never heard about him before, which to her way of thinking was a serious oversight on their part. Then again, her brothers had always been weird about her dating their friends. And by *weird* she meant that they'd forbidden their friends to so much as look at her as an available female from the time she'd started high school.

Unfortunately, nothing had changed in the past fifteen years. Alec, Harry, and Drake were more adamant than ever that no one was good enough for her, especially not the guys they hung with. For the most part, she couldn't argue. Not when Alec had a reputation as one of the biggest bad boys in the city—so if he called someone else a *player*, it meant the guy was pretty darned awful.

Suzanne wasn't at all averse to pleasure. But at thirty-one, she wasn't particularly interested in one-night stands anymore either. She wanted what Drake and Rosa had found—a love that was deep, true, and strong.

Despite Roman's good looks and the confident way he held himself, he didn't strike Suzanne as a player. He seemed too watchful, too alert to everyone and everything around him, to be a guy out on the prowl.

She knew that feeling, having spent a great deal of her life on the outside of the crowd, watching. Kindergarten had been the first time she'd realized she wasn't like the other girls. She'd been more interested in building and creating things than giggling on the playground or playing dress-up with dolls. Her outsider status had only intensified as she'd grown older. Where dreaming of boys had consumed the other girls, she'd fallen head over heels for electronics and coding. Her best friends had been the other kids in the computer club, and her first kiss had been with a fellow geek when she was a sophomore in high school—more of an experiment on both their parts than actual romantic interest. During college, she'd finally learned how to pretend to be "normal" with some major coaching from her female cousins, but it was always a huge relief to head back to her computers. She wasn't a virgin by any means, but she'd never had a serious relationship either. She supposed the phrase *married to her job* wasn't too far off the mark.

Just then, Roman's eyes met hers...and every thought in her usually jam-packed brain dropped away. As lucidity slowly came back, she realized she'd never seen eyes so intense.

The best kind of intense, she thought as attraction continued to spark, even from across the room. He was looking a little too long, and a little too hard, but it wasn't disconcerting.

It was *hot*.

Hotter than anything she'd felt in a very long time.

Suzanne had never learned how to play coy. So she didn't even bother to keep the smile from her lips. It wasn't a come-hither smile. She hadn't ever really learned how to flirt either, regardless of how hard her cousins Mia and Lori had tried to show her the ropes. But instead of smiling back, Roman's gaze grew even more intense. Even more heated.

Suddenly, she wished she'd had time to change out of the black jeans, T-shirt, and boots that were her standard workday clothes. Especially given that all the other women in the gallery were wearing bright dresses with short hems that sparkled and shone.

As she instinctively took a couple of steps forward, she realized he was moving toward her too. Everyone else in the crowded room fell away, until it was only the two of them. And then, there he was, so close that all she had to do was reach out.

She could touch him if she dared.

"Suz."

Alec's voice jolted her. She hadn't realized that her brothers had crossed the room with Roman, hadn't been aware of anything but him.

"We want you to meet our friend Roman. Roman, this is our sister, Suzanne."

"Hello, Suzanne."

God. His voice was as sexy as the rest of him. Especially when he rumbled her name in that deep tone. She wasn't the most visual person in the world, unless she was reviewing lines of code. But she couldn't stop the images that started dancing through her mind, visions of his mouth and hands on her bare skin, and hers all over his…

She swallowed hard at the vivid mental pictures. It didn't matter that she was in her thirties. Her brothers would lock her up in a tower and throw away the key if they knew what she was thinking right now.

Still not sure she had herself—or, more specifically, her hormones—totally under control, she paused for a moment to pull herself together. When her pulse had lowered to a slow gallop, she put out her hand. "It's nice to meet you."

Roman gripped her hand for only a handful of seconds. But his electric touch on top of his sexy voice and intense gaze was more sensuality than she was prepared to withstand. Especially with her brothers watching her every move.

"How do you know each other?" Her voice sounded chirpy. Too high-pitched. Fortunately, neither Alec nor Harry seemed to notice.

"Roman has done some work for me," Alec said.

"He's not bad at jousting either," Harry put in. It was nearly the highest praise her brother could give someone, given that he was a world-renowned expert on medieval history, with a museum-worthy collection of armor.

At long last, here was a guy her brothers obviously approved of. Could they have brought him over to her tonight in the hopes that she and Roman would have a connection?

"I am friends with your brothers," Roman said, his deep voice resonating through every cell of her body. "But that isn't why I'm here tonight."

She nearly swooned. The computer geek who had never even come close to falling into a man's arms was right on the verge of toppling straight toward his big, broad chest. And maybe, if her brothers were finally ready to see her happy with a great guy they were friends with, it would be okay if she did.

"Why are you here, then?" she asked, barely able to keep the breathlessness from her voice.

His dark eyes held hers. "I'm your new body-guard."

CHAPTER TWO

"My new bodyguard?" Suzanne gaped at Roman. "That's impossible."

He wasn't surprised by her reaction. Her wide eyes and shocked gasp made perfect sense given that her brothers had hired him to protect her without informing her of their decision...until now.

The only thing Roman was surprised by tonight was *his* reaction to *her*.

The second he'd walked into the gallery, he'd noticed her. Not just because she was a stunningly beautiful woman whom any man would take a second hungry look at in the black jeans and T-shirt that clung to her curves in the sexiest way possible. But simply because every cell in his body had gone on alert just from being in the same room with her.

Careful not to give his reaction away, he hadn't let himself stare. His clients had often commented that he must have eyes on all sides of his head, because he never missed a thing. Nights like this, he was especially glad for that skill. It meant he could watch her without anyone knowing it.

Her brothers had told him that Suzanne was a brilliant software developer who was running into trouble lately and was too trusting for her own good. The research he'd done online had filled in the blanks on just how successful she was. But it was what everyone had left out that knocked Roman sideways.

He'd been with plenty of attractive women, enough that he should have been able to keep himself together tonight. Only, he couldn't remember the last time a woman had seemed so sweet *and* so sensual at the same time.

Not to mention as far off-limits as any woman had ever been.

First off, she was his new client, and the boundaries between bodyguard and client were sacrosanct. Second—and equally important—her brothers would kill him for so much as looking at her wrong. And he couldn't blame them.

The last thing he would want was for a little sister, if he'd had one, to end up with a guy like him.

Throughout the handful of minutes that he'd been talking with Alec and Harry in the gallery, Roman had been silently reminding himself that he was a consummate professional who was trained to shut off his emotions and do his job. Especially when it came to women. He'd never been the slightest bit tempted by one of his female clients, even the ones who had paraded naked in front of him to try to get him to bend his solid-steel rule about maintaining a professional relationship.

By the time he finally let himself look directly at Suzanne, he'd been certain his steel mask was back in place. But then she'd smiled...

One bright, beautiful smile was all it took for the bottom to drop out of his ironclad control.

Taking this job is a bad idea.

The thought had hit him hard, right in the solar plexus. Hard enough that he'd considered bowing out of the job. Unfortunately, that was right when Harry had said, "Suzanne's safety means everything to us. We can't thank you enough for doing this."

He couldn't let his friends down just because he was awed by her beauty. And he didn't like the idea of letting her down either. Not when, from everything he'd learned so far, she needed his services more than she wanted to admit.

Right now, however, she was clearly pissed beyond measure. Steam was all but coming out of her ears as she glared at him. Wanting to head a public family argument off at the pass, he suggested, "Why don't the four of us go somewhere more private to discuss this?"

She all but snarled, "No." And then she shut him down completely by turning to her brothers. "What the hell are you two thinking? Did you really think you could just up and hire a bodyguard for me and that I'd say, *Okay, whatever you think is best, big brothers?*"

Roman was impressed by the way she went toe to toe with her brothers. She was no shrinking violet, that was for sure. Still, that didn't mean that she wasn't in need of protection. Even the strongest people needed backup sometimes.

Neither Alec nor Harry looked the least bit surprised by her response. And it didn't look like they were going to back down any time soon either, as Alec said, "We know what's been happening with the countless calls and the attacks on your servers. Who knows when it will escalate to an attack on you? You've got to be smart about this, Suz."

"*Smart?*" If Roman thought she'd been furious before, he hadn't seen the half of it. "You think I'm not being *smart?*" It was as though Alec had just thrown down the ultimate gauntlet. She poked a finger of each hand into both brothers' chests. "You're the ones who are missing brain cells if you think I can't take care of myself."

After having worked with Alec's company a dozen times on security detail for the rich and famous people who rented Alec's private planes, Roman knew his friend could be a hothead. Despite that, Alec was the first billionaire with whom Roman had ever been friends. He was cocky, but he wasn't an ass. In fact, he was surprisingly normal, for all his money and family connections with movie stars and pro athletes.

Roman had grown up hanging with the lowest guys on the totem pole. Now, though he'd carved out a lucrative career working for the highest ones, he'd always be a fighter kid from the Bronx. At events like this, he often had to stop himself from tugging at a tie that felt like it was on too tight.

"Suz," Harry said, looking a little guilty, "we didn't do this to upset you."

Roman had first met Harry at one of Alec's parties a couple of years ago and knew he tended to be more measured in his approach to life than Alec. That didn't mean he was a wimp, though. On the contrary, Harry had skills he'd learned from his hands-on study of medieval combat that put regular fighters to shame.

"We know you can take care of yourself," Harry continued, "but wouldn't it make you feel better to know there was someone looking out for you while you get to the bottom of whoever has been harassing you and why?"

"I already feel great about things, thank you very much. And we all know that you haven't hired him"— she hooked an irritated thumb in Roman's direction— "to make *me* feel better. You hired him to make *yourselves* feel better. I've told you a million times that

I'm handling things. I don't need you making decisions about my life. And I definitely don't need a body-guard!"

She spun on her boot heel and headed for the door. Alec and Harry started to follow her, but Roman stopped them. "I'll take care of things from here."

Harry still looked conflicted about the way they'd handled it, but if anything, Alec looked more con-vinced than ever that his sister needed a bodyguard. "We know you will."

Suzanne was fast, but Roman had professional practice at chasing people down. By the time he got outside, she was burning up the sidewalk, so angry that strangers were having to jump out of her way so that they didn't get mowed down. People made bad decisions when they were angry, something Roman knew all too well. Somehow, he needed to make her see that having him around wouldn't be a bad thing.

He had nearly caught up when she stopped on a dime and spun around so quickly that Roman found himself nose to nose with her.

"Stop following me!" Her eyes were spitting fire. "Weren't you listening? I don't need you to watch over m—"

The taxi came out of nowhere, speeding around the corner so fast that the driver momentarily lost control, aiming straight for them on the sidewalk.

Roman pulled Suzanne into his arms and threw her as far off the sidewalk as he possibly could before leaping in the same direction and covering her body with his so that they were pressed tightly to the brick wall.

The driver finally hit the brakes when the vehicle was a hairsbreadth from Roman's left heel.

As close to Suzanne as he could be outside of a bedroom, Roman could feel her heart pounding as fast as his. Her chest was heaving, but she wasn't crying the way anyone else would have been.

"Thank God."

He couldn't hear her words clearly at first. Couldn't possibly process them with blood rushing like class-five whitewater in his ears. But when he heard the taxi shift into reverse and pull away from them, he realized that the danger had passed.

Which meant he needed to let her go.

He'd protected his clients with his body dozens of times. But he'd never been so reluctant to move away from one of them. Never felt a desperate need to run his hands over every inch of their bodies, head to toe, to make sure they were truly all right.

"Suzanne." He finally drew back enough so that he could look down at her face. "Are you okay?"

"I am." She swallowed hard as she blinked up at him with eyes so clear and pretty that they would have stolen his breath away if he'd had any left after the near accident. "Because of you."

How, he wondered, was she managing to smell like a spring morning in the middle of a dirty Manhattan sidewalk? And why the hell was he letting himself even notice something like that about one of his clients? A completely reluctant client, no less.

Roman never liked taking on jobs this way. It was always better to be hired directly by the client rather than by a third party. But at the same time, he understood her brothers' concerns. Keeping Suzanne safe was the most important thing—even if it meant a little extra work persuading her to see things clearly.

He wasn't at all glad that the taxi had almost taken them out on the sidewalk. There might be a silver lining, however, if she was now convinced that he could keep her out of harm's way, regardless of what kind of harm it might be.

He was just taking a step back when she put her hand on his arm. "What about you? Are you okay?" When she licked her lips, he couldn't look away from her glistening mouth. "The taxi came so close. I was sure that you would be—"

"I'm good." The two words came out more gruffly than he intended as he made himself put a good couple of feet between them. It would be a fine line with Suzanne—to stay close enough to protect her no matter what happened, while never getting close enough to lose control. "So now you see why having me around is a good thing."

Just moments after they'd nearly been crushed by a taxi, the last thing he expected her to do was to snort. "Thank you for saving my life. I totally owe you for that. But it was just a freak accident. No matter what you or my brothers think, I still don't need a bodyguard." She pushed away from the brick wall. "Good night, Roman."

Though her brothers hadn't prepared him for her stunning beauty, they had prepared him for her stubborn streak. And from his research, he understood that trait had undoubtedly helped her build a technology company that was growing at a rapid pace.

"My night's not over yet," he informed her. "I'm going to have to walk home with you."

She didn't so much as break stride. "Free country. If you want to walk on the same sidewalk in the same direction, be my guest."

He never got personal with clients, and always made sure to keep his emotions out of it, but he could barely stifle a grin. Her brothers had told him she was feisty—but they'd left out just how likable she was. Problem was, he didn't think she was going to be much happier with any of them when she found out where he was now living. Knowing he needed to break that news to her took away his almost-smile in a flash.

Deciding that blunt was his best option, he said, "I'll be staying in the apartment next to yours while I'm working with you."

Again, she stopped dead on the sidewalk. For a few long seconds, she didn't say anything, just stared at him as if he'd grown three heads and each of them was speaking a different language.

"I'm going to kill my brothers." Each word was precise. And icy cold. When she turned around, he knew she must be planning to head back to the gallery to hunt them down.

"Suzanne," he said as he moved to block her path, "I understand you don't want me around. But your brothers didn't hire me to hurt you. Hurting you is the very last thing they want. I've protected a lot of family members over the years, but I can see that they care about you more than most people are ever cared about their whole lives." He ran a hand through his hair. "I worked for Ford Vincent for a while during one of his concert tours, and he said the same thing—Sullivans stick together and have each other's backs, no matter what." He hoped some of what he was saying was making a difference. "Alec, Harry, and Drake just want to make sure they've got your back."

"Damn you." Her words were softly spoken, but passionate nonetheless. "How did you know exactly what to say?"

Because I know you.

The crazy thought came at him from out of the blue. They'd only just met tonight, so it didn't make any sense. Barely bridled attraction was obviously twisting things up inside his usually perfectly rational mind.

Working to shove *crazy* completely away, instead of answering her question, he said, "My job is to make sure nothing happens to you. But it's a hell of a lot harder to keep you safe if you're fighting me at every turn."

"That's too bad, because I'm not going to stop fighting," she told him. "You might have taken round one by saying exactly the right thing at exactly the right time, but I guarantee the next round is going to me."

With that, she took off at a brisk pace in the direction of her apartment. Knowing it would be wiser not to poke at her any more tonight by trying to walk beside her, he stayed a step behind. Close enough that he could smell her fresh scent wafting back to him—and had to work really hard not to stare at the curves outlined in her black jeans.

When they got to her building and he headed into the elevator with her, she muttered, "Note to self: Never live in a building owned by family. Especially when they don't seem to know the meaning of the words *privacy* or *autonomous*."

The second the elevator opened again, she shot toward her front door, clearly intending to dash inside and lock him out.

"Suzanne." She wasn't going to like this, but it still had to be done. "I need to do a quick search of your apartment to make sure there are no threats inside."

He didn't need to see her face to know how furious he'd just made her. Her body language alone said it.

"Fine." She punched in her code on the electronic lock and all but kicked open the door.

His search was as quick as he could make it. Unfortunately, he couldn't help but notice Suzanne's mark on everything in her apartment, from the stack of computers and tablets on the coffee table, to the bright quilts and blankets that he guessed had been made for her by relatives, to the huge wall of family photos in the hallway to her bedroom.

Sweet Lord, if that wasn't the most difficult room of all to walk into. Knowing that she'd soon be taking her clothes off and getting into her be—

Damn it. He couldn't let his brain go there.

She was standing in the middle of her entryway looking irritated when he finished his search. "Everything's clear."

"Of course it is." She opened the door for him. "Good night."

Again, he couldn't help but admire her fiery personality. "Good night, Suzanne. I'll be waiting outside in the morning."

She didn't reply, simply shot fire at him from her eyes, then slammed the door shut in his face.

Roman wouldn't be surprised if her cousin Ian, the billionaire Seattle businessman who owned the building, got some heat from Suzanne tonight for renting Roman the apartment next door. But for all her grumbling, he knew she had to appreciate her family. He sure as hell would have if he'd grown up with anyone watching out for him the way they were watching out for her.

He wouldn't let Alec, Harry, or Drake down.

Roman had begun by making sure Suzanne got home safely. He'd continue by keeping his mind out of the gutter...and his hands off her.

No matter what.

CHAPTER THREE

Suzanne was good at ignoring distractions.

Scratch that. She was a *master* at it. Complete and utter focus was what made her so good at coding. She never let her plans be swayed. If she wanted the new software that she was creating to work, she made it happen, no matter how many hours she needed to put in at her computer.

But her big goal for today didn't have anything to do with code. Instead, she was aiming to get rid of her bodyguard as quickly as possible. Not only because the entire idea of having a bodyguard was ridiculous—but also because it was going to be damned hard to concentrate on everything she needed to get done with Roman standing guard over her, looking way too tall, dark, and handsome for her peace of mind.

She'd been up late the previous night thinking through her best plan of attack. Working to convince her brothers that they were being ridiculous was obviously a dead end. And Roman had already proved that he was tough and smart enough to deal with her anger and frustration, so there was no point in wasting her time and energy storming around like a brat.

So, what was the one thing that would guarantee Roman's resignation?

She'd nearly paced a hole in her living room rug trying to figure out the answer. And also to burn off her irritation at having been attracted to him. Every time she thought about her drooly reaction when he'd first walked into the gallery, she grew more angry at herself.

Around two in the morning, she'd fallen into a fitful sleep, only to dream of him the second she let her brain go. Her dreams had revolved around hot, sweaty, impressively acrobatic sex, and she'd awakened with a jolt to her six a.m. alarm, even more irritated than she'd been the night before.

Of all the guys to feel a spark with—of all the guys to have sexy dreams about—how could she have picked *him*?

She was stepping into the shower when the solution to her problem hit her like a lightning bolt, the way so many answers did when warm water was spraying over her. Given that Roman seemed close to her brothers, he had to know they would kill him for trying anything with her. So while she might not be able to scare her bodyguard away with reason or anger, she suddenly realized she had one great big thing in her corner.

Sex.

Suzanne knew she wasn't the most normal woman in the world, given that her workaholic tendencies meant she didn't have much time for dating. But that didn't mean she couldn't recognize attraction when it flared in a man's eyes. Last night at the gallery, she was positive she hadn't been the only one feeling sparks. Roman had too.

Not once in her life had she used her feminine wiles to get something. Her brain had always been her best tool. But drastic times called for drastic measures. As drastic as making the bodyguard she'd never wanted in the first place so uncomfortable with the sexual pull between them that he'd have no choice but to quit.

Once Roman was gone, she had no concerns whatsoever about being able to make any replacement bodyguards her brothers sent in run with their tails between their legs within hours of meeting her. Very few people could have pulled off what Roman had last night, when he'd got to her with his speech about how her brothers cared so much about her.

Feeling much better now that she had a workable game plan, Suzanne stepped out of the shower, wrapped a towel around herself, and opened her closet. She wasn't particularly into clothes, but when her cousins Lori and Mia came to visit from San Francisco and Seattle, they always dragged her away from the office and into the city's best boutiques. It wasn't enough for her to keep them company while they shopped, however. They also insisted that she try on and buy the expensive dresses and heels they hand-picked for her. Early on, she'd learned that it was easier to humor them than to bother insisting she didn't need the new clothes. Despite the fact that her standard work outfit consisted of dark jeans and T-shirts, because of her cousins, she had a lot of really nice outfits when she needed them. And the truth was that the pretty dresses and shoes that they'd browbeaten her into purchasing had come in handy many times during the past five years at all the family weddings and baby showers.

But she wasn't looking for pretty today. She was aiming for straight-up sexy. Borderline inappropriate would be even better.

She knew exactly which outfit would fit the bill.

Still, she found herself hesitating as she reached for the formfitting, light purple dress that Lori had insisted she buy even though Suzanne knew she'd never wear it outside of the boutique's dressing room. Though she shouldn't feel guilty about thwarting her brothers' annoying sister-sitting plans, a part of her did anyway. Roman had been right when he'd said they only wanted the best for her, even if their way of showing it was sorely misguided.

Suzanne forced herself to shake off the guilt. This was her life and she'd live it exactly the way she wanted to. Especially since she knew how poorly her brothers would take it if she ever tried to do something like this to one of them. They'd brush off her concern the way they would a fly buzzing through the air. *Men.*

Sliding the dress off its hanger, she braced herself to be brave enough to slip it on, along with the nude heels Mia had insisted she buy with it. Turning to the full-length mirror, Suzanne nearly gasped aloud.

She'd forgotten that the silk was so fine it clung to her curves like plastic wrap. On top of that, it was short enough that she'd have to be careful not to flash everyone her underwear when she sat down. Suzanne didn't deliberately try to hide her figure, but she rarely put it on display like this. Simply taking the elevator from her apartment or walking down the sidewalk was going to feel strange.

But hopefully, if she played her fake-seduction cards right, Roman would break before she did. Especially given that walking for any prolonged amount of time in these heels was going to hobble her.

Carefully, she made her way over to the drawer in which she kept her rarely used makeup and hair dryer. Though she usually tied her hair back into a ponytail and couldn't be bothered with blush or mascara, she never went into a plan half-cocked. Either she did this right, or she didn't do it at all.

By the time she was done blow-drying and making herself up, she barely recognized herself. When she walked into the Sullivan Security headquarters in an hour, her employees were going to take one look at her and wonder if she had a screw loose.

But it would all be worth it if she achieved her goal of getting Roman so hot and bothered that he freaked out about betraying his friendship with her brothers— and left her the hell alone.

Strangely, by the time she'd finished eating breakfast and transferred her laptop from her faded computer bag into a sleek leather bag that had been a gift from one of her cousins in Maine, she was almost looking forward to coming face-to-face with Roman again.

Would he be a worthy opponent? Or would he crumble at the first sign of trouble?

Instinct told her to lay odds on *worthy*.

★ ★ ★

One silent curse after another streamed through Roman's brain as Suzanne walked out of her apartment and he breathed in her delicious scent.

Damn it. He needed to stop noticing how good she smelled. And he sure as hell needed to stop being bowled over by her beauty.

She'd been a stunner last night in black jeans and boots, and he'd done enough security in the tech world to guess that she must have come straight to the gallery from her office. But maybe he'd been wrong, because this morning she'd poured herself into a purple scrap of fabric that had his eyes bugging from his head like a cartoon character's.

He didn't know where to look. Or where *not* to let himself look.

Tall and curvy, Suzanne definitely wasn't some scrawny computer geek. If he'd been asked to define the looks of his perfect woman, she'd be standing right here in front of him.

Her long, dark hair fell like silk down her back and over her chest. His mouth watered and he swallowed hard as he averted his eyes from her gorgeous breasts...only to be hit with a view of tanned, toned legs that were a mile long.

"Good morning." The two words drawled from her lips in a way that reminded him of her brothers' innate confidence. Brothers who would tear him into a million little pieces if they knew he was having sexual thoughts about their sister.

When he finally managed to drag his gaze back to hers, one corner of her mouth was slightly lifted, as if she knew exactly what he was thinking despite his attempts not to.

"Ready to go?"

Her tone was surprisingly cheerful. But she couldn't have flipped to her brothers' viewpoint this quickly. Not after how furious she'd been last night. Unfortunately, his brain was addled enough simply from being this close to her that he couldn't work out her motives this morning.

Giving her a strictly professional smile, he gestured to the elevator. "After you."

Too late, he realized he should have rethought the smile. Because when she smiled back at him, for the first time in his life he lost his breath just from standing in a hallway. He could scale a mountain without so much as breaking a sweat, but her smile was that blindingly beautiful.

Distance. He needed to try to keep some distance between himself and his new client. But that was the very opposite of what he'd been hired to do. Where Suzanne went, Roman would go too. No matter how much being close to her messed with him.

When the elevator came and they stepped inside, he was palpably aware of what a small space it was. She didn't just smell good—she smelled downright amazing.

Another string of silent curses let loose inside his head. *Enough.* He was a professional. It was time to start acting like one again.

In a normal bodyguard/client situation, they would already have sat down together so that she could detail the threats against her. But in this case, since she'd made it clear last night that she didn't want him around, he decided it was wiser to wait until she was more receptive to his being there before he pushed for the information.

"Did you sleep well?" he asked, an innocuous enough conversation starter.

"I had some work to take care of for a few hours, but I finally found my way to bed." She nearly purred the word *bed,* which made his brain short-circuit again. "By the time I woke up this morning, I had a great idea for how to achieve one of my biggest goals."

Though it was taking most of his focus to corral his brain—and body—away from thoughts of Suzanne slipping naked between her sheets, he said, "Sounds like you're off to a good start."

"Oh yes," she said in a slightly husky tone that went through him like a shot of the finest Scottish whisky. "I have a really good feeling about how things are going to go today." She licked her lower lip, leaving it looking just kissed. "On all fronts."

Working like hell to force all thoughts of kissing away, he said, "I'd appreciate it if you could take me through your plans for the day."

They walked out of the elevator, through the lobby, and onto the sidewalk, where she raised her arm to hail a cab. He found it interesting that a woman as successful as Suzanne leased an apartment from her cousin and took a taxi to work. Anyone else in her financial position would own a multimillion-dollar home with staff to cook and clean, and have a full-time driver who jumped at her every whim. It was almost as if those trappings of wealth and power didn't mean anything to her, and she was happy just to put her focus into her work instead. If that were actually the case, she would be the most unique woman he'd ever known—he'd never met a woman whose head wasn't turned by money and power.

"I have a meeting with my investors this morning, and then I'm going to try a couple of different things with the new software I've been working on."

The taxi skidded to a stop in front of them, and a few moments later she was sliding into the backseat. Only a monk would have been able to keep from noticing the way her barely there dress tightened over her hips, then rode up her thighs when she sat. He was gritting his teeth hard enough to break a molar when he got in beside her.

If only she'd pull the dress down. But she didn't seem to notice that she was displaying nearly as much skin as she would have in a pair of short shorts.

If this was what she wore to the office, what the hell would she wear out on a date? He prayed she wouldn't have too many hot nights out planned while he was working for her. He didn't want to rip the throats out of too many guys for daring to touch her.

Thinking about all the guys he'd likely have to restrain himself from tearing apart over the next weeks— or months—that he worked as her bodyguard made it difficult to keep the growl out of his voice. "After that, will you play the rest of your day by ear?"

She nodded. "If there are fires to put out with my employees or customers, I'll put them out. And then I have a meeting with Rosa Bouchard and the staff of her new nonprofit tonight at eight."

Roman was impressed that Suzanne was running such a big, powerful company at only thirty-one. Investors, employees, customers—she had so many people to keep happy. Sullivan Security was one of the hottest tech firms in the world.

No wonder she was a target.

"Although," she continued, "if everything is cooking along well, maybe I'll try to squeeze in a run through the park at some point during the afternoon." She paused, and from the look on her face, it almost seemed as if she had suddenly remembered something important. A moment later, she turned her gaze back to him, then ran it slowly from his torso down the rest of his body. "You look like you work out a lot."

Jesus. She hadn't even needed to touch him to send him straight to the edge of losing his mind. He'd worked for a lot of tough clients, but he had no doubt that Suzanne was going to be his toughest yet. He'd take being screamed at and treated like dirt over trying to corral an impossible attraction any day. What's more, most clients didn't ask him questions. Primarily because they didn't give a crap about him. And that was just fine with him. He wasn't interested in opening himself up to his clients. Better to keep his past buried deep where it belonged.

But since she was obviously waiting for him to reply, he said, "I make sure to keep in shape so that I can do my job."

She raised an eyebrow, and even that simple movement was sexy. "Your version of keeping in shape seems different from most people's. I've never seen anyone with muscles like yours."

Her skin flushed, as if she wasn't used to saying anything quite so direct. The innocence of her blush didn't match either the outfit she had on this morning or the way she'd just been looking at him, as though she wanted to eat him up. Suzanne Sullivan was more of a puzzle than he'd thought. A puzzle he was far too interested in solving.

"When do you even get a chance to go to the gym

if you're stuck shadowing your clients all the time?"

"I don't need a gym to stay in shape. I can do everything I need wherever I am, no weights, no machines, just by using my own body weight for resistance."

"I'd like to learn how to do that. I'm in my office more often than I'm not. And I usually can't get away." She half smiled. "Okay, I probably could get away, but I don't want to, especially when things start clicking with my code. Which I'm always convinced is going to happen any second if I only keep at it for another five minutes."

Her half smile shifted into another brilliantly beautiful grin. Though he tried to brace for impact, it didn't do any good. Every time she looked at him like that, his heart raced as though he'd just sprinted around a track at full speed.

"If there were things I could do to get my heart rate up while I'm waiting for my code to compile or thinking through a bug fix, that would be awesome."

"I can show you."

Wait. *What the hell was he saying?* The last thing he needed to do was offer to get sweaty with her. It was her smile. It messed with his head so much that he couldn't think straight.

Before he could take it back, she said, "Great!" Her grin turned the sunshine up another notch inside the dirty taxi.

"So your brothers were right when they said you work around the clock?"

At his mention of her brothers, her smile fell away. "I'd appreciate it if you could leave them off our list of discussion topics. I still haven't forgiven them for their underhanded, low-down, ridiculous—" She stopped, paused, breathed. "Sorry, you were asking about my work schedule. I do work a lot, but it's because I really love what I do. I love knowing that my digital security software helps people. I always feel like I have a purpose. As long as I have my work, I'm not going to just float away one day, not going to feel lost."

In his line of work, Roman made sure to pay close attention to absolutely every cue—both from his clients and the strangers around him. He couldn't miss the passion in Suzanne's voice when she spoke about her company and about having purpose. Her word choices were interesting as well, considering that he couldn't imagine her ever floating away or being lost. And yet, those seemed to be concerns for her.

"My brothers are all workaholics too," she said, temporarily forgetting that she'd banned them from the conversation. "I'm pretty sure we get it from my dad. I'm assuming you know who he is?"

Roman never took on a job without researching his prospective clients. Due to the jobs he'd taken with

Alec's company, he already knew the public information about the Sullivans. "Your father is a famous
painter."

"He was. Until my mom—" She inhaled a breath
that shook slightly in her chest. "You've been friends
with Alec and Harry for long enough that you probably
also know what happened to her, don't you?"

Her brothers didn't talk much about their past—
none of them did, which Roman appreciated, since he
didn't plan on sharing the past he'd put behind him
with anyone. But Suzanne's past wasn't something that
could be hidden, not when her father had once been
such a worldwide sensation in his field that he'd ended
up on the cover of *Time* magazine.

Neither Roman nor Suzanne had grown up with
mothers. But where Roman's father had kicked his
mother out for lying and cheating, Roman had learned
on Wikipedia that Suzanne's mother had taken her
own life when Suzanne was only a toddler.

"I'm sorry for your loss, Suzanne."

"It was a long time ago. I barely even knew her
when she left." The driver came to a stop in front of a
skyscraper, and he could see the clear relief on her face
that she could now drop the subject. "We're here."

He paid the cabbie before she could, and when he
got out of the car, it was instinct to reach out. He
didn't realize the miscalculation until she pressed her

palm against his. Still, it might have been nothing but a split-second shock of electricity if one of her high heels hadn't caught on the uneven curb.

She tumbled into him, and the press of her curves against his hard muscles was almost enough to make him forget.

Forget how to do anything but stare into her eyes.

Forget that she was the very definition of *off-limits*.

Forget that he didn't have it in him to do more than take a woman to bed and then leave her in the morning.

Forget everything except how much he wanted her. More than he could ever remember wanting anyone or anything before.

CHAPTER FOUR

It was only through sheer force of will, honed by years of training himself to turn the heat at his core to ice, that Roman was not only able to remove his hands from Suzanne's hips, but also to put a good foot of space between them.

Suzanne didn't move away immediately, however. Instead, she stared at him as though she were seeing him for the very first time. The little flecks of gold and amber in her eyes mesmerized him for just long enough that several moments passed before he could get his mouth—and brain—to cooperate.

"What floor are we headed to?"

"Floor?" She blinked as if her brain was having just as many problems. Then, with a shake of her head, she said, "My office is on the tenth floor."

He had assumed she'd be on the top, like most founders and CEOs, not in the middle of the building. It was a good reminder that he shouldn't make the mistake of assuming anything where Suzanne Sullivan was concerned.

As she headed toward the glass entry doors to the building, the heels she was wearing seemed to trip her up a bit. Yet again, he wondered why she was dressed in such markedly different clothes than she'd been wearing at the gallery. Was there a guy she was interested in? His gut had absolutely no business tightening in jealousy.

He'd been in high-tech workspaces before, and the lobby, hallways, and break rooms of Sullivan Security were just as bright and engaging as he would have expected after meeting the company's founder. But though he wasn't surprised by the workspace, he was surprised that when they passed one of the Ping-Pong tables and an employee asked her to play, Suzanne instantly put down her bag and jumped into the game.

She laughed as she hit the first ball into the net, then cheered when she scored a point. Roman expected her employees to throw the game. After all, she was the big boss and held their careers in the palm of her hand. But no one seemed afraid of her, even though the net worth of her company had a hell of a lot of zeros.

The puzzle that was Suzanne Sullivan continued to grow. Especially when a twenty-something woman in a red hoodie, jeans, and sneakers said, "I didn't think you'd play this well with those heels on. What are they, five inches?"

"Try eight. At least, that's what they feel like."

"I didn't even know you owned heels," the woman said with a shudder that made it clear what she thought of them. "Must be a pretty special event for you to be so dressed up."

Suzanne shot a glance at Roman, her expression freezing as though she'd just been caught out at something. But then she shrugged. "I figured I should wear some of the stuff collecting dust in my closet."

Though the woman nodded, she still looked confused. They all did, actually. What was more, every guy in the room was trying to act like they hadn't noticed their boss's figure in the dress.

Roman wished them luck. Lord knew each and every one of them needed a truckload of it right now.

"Do you want to play?" the woman said, holding out a paddle to Roman.

He shook his head. "No, thank you."

Despite the fact that she didn't want him there, Suzanne politely said, "This is Roman." She rattled off the names of the dozen people closest to them, and he quickly memorized them. Given that the threat could just as easily be coming from inside her company as outside of it, he needed to be as watchful here as anywhere else he went with Suzanne.

"Are you going to be joining our R&D team?" a guy with thick-framed black glasses asked.

"No." Roman looked to Suzanne, knowing it would be best if he let her field questions about his job title.

Her expression tightened for a split second before she smoothed it out and gave her employees a forced smile. Unlike her brother Alec, she didn't have much of a poker face. Everything she was thinking and feeling seemed to be written there. Hopefully, her transparency would make this already difficult job a little easier.

"Roman works in security, but not digital. Personal."

A blonde peeked her head out from around a gray cubicle wall. Her eyes were big as she asked, "You're a bodyguard?" When he nodded, her eyes went even wider. "For who?" She turned to Suzanne. "Is your cousin Smith coming here today? His last movie was *fabulous*."

Suzanne half laughed, half groaned. "No. Roman isn't here to protect Smith." She pressed her lips together as if she didn't want to have to say it. "He's here to protect me."

"*You?*"

The word came from a chorus of voices, all similarly incredulous.

He expected Suzanne to say she agreed with them and that she most certainly did not need a bodyguard. Instead, she simply nodded. "Yes, Roman is here to work with me. It's a long story, and I don't want to bore everyone with it, but don't worry. Everything's fine. I'm fine." Everyone looked from her to him, clearly wondering why he was standing there if she was truly *fine*. "I've got a meeting with the Mavericks in a few minutes, but I'm hoping to spend the rest of the day working on code, so I'll be around if anyone needs me."

With that, she continued down the hall and around the corner to the back of the building. "Good morning, Jeannie," she said to a petite woman with red curls who was sitting behind a big computer screen. "This is Roman. He's my bodyguard and will need complete access to the building. Could you please make him a badge?"

"Absolutely." Suzanne's assistant barely blinked at the request, nor did she react in any outward way to her boss's outfit. "The Mavericks have confirmed they're on for your meeting in ten minutes. There are several messages on your desk for you to take a look at before the meeting begins, and I've highlighted your highest priority emails in your inbox." Jeannie paused before adding, "Nothing urgent or out of the ordinary."

Relief flashed across Suzanne's face. "Great, thank you."

Roman wanted to understand more about what *out of the ordinary* looked like for Suzanne. But as she was about to head into a meeting—and he still wasn't exactly sure where she now stood on the whole bodyguard thing—he figured it would be best to watch everything carefully for the time being.

Though her office wasn't huge, it had a great view of Central Park. She had a big desk, a leather couch, and a glass table in the corner for one-on-one meetings. The big difference from other CEOs he had worked with was that more than a dozen computers, tablets, and phones were strewn throughout the room—on her desk, her coffee table, her glass tabletop, her shelves.

"I need to test my software on every possible device," she said in answer to his unspoken question. "You're not the first person to wonder why I've got enough in here to stock an electronics store. Plus," she said as she ran her hand over one of the PCs, "computers are my drug of choice."

"As far as drugs go, these seem like pretty good ones to get hooked on."

"Can you please tell that to the last guy I dated? He took one look at my office and mentally committed me."

"If he didn't get it, he didn't deserve you."

Her hand stilled over the computer. "Do you?" She licked her lips. "Get it, I mean?"

Telling himself her question shouldn't feel as weighted as it did, he nodded. "Of course I do." She might be a puzzle, but she was an open book when it came to things she loved—the top two obviously being her family and computers.

The large screen directly across from her desk began to buzz. "My meeting is about to start. You can take a seat anywhere you'd like."

"I'd prefer to stand." Any bodyguard worth his salt could easily spend twelve hours a day on his feet without feeling it. You could react far more quickly to potential threats if you were already standing.

"Suit yourself," she said with a shrug, "even though I can guarantee no one is going to come busting down my door with a machete." With that, she sat in her leather office chair, kicked off her heels with what sounded like a moan of appreciation, then clicked on a remote to accept the video call. She smiled as four men appeared in four different frames on the screen. "Good morning. It's an early one for those of you in California."

One of the men laughed. "Five a.m. meetings are a good excuse to catch the sunrise."

"Are you sitting out on your deck, Will?" He turned his camera around so she could see that her guess was correct. "That's quite a view," she said as she took in the tall redwoods and the rolling hills and ocean beyond it.

"Harper and Jeremy are hoping you'll come out to

visit us soon," Will replied. "Hopefully, this will entice you."

"Charlie is angling for the same thing," another man said. "Would it seal the deal if she threw in a sculpture?"

"And Noah is dying to show you how well he can swim now that his water wings are off," another of the Mavericks put in.

"I'm not going to turn down your stunning views, Will, or one of Charlie's incredible pieces of metal art, Sebastian. And let Noah know that I'm dying to swim with him, Matt. I don't need any bribes to come spend some time in Northern California with you. Just a little more downtime."

"I hear you," a man with a beard agreed. "I keep thinking I'm going to be able to get to Lake Tahoe to work on my cabin, but somehow I never quite seem to make it into the woods."

Roman recognized him as Daniel Spencer, the founder of Top-Notch DIY, a chain of home improvement stores. He recognized each of the Mavericks, as their rags-to-billionaire stories had made the five men famous over the years. Their trajectory was impressive enough to have helped fuel the determination of a guy like Roman, who also came from a rough place.

Few people from his world made it out—and even if they did, they still couldn't dream of making the kind of money he had. As an adult, he'd worked hard to cage the part of him that had been trained to win at all costs, no matter the danger, regardless of the consequences. But the fact was that with his size and boxing background, being a bodyguard had been the best way to get out of a bad neighborhood and into a better one.

Billions of dollars would be nice, but it was more than enough right now for Roman to feel he was doing the best job he could for the people who needed his help. People like Suzanne and her brothers. Fortunately, he'd saved enough, and invested well enough over the years, that he didn't need to work for dickheads anymore.

Interestingly, for all their money and power, the Mavericks didn't seem like dickheads. And they clearly weren't just investors to Suzanne either. With the attached guys, she'd talked about kids and significant others. But the single Maverick didn't give a whiff of anything other than friendly affection, and neither did she. It would have been the perfect "arranged" relationship—a Sullivan marrying a Maverick—but clearly those kinds of sparks weren't there.

Roman was relieved despite himself. Despite the fact that Suzanne would never, and could never, be his.

"Should we wait for Evan before I bring this meeting to order?" she asked.

The four Mavericks seemed to share a look with

each other on the screen before Will replied. "He's going to have to sit this one out. But we'll fill him in. So tell us, what news do you have for us on MavG1?"

"All good." Her grin lit up her face. "We've got a few finishing touches to make the code a little prettier, and then we're ready to jump into our first round of beta testing. I'm thinking we'll be in beta by Friday at the latest."

Sebastian whistled. "You're a good six months ahead of schedule."

"Not to mention you've already done the impossible by even taking this on when everyone said it couldn't be done," Daniel noted.

"Everything just clicked." She looked extremely pleased about it. "In fact, I'm already jotting down some notes on how to make this product even more affordable."

For the next ten minutes, Roman watched as she proceeded to blow each of the Mavericks' hair back with her ideas. Obviously technologically savvy themselves, they asked good questions and were impressed with the answers she gave.

"Only you could have pulled this off, Suzanne," Matt enthused. "Your mind is a marvel."

"You know I love it when you blow smoke," she replied with a grin, "but how about I make back your investment on the new product before you deem me to be a digital security superhero."

They chatted a few minutes longer about how her brothers and father were doing, and then when she clicked off, Jeannie buzzed in. "I have the head of IT from the Kaizen Group in Japan on the line if you're free."

"Put her on."

Suzanne settled deeper into her seat as she put on her headset to take the call while lighting up several of the computer monitors on her desk. She was so deeply in her element that he got the feeling she'd forgotten he was even there at all as the first two meetings of the day turned into half a dozen more.

It was his job to disappear into the background, but he didn't like having to admit that it almost hurt his masculine pride knowing how easy it was for her to tune him out. Especially when he was doing a damned poor job of tuning out one single thing about her. It was more than just how spectacular she looked in her little slip of a dress, or how long her legs were.

Her brain, he was surprised to realize, was at least as alluring as her body. And when she laughed?

Hell. He didn't know how to deal with the way her laughter moved through him. All he knew was that more than ever, he wanted to make sure nothing frightened or harmed her, just so she could keep laughing like that.

CHAPTER FIVE

How the heck was Suzanne supposed to concentrate with Roman standing guard in the corner, watching her every move?

Every time she lifted her hair from her shoulders, his eyes seemed to graze the bare skin of her neck. Every time she laughed, it was as though he leaned in closer. And every time she shifted in her chair to cross her legs on the other side, she started to feel a little too hot all over.

She'd opened her door this morning to find him standing there looking beyond gorgeous in his dark suit, his crisp white shirt perfectly setting off his tanned skin. Honestly, it had been all she could do not to beg him to come inside and christen the new sheets she'd bought a couple of weeks earlier. The sexy dreams she'd had about him sure didn't help any.

Of course, she'd kept her composure and made herself launch into her seduction plan. But it hadn't gotten any easier to rein in her hormones as the hours ticked by.

At the end of her call with a strategic partner in Germany, Jeannie popped her head in. "You've been in back-to-back meetings for five hours straight. I'm holding all calls for you for the next ninety minutes." The executive assistant Suzanne couldn't live without jerked her thumb over her shoulder. "Get out of here. And don't come back until you've had a little sun and something to eat."

Suzanne grinned at Jeannie. Anyone who thought the petite woman with the angelic-looking red curls was a meek pushover was a fool. "Aye-aye, Captain."

Jeannie looked at Roman. "I'm counting on you to hold her to it."

Roman nodded. "No problem."

Suzanne shoved away from her desk. Perhaps she shouldn't be irritated by that overly confident *no problem*, as if corralling her into behaving would be no sweat. But five hours of trying to get her brain to work straight and her hormones to settle down while he was watching from the corner had tried her patience.

"I'm going for a run."

She nearly slammed her bathroom door behind her when she went to change into her running gear, but she managed to temper her irritation at the last second. Her plan to fake-seduce Roman into quitting would be no good if she couldn't even hold her smiles together past lunch. No doubt about it, a good, hard run would help burn off some pent-up energy.

She wished she could reach for her usual T-shirt and shorts, but after a long morning of working to fight her instinctive feminine reaction to Roman, getting him to quit quickly was more of a necessity than ever. Which meant that instead of throwing on a T-shirt and shorts, she had to reach for a bright blue sports bra and matching spandex. She tried to tell herself that compared to the silk dress she'd been wearing, it wasn't much more revealing. But it was hard to believe it when outfits like these were *so* not her.

Deep breaths. That was how she was going to get over the tough parts of her plan—with lots of deep breaths and a bottomless well of determination.

She emerged from the bathroom, surprised to see that Roman had changed into running clothes and shoes as well, which must have been in the leather bag he'd brought with him. She'd hoped to make his eyes bug from his head when he saw her in her tiny little running getup, but she was the one who had to work to hide her own reaction.

He'd been incredibly handsome in his dark suit. But in a T-shirt and shorts, with all of his muscles on display, she needed to take plenty more deep breaths. She also needed to work like crazy to stop her drool reflex from going into overdrive.

She gave her head a shake to try to clear the help-less-attraction nonsense from it. "I take it you're running with me?" She was proud of how normal her voice sounded. Not at all as breathless as she felt just from standing in the same room with him.

"My job is to protect you, no matter what you're doing."

"Seriously? You're planning to be with me every second, no matter what? Nothing is off-limits?"

"Not if it means keeping you safe."

"What if I've got a date?"

He didn't so much as blink at her pointed question. "I won't leave you alone with anyone I haven't thoroughly checked out."

"So you're saying that if no guy checks out well enough for you, I have to be a nun?"

Finally, she thought she saw a chink in his armor. "Like I said, if your dates check out, I won't stand in your way."

It was entirely beside the point that she had no dates set up, nor was she looking for anyone to sleep with. What bugged her was if Roman thought he could control her in this way. In any way at all.

Momentarily forgetting her plan to seduce him into misbehaving and quitting, she said, "If I'm going to sleep with someone, that means *I* have already checked him out." She held up a hand before he could argue with her. "I'll let you stay in the apartment next door and stand in my office all day. I'll even let you go on a run with me. But what I do with my body in the privacy of my own bedroom is my decision. Period."

With that, she strapped her phone to her armband and headed out the door. Now she *really* needed a hit of fresh air to her brain, if only to cool off her temper and get back on plan.

Jeannie hadn't reacted to Suzanne's dress and heels that morning, but the sports bra and spandex without an oversized T-shirt to cover it all up had her assistant cocking her head in question before she could stop herself. Suzanne shot her a look that said, *I'll explain everything later.* Fortunately, they'd been working together for so long that they could have entire conversations without saying a word.

By the time Suzanne and Roman had left the building, crossed the street, and entered the park, she was beyond ready to spring off the starting block. She usually let herself warm up a little bit, but because she was desperate to try to outrun both her irritation and her unacceptable attraction to the man who seemed determined to keep her a prisoner in the name of safety, she all but sprinted down the paved pathway.

Roman had no trouble keeping up with her, and she was impressed despite herself. Her brothers were all in great shape, but she could run rings around them. As far as she could tell, Roman was barely even breaking a sweat. Not that she was going to let herself sneak too many looks at him out of the corner of her eye, of course. Right now, she had to be totally focused on getting her brain—and body—back on track.

It took a few minutes of running full speed for her mind to clear. But relief was short-lived. Because once she could think straight again, she finally remembered that she was supposed to be doing whatever she could to entice Roman into overstepping the boundaries of professionalism.

If her brothers hadn't been such meddling, overbearing *men* who thought it was okay to sic a bodyguard on her, she wouldn't even be in this situation. One day, she hoped Harry and Alec met women who would knock them down a peg. Mostly just Alec, since Harry was a sweetheart most of the time. Alec, on the other hand, needed his heart served to him on a platter by someone who drove him positively nuts. If she'd known the right woman, Suzanne would have gleefully introduced them already. Unfortunately, she didn't know a single woman capable of wrapping Alec around her finger.

Speaking of which, Suzanne needed to get back to her plan, ASAP. Which meant being sweet to Roman instead of sour. It was time to buck up and get the job done. Time, she sensed, was of the essence with Roman. Because if she let him stick around too long, she was very much afraid it wouldn't be attraction that would do her in, but the fact that she'd enjoyed talking with him this morning in the taxi.

"Do you have a girlfriend?" she asked in what she hoped was a sultry tone. Granted, it was hard to sound sultry when she was running this fast.

She could have sworn he almost stumbled on the path before he said, "No."

"Mmm." She made sure to draw the sound out in a husky tone she'd never used before. "It must be hard to go out on your own dates when you're with clients nearly twenty-four seven." She turned her gaze to him and let it linger longer than it should. "Somehow I can't imagine you living as a monk, though, do you?"

His expression didn't change, apart from a muscle that began to jump in his jaw. "Most clients aren't interested in my personal life."

"Sure they are," she responded. "They're just too afraid of that forbidding expression you wear all the time to ask. But I've been around enough men my whole life to see right through it. Icy exteriors always melt." The muscle was jumping even faster in his jaw as she forced herself totally outside of her comfort zone. "Besides, if we're going to be with each other practically every second of the day and night, don't you think we should get to know each other?"

"No."

Her laughter came unbidden. Real laughter, not fake I'm-trying-to-seduce-you laughter.

It was a majorly bad idea to think that the bodyguard she didn't want was cute, but in that moment he'd sounded like a stubborn little boy who was upset that he wasn't getting his own way. All because of a client who wouldn't respect professional boundaries and stop poking into his personal life. Of course, his response only helped to egg her on more. After all, she had never liked being told what she could and couldn't do.

"I'll start," she offered as if he hadn't said no. "I was born in April, and I'm an Aries through and through. All fire, all the time. What month were you born?"

He didn't reply for a few moments, but then when he must have figured she could look up the information, he said, "November."

"A Scorpio." She wasn't at all surprised. "I recently read this article about the sexiest astrological signs. Aries won big points for passion, although we can also be quite impulsive. Do you want to know what the researchers said about Scorpio?"

"No," he said again, but it was resigned and half-hearted this time.

"It said you're dark and mysterious and utterly addictive." She tried to tell herself that her heart was only beating fast because they were running, before making herself go even further with it. "Does that sound right to you? Because from what I've seen so far, I'm thinking it's dead-on."

Finally, he turned to her, and she held her breath waiting to hear what his response would be. Would he finally flirt back? Or had she not managed to break down his professional walls at all with her sexy banter?

Unfortunately, it turned out that combining held breath with running that fast was a bad move. A side cramp hit her so hard she doubled over.

"Suzanne." She could hear the concern in his tone. Along with the clear promise that he'd take care of her. No matter what. "What happened?"

"S...si...side cramp."

"Don't try to talk. I know it hurts, but I want you to breathe as normally as you can."

She felt his arms going around her as he spoke in a gentle voice while helping her move off to the side of the path and over to a water fountain.

"Drink. Slowly, or it will make the cramp worse."

She wanted to guzzle the city's entire supply of water. But she knew he was right and only let herself have one small sip, and then another, until the cramp finally started to ease.

"Thank you, the water was just what I needed." And, she had to admit, the feel of his strong arms around her was nice too. So nice that when he finally deemed her okay enough to stand up on her own and let her go, she missed his touch. More than she wanted to admit.

A part of her wished she could apologize for making him so uncomfortable with her personal—and deliberately sexual—questions. But though he had helped her so sweetly, she couldn't let herself go soft now, could she?

Besides, she wouldn't have needed to sprint as if her life depended on it if his presence hadn't been stealing her every coherent thought this morning in her office.

"I'm okay to run again now."

She could still read concern on his face, but he didn't try to stop her from jogging down the path, simply kept pace with her as he had before. She knew she should start back in on her sexy questions, but in the wake of his gentle voice and comforting hands, it was hard to find the motivation. Soon, she'd force herself to get back on task, but for a few minutes would it really be so bad to let herself enjoy his company as they ran through the park on a lovely day? Because no matter how much she wanted to deny that she felt safe with Roman, the truth was that when he was around, she felt almost bulletproo—

The SOS ringtone trilled from the phone she'd strapped to her upper arm. The harsh sound couldn't be ignored. Even passersby turned to look at her with alarm.

"Damn it." She'd been so hopeful that she was done with the nonsense her brothers were so worried about. Not only because she was tired of wasting so much time dealing with the online attacks, but also because it would also prove to her brothers that she didn't need a bodyguard. Unfortunately, this ringtone meant there was a big problem at Sullivan Security. One that she needed to deal with as soon as humanly possible.

"What's wrong?"

"It's my office." She'd already turned around on the path. "We've got to head back, immediately."

So much for being bulletproof.

CHAPTER SIX

Suzanne was crazy fast on those long legs. Roman had never found anyone who could outrun him before, but just minutes into their run, he'd realized he might finally have met his match. When she got the emergency call from her office, she all but blazed back through the park—while protectiveness blazed within Roman.

It wasn't simply because his job was to make sure nothing happened to her. After seeing her interact with both employees and business partners today, and her family the night before, he now knew for sure that she didn't deserve to be treated poorly. Not by anyone.

He'd planned to wait until she was more comfortable with him before questioning her about the email, phone, and corporate server attacks that her brothers had informed him about, but time was now of the essence. Shoving aside his heated physical reaction to the way she'd said, *"You're dark, mysterious, and utterly addictive,"* minutes before—when it had seemed strangely like she was trying to flirt with him—he focused his full attention on the current threat.

"What's going on?"

"Our main server farm has been attacked. It's not completely taken down yet, but we've got to act fast to keep it from collapsing." Her expression was full of grim fury. "We have too many individuals, too many businesses around the world counting on our software to let it go down for even a second."

"Your staff is already on it, aren't they?"

"They are. And I need to get back in there and get into the trenches with them."

He had seen enough to understand that while Suzanne would never say it herself, one of the reasons her staff needed her in the trenches with them was because her brain worked at unmatched speeds. If anyone was going to be able to come up with a solution to this problem quickly, it was likely to be her. She was miles more intelligent than any woman—or man—he'd ever met. And yet, she never shoved her brains in your face.

But he was pretty sure she was sprinting back to her office for more reasons than that. She also seemed to be the kind of person who was determined to fix every problem all by herself. Take the way she'd rejected her brothers' attempts to help, for instance. It wasn't that she wasn't a team player. It seemed more that she might believe accepting help meant she was weak. Whereas Roman had learned a long time ago that sometimes letting someone else help you out of a rough spot was the very best choice you could make.

"How many times has this happened?"

They were running so fast neither of them should have been able to say much, but her answer was perfectly clear. "Too many." She made a little growling sound. "We put in several new safeguards for our servers. This shouldn't have happened. At least not this quickly—unless someone knew exactly where to look, exactly what to aim for."

Her statement brought his earlier thoughts about digging into her employees' backgrounds back to the forefront. "Do you think someone from inside your own company could be doing this?"

She shot him a horrified look. "*No.* No way. That's not what I'm saying, not at all. My employees would never betray me."

She was obviously disgusted with him for even suggesting it, but it seemed like an obvious question. At least for a guy like him, who had made the mistake of trusting the wrong person before. Honestly, he couldn't imagine what it would be like to have trust like hers, but he wouldn't press his point now. Instead, while she worked on getting the servers back to a hundred percent again, he'd start doing some digging of his own.

"I don't know who's doing this, but whoever they

are, they're damned smart if they could unravel our systems in less than twenty-four hours. Which means we'll have to up our game."

Right alongside the anger was a competitive edge. It was almost as if she welcomed the chance to spin her game up another level. By the hour, his respect for her grew. Respect that could be dangerously close to turning into something more if he didn't lock his usual ironclad self-control back into place.

Roman was panting by the time they pushed through the front door of Suzanne's building. She was too, but that didn't stop her from sprinting up the stairs instead of taking the elevator.

Without pausing, she ran straight toward what he assumed was command central for her corporate servers. She didn't seem to remember that she was still in running clothes, nor did she seem to notice that she was dripping with sweat as she quickly conferred with her employees. To Roman, it was almost as though they were speaking a foreign language. Seconds later, she was sliding into a chair and opening the laptop her assistant had brought for her.

No break. No transition or cool-down time. She simply went straight from the hard run to her even harder job with absolute focus, and not one second of complaint. There was work to be done, and it was obvious to Roman—and to each and every one of her employees—that she would do it.

Suzanne Sullivan impressed the hell out of him.

Despite his father raising him never to make the mistake of trusting a woman, he knew better than to underestimate women. More than once in his line of work, the threat had been female. The women he'd dated hadn't been dingbats—not all of them, anyway— so he understood that brains combined with beauty weren't an impossibility.

But he'd never met a woman like Suzanne.

* * *

It wasn't easy, and Suzanne wasn't happy that her employees' work plans for the day had been upended yet again, but that didn't make it any less satisfying to finally get all the servers back up and running. Even better, while they were at it they mapped out a new plan to make their system even more impervious to attacks.

She looked down at her watch, surprised to see that it was almost seven thirty. "I didn't mean to work everyone so late." Just because other tech companies operated around the clock, didn't mean hers did. Sure, she worked a zillion hours, but that was different. This was her company. It was her responsibility to make sure she took care of everyone, no matter what. "Please apologize to your families for me."

Everyone told her they were more than happy to work late, but she knew they must all be starved and ready to head home. Lord knew she was desperate for a long soak in the bath with a big glass of wine.

Finally pushing back her chair, she belatedly realized she was still wearing her running clothes. She could hardly remember even going for a run. Only the feel of Roman's arms around her in the park remained.

She spun around on her swivel chair and found him standing nearby. Everyone else was already gone. "Have you been there the whole time?"

"I briefly stepped away a couple of times, but you were always in my line of sight." She should have been indignant at being watched like a toddler who couldn't be trusted not to stumble into danger, but Roman was so unobtrusive that it was getting more and more difficult to muster up any anger at him for doing the job her brothers had hired him for.

When it came to her brothers, on the other hand, she could still be furious. And she was. One day, she'd pay them back for trying to take over her life like this. Preferably when they didn't see payback coming.

Her phone alarm went off and a message popped up on her screen: *Rosa's online bullying meeting, 8 p.m.*

"I have a meeting in thirty minutes."

"Another meeting?" He frowned, looking more forbidding than usual. Sexier too, she thought with a small sigh. She hadn't yet figured out how to stop feeling weak in the knees—and hot all over—around him. "You've had a long day already. Can you reschedule?"

"No. I really need to be there. Which means we've got to take the world's fastest shower." She blushed as she realized the way that sounded—as if she were suggesting they shower together. "In separate showers, I mean," she clarified before she belatedly remembered that letting her accidental suggestion of a co-shower linger would have been perfect for the mock seduction she was supposed to be staging.

"I knew what you meant."

Was it her imagination, or did his voice sound a little strangled? As though the thought of the two of them in the shower together had the same effect on him as it did on her—instantly heating up every cell in her body.

"I'll show you where the men's showers are on the way back to my office."

He shook his head. "I can't leave you alone in the building for that long."

She was too tired and hungry to keep herself from snapping, "So that means we really do need to shower together, don't we?"

"I'm fine like this, Suzanne."

He always said her name like that—so serious and

sober, and yet warm and rumbly too. It made her blood heat up more each time he said it. Worse, no matter how much she tried to deny it, she couldn't help but want to find out exactly what it would sound like if he said her name when they were sweaty and barely dressed...and not from a run.

"If you feel anywhere near as gross as I do right now," she said, "it wouldn't be fair to make you stay this way. You can use my private shower." Before he could protest, she said, "I won't leave my office while you're in there. Scout's honor."

"Let me guess," he said as they headed toward her office. "Instead of selling Girl Scout cookies on the corner, you masterminded a computer program that did it for you."

"Sometimes the simplest way of doing something is best." She smiled, thinking back to how much she'd enjoyed working on this at school. "But that definitely doesn't apply to selling Girl Scout cookies. It was a lot of fun figuring out not only how to sell enough boxes to make lots of money for charity, but also how to win the grand prize for our local troop." They'd reached her office by then, so she said, "I need to send a couple of quick emails, so why don't you shower first?"

She'd barely finished composing her first email by the time he stepped back out of the bathroom, looking and smelling deliciously clean. Not to mention as drop-dead gorgeous as always in his white shirt and dark suit. Her jaw was going to dislocate soon if she kept letting it fall open like this.

"Your turn," he said, and even the way he turned his left wrist so he could button his cuff with his right hand made her melt inside.

She tried to play it cool and unaffected as she headed into the shower, but it didn't help that the room was all steamy and smelled like Roman. Her skin felt extra sensitive as she ran the bar of soap over herself. He was right that it had been a long day already, and not just because of the back-to-back meetings and server attack. What had mixed her up the most were all those hours with his dark eyes on her, especially when she couldn't quite seem to rein in how much she liked having him so close.

The problem was, letting Roman stay would mean her brothers won. And since she absolutely couldn't allow that to happen, she needed to stick to her game plan without letting a foolish attraction derail her.

Still, she had to force herself to put the skimpy dress back on. She wasn't looking forward to having to wear another super-sexy outfit tomorrow morning—if she wasn't able to convince him to kiss her and resign by then, that was all the more reason to work harder to get to her plan's finish line.

"Do you have a jacket?" he asked when she

emerged from the bathroom. "The temperature outside is bound to have dropped by now."

She did, but she couldn't risk covering up now and blowing her chance to tempt him over the line. "I'll be fine."

But she hadn't counted on how hard the wind was blowing when they headed outside to catch a cab. By the time a taxi pulled over to the curb, it was impossible to hide how cold she was.

Warmth suddenly enveloped her, along with the scent of clean male, as Roman draped his jacket over her shoulders. She knew she should give it back to him, but couldn't resist wrapping it around herself like a blanket instead.

"Thank you," she murmured as he opened the taxi door and she slipped into the backseat.

She gave the driver the address, then told Roman, "Looks like we've got just enough time to get to Rosa's if traffic isn't too bad."

Her growling stomach nearly drowned out her last few words. God, she was starved. She really hoped Rosa wouldn't mind her raiding her kitchen. Suzanne felt a pang of guilt as she realized that if she was this starved, Roman must be desperate for food, given that he had to have a good fifty pounds on her. All of it muscle. Seriously sexy muscle...

"You need to eat," he said, clearly expecting her to

argue with him.

But even if she could go without food a little while longer, she knew he couldn't. "We both do." She got the driver's attention. "Change of plans. Can you pull over at that pizza place on the corner?" Turning to Roman, she said, "It's a hidden gem. They make this one pizza that's the best I've ever had. It's called the—"

"New York Classic." His unexpected smile made her heart temporarily stop beating. God, he was good looking. Especially when his man-of-stone mask fell away.

"You know it?"

"I used to work there. In high school." He almost looked a little bashful as he admitted, "I came up with the toppings for that pizza."

It was one of the first personal things he'd told her about himself without her pushing him to share, and the knowledge was strangely sweet.

"Amazing," she said, not quite sure at the moment if she was talking about the fact that he'd created her favorite pizza...or about the connection that seemed to be growing between them by the second. "You grew up in the city?"

"The Bronx. But a friend's uncle owned the place, and all the free pizza I could eat was a big lure."

She couldn't quite put her finger on why it felt like there was more to his story than just a high school kid working to earn some extra money. Maybe it was the hint of emotion he hadn't quite concealed when he'd mentioned his friend's uncle. Or maybe it was the interesting mixture of anticipation and dread on his face at the thought of getting pizza with her there tonight.

Given that she was supposed to be working on a plan to get Roman out of her life as quickly as possible, she shouldn't be so intrigued by him. Shouldn't be trying to figure out what made him tick. But she'd never been one to turn away from something that didn't quite add up.

Especially when that something looked as good in a suit as he did.

The cab stopped, and Roman gave the driver a twenty before she could take care of it. "You don't always have to pay," she said. "In fact, you never should, since technically you work for my company."

But he acted like he didn't hear her as he opened the door to the restaurant. When, she wondered, was the last time she'd been with a guy who had held the door for her to any room but a bedroom?

Not, of course, that she was *with* Roman. She needed to remind herself of that, because coming here almost felt like a date. None of the guys she'd been out with would have considered this little hole-in-the-wall pizza place up to their standards—not when they were all trying so hard to impress everyone with their fancy suits and expensive watches. Didn't they realize that it was guys like Roman who truly impressed, in large part because he didn't have to try at all?

Seriously. She needed to stop letting her hormones get the best of her. But it wasn't easy to stop feeling all the feelings when the guys behind the counter saw Roman and couldn't contain their excitement.

"Roman, dude, it's you!" The kid at the register yelled back to the kitchen, "Roman is here!"

A gray-haired man in a white chef's cap came out of the kitchen, his face split in a wide smile. "Mr. Huson, it's been too long."

The two men did the one-armed, shoulder-to-shoulder hug Suzanne had seen her brothers do a million times. In an instant, she could see that they were more than friends. They might not be related by blood, but they were clearly family. Again, she wondered what the full story was.

"Jerry," Roman said, taking a step to the side, "this is Suzanne." She recognized the gleam in Jerry's eyes. It was the one every matchmaker had when they thought they were looking at a happy couple. Evidently, Roman saw it too, because he quickly added, "I've recently begun working with her."

Jerry's face fell slightly at the news that Cupid hadn't struck Roman with an arrow, but his smile was still completely genuine as he shook her hand. "It's a pleasure to meet you, Suzanne."

"I absolutely *love* your pizza," she said, hoping that would help take the sting out of the fact that she and Roman were most definitely not a couple. "When I was in high school, my friends and I always used to be late back from lunch because we couldn't stand to waste even a bite."

"Beautiful *and* with great taste." No one could have missed the look Jerry shot Roman. One so obvious that she found herself blushing.

"Suzanne has a meeting in a few minutes," Roman said in a more brusque tone than he needed to, given that everyone in the restaurant clearly thought the sun rose and set on every move he made. "Is there any way you can fast-track a New York Classic for us?"

"Sure thing." Jerry turned back to her. "Don't let him fool you, Suzanne. All that growling is just for show. And we've renamed that pizza." He grinned. "It's the Roman Classic now."

Suzanne was pretty sure Roman might have growled if Jerry hadn't hightailed it back to the kitchen just then. "Why don't you go say a few words to your fan club while I grab a table? I'll barely be a few feet away, right in your line of sight."

Before she even sat down, he was surrounded by a handful of teenage boys. They were all talking to him at once, and while she could tell that he was listening, she knew he was also keeping perfect track of where she was and what she was doing.

No man had ever been so aware of her—and she'd definitely never been this aware of a man. Unfortunately, while he was being paid to pay attention to her, she was simply exhibiting a serious and pathetic lack of self-control.

A few minutes later, he sat down. "Sorry about that. I've known Jerry for so long, and he's desperate for me to be hap—" He cut his sentence short. "I apologize that he thought you were my girlfriend."

Suzanne tried to ignore the twinge of longing for that to be true. "You don't have to apologize for anything. He's very sweet. He obviously wants you to find a nice girl to settle down with."

He frowned, looking even more uncomfortable than he had just seconds before. "He knows better."

"Why would you say that?"

Her too-intimate question sent Roman's impenetrable mask falling right back into place. "Trust me, you don't want to know."

Of course she wanted to know. She was *dying* to push. To poke. To dig until she got answers. Until she uncovered the man behind the always professional bodyguard. But she'd lived with her brothers long enough to know that a direct hit was rarely the way to get what you wanted. It would be better to try to loosen him up again before fishing for more.

"This must be a pretty boring job for you, watching a bunch of computer geeks all day, isn't it?"

He looked momentarily surprised by her change of subject. "I'm not bored at all. It's my job to deal with physical threats, but the kind of threats you're protecting people from are coming faster and darker all the time. What you're doing with your digital security software, it's important. And plenty interesting."

She was surprised that he truly did seem to find her job interesting. Most guys she'd dated outside of her industry were either bored to tears by her career or threatened by her being the CEO.

"What kind of people do you usually work with?"

"Athletes. Politicians. Actors. Musicians."

"So I'm your first nerd girl, huh?"

When he stopped in mid-sip of his water, she realized it had sounded like yet another double entendre. One she hadn't meant despite her whole seductress plan.

Or had she? Because somehow the idea of being Roman's first nerd girl didn't sound all that bad...

He recovered first. "Definitely the first who keeps calling herself a nerd and a geek. Less than that got you a black eye back when I was in school."

"In my world, *nerd* and *geek* aren't insults. As far

back as I can remember, I was always the president of the computer club. And honestly, there's always been so much gossip about my family that a bunch of kids throwing those words into it wouldn't have made much difference."

His face was often a mask that she couldn't read, but in that moment, she saw what looked like empathy for her past. Maybe even commiseration, as if his own childhood hadn't been a bed of roses either. Yet again, she wanted to shift from patiently waiting for him to open up, to asking direct questions that would help her better understand all of Roman's many intriguing layers.

One of his teenage fanboys brought over their pizza. "Here you go, Roman. Hope you like it."

The kid kept standing there until Roman took a bite and said, "Best one I've had in years."

"Thanks, man." The smile on the kid's face made it look as if he had just won the lottery. He scooted back to tell the rest of the staff.

"They really do love you here."

"They're good kids, but they've heard too many stories." She wanted to ask him to tell her those stories, but before she could, he said, "Not like with your employees. Today, when you were working with them, you were the sun everyone was revolving around while you made magic happen with the servers."

His compliment made her insides feel all warm and fuzzy. "My team is great. Super smart. Nice too. Any one of them could start their own company. It's an honor to have them working for me. Especially when we're tackling difficult puzzles like we were today."

He studied her as if he was confused about something. "The puzzle of what you were working on appealed to you despite the reason for the extra work and how angry you were about it, didn't it?"

Most people could know her for years and not understand this. But Roman had gotten it inside of one day. She couldn't help but think back to what he'd said, about how the last guy she'd dated hadn't understood her. Roman clearly did.

"I'm not at all happy about the attack, of course, but figuring out how to thwart the bad guys is always interesting. It's part of the reason I decided to focus on digital security as opposed to building other kinds of software applications. That, and the fact that I want people to feel safe whenever they're online."

Somewhere in there, she realized what a terrible job she was doing of seducing him into breaking his bodyguard rules. She should be talking about anything but software applications. If only her female cousins were here right now to give her a refresh on their flirting lessons from all those years ago.

What was it they had said? *Lean in close, then flatter him.* And if that didn't work—*Pretend he has something on his mouth and reach over to help him clean up.*

Scooting her chair closer, she looked deeply into Roman's eyes. "I know this may come as a bit of a surprise, but you make me feel really safe." She'd meant to say it as mere flattery, but as soon as the words left her lips, she realized she meant them. She still didn't need a bodyguard, but that didn't mean she hadn't noticed feeling extra secure whenever Roman was near.

He didn't say anything for a long moment. Finally, he replied, "I'm glad."

The moment hung between them, heavy with exactly the kind of sparks she'd previously told herself were integral to succeeding in her plan to make him quit. Only, it didn't feel so much like a plan anymore.

No, the heat between them felt *real*.

Real enough that she instinctively reached up to touch his jaw, and not because there was anything to wipe away. As her fingertips made contact with his warm, tanned skin, *she* was a hairsbreadth away from kissing *him*.

Before she could, he shoved his chair back from the table and stood up. "If you're done, we should go to your meeting."

Disappointment rang through her at the way he'd

leaped up to get away from her. Even though he was right. Her fake-seduction plan was supposed to lead to a kiss—but not a real one.

He'd just narrowly saved her from screwing up her own plan.

"Right." She pushed away from the table too. "Let's go." She forced a smile for Jerry and his teenage staff. "Thank you for the great pizza."

"I hope to see you two again soon."

Keeping the smile frozen on her face, she nodded. "Bye."

Roman hung behind for a few moments as Jerry said something to him in a low voice. By the time Roman hailed them a cab, his face had returned to looking like thunder. And the truth was that Suzanne's insides suddenly felt just as stormy.

Because though she had absolutely no intention of falling for the bodyguard she'd never wanted in the first place, she couldn't help but wonder if she was really as in control as she'd originally planned to be.

CHAPTER SEVEN

Don't let this one slip away, Roman. She's perfect for you.

Was Jerry nuts, saying that right as they'd been walking out of the restaurant? Clearly, the man had taken one look at Suzanne's pretty face and lost his mind.

Couldn't he see that she was as untouchable as they came? And not just because she was too smart and successful for a guy like Roman, whose only teenage refuge had been working in a pizza joint. Suzanne deserved a guy who could give her a solid relationship. A guy who had grown up learning how to love from two parents who were happy together.

Roman would never be that guy.

It shouldn't matter that he wasn't. He was her bodyguard, not a blind date set up by her brothers. But after spending an entire day being more impressed with her by the minute, for the first time in a very long time, he found himself wishing that things were different. That *he* was different.

At thirty-six, Roman was old enough to be brutally

honest about who he was. He'd enjoyed the company of plenty of women. But he never let things get serious with any of them. Huson men didn't do serious. Not after Roman's father had made the mistake of falling in love with a woman with a white-collar upbringing who'd slummed it with him for long enough to have Roman, then she got bored, cheated, and left. Tommy Huson never missed an opportunity to hammer these facts home, and he insisted that his son not make the same mistake. Roman had made other mistakes in the past three decades, but trusting a woman with his heart wasn't one of them.

Their taxi ride was a silent one, as Suzanne also seemed to be brooding. He enjoyed talking with her more than with any other woman, but this silence was better. Safer. For both of them.

They soon arrived at Drake's loft. "Remind me, what's this meeting for?"

"Rosa has recently launched a foundation to fight online bullying, and I'm helping her out in my spare time."

"Spare time?" He nearly laughed out loud at her even using those words. "When do you get some of that?" After only one day, he could already see how tightly she was stretched. No wonder her brothers wanted someone to take care of her. Roman wasn't sure she would ever take the time to take care of herself—not when others needed her.

The door opened before she could reply, and she was swept up into a hug. "Sorry I'm late, Rosa."

Of course, he recognized the woman hugging Suzanne. Rosalind Bouchard was unarguably the most famous reality TV star in the world. He'd heard she'd recently left the business—he supposed it had come in the wake of her nude-picture scandal. He didn't know much about her beyond the headlines that popped up on the Internet, but he felt for anyone who'd had to go through that kind of unwanted exposure.

He knew all too well how much it sucked to have someone peddle you out for their own gain—especially when the last thing you wanted was to be used that way.

"I'm glad you were able to squeeze us in at all, Suz." Rosa held Suzanne at arm's length. "Wow, you look amazing in that dress. Do you have a date later tonight?"

"Dates? What are those?" Suzanne joked, but by now he knew the different tenors in her voice well enough to recognize the tiny bit of sadness that hung behind the humor when she spoke about being single.

Rosa suddenly noticed him. "Oh, hi!"

"Rosa, this is Roman." Before the other woman could make any wrong assumptions, Suzanne added, "He's my bodyguard. I'm sure Drake told you all about what they did behind my back, right?"

"He did, and I was really mad at him." She scowled. "I told Drake they shouldn't have hired a bodyguard without your permission."

"I agree. But as you can see"—Suzanne nodded toward Roman—"what's done is done."

"You're being much nicer than I'm afraid I would be," Rosa said. She turned again to Roman. "In any case, it's nice to meet you. Come on inside and make yourselves comfortable. There's plenty of food and drink. Let me introduce you both to everyone."

Five minutes later, Roman had memorized another half-dozen names and faces. He'd make sure to look them all up tonight to ensure that none of them posed a potential threat to Suzanne.

Drake wasted little time in taking him out on the patio so that they could speak in private. Roman made sure to stand where he had a clear sight line to Suzanne.

"So, how's it going with Suz? You're still here at the end of day one, so that's something."

"She's not happy about having me around, but she's been so busy today at work that I don't think she's had time to do much about getting rid of me."

"She's smarter than all of us combined," Drake said, obviously immensely proud of his sister.

"No offense to you and your brothers, but I've got

to agree with you there," Roman said. "I've never seen anyone's brain work so fast. Her colleagues are constantly racing to try to keep up."

"I'm not much of a computer guy, but the stuff she works on is really interesting, isn't it?"

"It is. Everyone in her company is young and energetic and undaunted. Most of all, your sister." Which was why Roman needed Drake to know something. "There was another server attack this afternoon. A bad one, from what I could gather."

With a low curse, Drake turned to look with concern at Suzanne, who was already knee-deep in planning with the others around the coffee table. "I'm assuming that since she's here, she's already fixed the problem?"

"She did."

"I know she's convinced it's just a little unimportant funny business, possibly from one of the many companies whose buyout offers she has repeatedly turned down—"

"Don't worry," Roman assured Drake. "Even if she's willing to look at these server attacks as more of a challenge than anything else, you can let Alec and Harry know that I'm not going anywhere until we've gotten to the bottom of things. I won't let anything happen to her."

Drake seemed to weigh his words for a few moments. "Alec said you're the best."

"I am." Roman might not be proud of some of the things he'd done in his life, but he was proud of the way he ran his security business. No one had ever been hurt on his watch. No one ever would. "I promise you, she's safe with me."

* * *

By the time they left Drake and Rosa's, Suzanne was way too exhausted to even think about putting on her "sexy" act. Heck, she couldn't even bother to put on her shoes at this point, carrying them instead as she tried to stay awake long enough to get into the cab.

She curled up on the seat, rubbing her feet and yawning. "I've got a six thirty a.m. meeting tomorrow, so I'll be heading out an hour before."

"Do you always move this fast?"

Her eyes had fallen closed and she couldn't muster up the energy to open them as she replied, "You mean sloth speed?"

She didn't hear his response, or remember the rest of the taxi ride. Only that she woke up to Roman's hand on her arm. "We're home."

Years ago, she had learned how to catnap during a nonstop day. She'd obviously just done that in the taxi. It always took her a good sixty seconds to come fully awake again, so she was really glad Roman was there to help her out of the taxi and into the lobby of her building, his hand on the small of her back to make sure she stayed on course in her sleepy state.

It was a little weird coming home with Roman like this. Not like being walked in by a date. But not as if he was just someone working for her either. In any case, she was too tired to make sense of her feelings right now.

As they rode the elevator up to her floor, she said, "Having you around today wasn't as bad as I thought it would be." Clearly, she was also too tired to keep her mouth shut.

The deep resonance of his unexpected laughter moved through her body like a sip of good red wine. Like he had the night before, he did a quick search of her apartment. But unlike last night, she wasn't irritated with him. Instead, a part of her wished he would stay a little longer.

"Good night, Suzanne." The way his voice wrapped around her name made her feel the same way his laughter had—warm all over. "I'll be waiting here in the morning."

"Are you sure five thirty isn't too early for you?"

"Any time you need me, I'll be here."

She understood that as her bodyguard he had to say that. But a secret little part of her couldn't help but wish he meant it as something more. Her family had always been there for her no matter what, but none of the guys she'd dated had ever wanted to step up like that.

He waited in the hall outside her door until she was inside. After putting her bag on her kitchen island and dropping her heels on the floor, she headed straight for her living room couch. The bed was too far tonight.

She'd fallen asleep in the taxi, but only because she knew Roman wouldn't let anything happen to her under his watch. Now, as she lay sprawled on the couch still wearing her purple dress, her brain slid back to that moment in the pizza place when they'd been close enough that she could feel his warmth radiating through to her.

When she'd touched his face, his eyes had gone so dark. So sexy. So intense. She would have bet money on his kissing her then—he'd seemed to want to devour her mouth as much as she wanted him to do it. But his control had been too good, too solid, and the moment had slipped away.

She'd lost her chance to see her plan through to its final conclusion tonight. But it was losing her chance to find out how Roman's lips would feel brushing over hers that she regretted most of all.

Had she been less tired, that realization would have shaken her to the core. It should have shaken her awake so that she could make even better plans to ensure that he'd resign soon. Because what she was feeling for Roman was crazy. And Suzanne didn't do crazy emotions with men. After all, look what had happened between her parents when they'd let crazy emotions get the best of them. Her mother had killed herself and her father had become a recluse.

But with all of Suzanne's defenses currently down tonight, she didn't have more energy to think clearly about how to protect herself from falling for a man who made her feel so many confusing, heated, conflicting things. All she could do was drift off to sleep dreaming of his kisses.

CHAPTER EIGHT

"Good morning, Suzanne."

She'd awakened more than a little horrified by the dreams she'd had about Roman. Just as sweaty and acrobatic as her dreams had been the night before...but also emotional now. In her dreams, they hadn't just been having a one-night stand. They'd been having a *relationship*.

Now, all it took was hearing the low rumble of her name on his lips for that familiar warmth to move through her.

Mustering up the energy for day two of her master plan to get him to resign as her bodyguard had been even more difficult than she'd anticipated. It wasn't the long hours she'd put in yesterday. She was used to keeping that kind of schedule.

No, it was the fact that she wasn't at all looking forward to trying to play the seductress again today. She was used to being herself, not pretending. Which was why she had barely been able to force herself to put on another sexy outfit this morning, when her T-shirts and oh-so-comfortable flats were calling to her.

Still, even if the off-white dress with the red pin-stripes was neither as body-skimming nor as short as yesterday's dress, she had a strong enough will to make herself wear red heels. In flats, she would have been dashing around the way she normally did, without a single thought for sex appeal. In heels, she'd at least have some swing to her hips as she walked.

And she needed to stick to her plan, damn it. No matter how much she liked seeing Roman first thing in the morning...and last thing at night.

Knowing that cranky and grumpy wouldn't get her any closer to completing her plan, she made herself smile as they stepped into the elevator. "Are you a morning person?"

"No."

His concise and rather heartfelt response made her laugh. Honestly, it was a relief just to let it flow through her. Maybe, she told herself, if she let herself relax a bit this morning, it might help her get things moving in the direction she needed them to go. Because she did still need to get him to step over the line with a kiss...

"You could have fooled me," she replied, laughter still in her voice. "Alec always stomps around in a pissy mood for a couple of hours if you wake him up early. Whereas you're quite pleasant this morning."

"I've never heard anyone refer to Alec Sullivan as *pissy* before," Roman commented dryly as the elevator doors opened and they headed through the lobby to catch a cab to her office. "Never heard anyone live to tell about it, at least."

"My brother works really hard at projecting that intimidating image," she said, "but the truth is that underneath it all, he's a pussycat."

"Pussycat?" She could tell Roman was trying not to laugh. "If you say so."

"Trust me, Alec might do the tough player act to perfection, but when he finally falls in love one day, he's going to turn to absolute mush. And it's going to be *awesome* to watch his downfall."

Roman finally let his own grin loose. "I know plenty of people who would pay good money to see that."

He was so handsome when he smiled that just sitting next to him in the taxi made all her girl parts flip around inside. Honestly, if he hadn't been a bodyguard foisted on her against her will, she'd be jumping him six ways to Sunday. Especially given her extremely long dry spell. A woman had needs, after all. A couple of times in the past she'd hooked up with a guy she knew from another company at a conference for a quick fix. Today, the thought of it made her scrunch up her nose. She didn't want anyone else. She wanted Ro—

God. *No.*

Soon, if she played her cards right, Roman would be resigning his position with her. And then she would be all alone again, with no one to wait outside her front door every morning. No one to laugh with about her brothers. No one with muscles to sneak glimpses of throughout the day. No one to tease by wearing the sexy dresses and heels her cousins had filled her closets with over the years. No one to tell her to grab some dinner instead of heading straight into her next meeting. No one to go running with her when she needed to shake off a morning of intense work. No one to put his arms around her when she needed just that.

Okay, so maybe his leaving didn't sound quite as good when she looked at things in that light. Nonetheless, she already knew all the reasons she needed to soldier on. Not only because she didn't need a bodyguard and couldn't let her brothers win, but also because Suzanne made it a point to keep her relationships with men neat and tidy, nice and calm—the polar opposite of her parents' destructive relationship.

But Roman pushed buttons in Suzanne that no other man had pushed before. He made her feel things she'd never felt before. So she couldn't let him stay. Couldn't take the risk of losing control of her emotions the way her mother and father had with each other. Which meant it was time to gear up for her seductress act again.

When it came to brainstorming software or new digital security plans, she couldn't turn her brain off. But trying to figure out what to say or do to be "sexy" made her mind go completely blank.

She would have laughed at herself if she hadn't been so irritated by her own ineptitude. But before she could either laugh—or groan—her phone rang. She pulled it out of her bag, and though she didn't recognize the number, she picked up anyway. There was no response on the other end.

She already knew how this was going to play out for the next several hours, damn it. One call would turn into a hundred or more. No one would ever be on the other end, and there wouldn't be any messages either. Unfortunately, even her fastest tracer software hadn't yet had any success, because the numbers were generated from all over the world. Once she had a few more business items checked off of her to-do list, she'd definitely be putting more effort into digging into the junk calls and server attacks.

But though she already had turned the phone from ringtone to vibrate, she couldn't put it away or turn it off. Not when someone at her company—or one of her family members—might legitimately be trying to reach her at the same time that the barrage of fake calls was coming in.

"This is what your brothers were talking about, isn't it?" Roman said in a dark voice.

She'd been so hopeful that this wouldn't happen while he was still around. But since her phone was currently buzzing like crazy, she simply told him, "It's irritating, but it isn't dangerous." She knew she sounded defensive, but she didn't want him to think a bunch of phone calls all coming one after another from random numbers meant she needed a bodyguard.

"Stalking often starts out as an irritation before it escalates." There was no hint of laughter left in his voice from their earlier conversation. "Especially when the target doesn't respond the way the stalker wants her to."

She didn't bother to hold back an eye roll. "I don't have a stalker. I told you, my business is highly competitive. And not everyone plays by the same rules."

"You would never play by these rules."

"No," she agreed. "And it's not just because I'm a woman."

"I never said anything about your gender. I'm talking about the fact that you've created a company that's the envy of everyone in the tech world. I'm talking about who you are."

The way he said that made her pause. It sounded as though he thought he'd already figured her out. And she liked the thought of Roman understanding her—

the real her—way too much.

"Just because I walk the straight and narrow with my business doesn't mean I'm naïve about the ones who like to skirt the line between right and wrong. They don't frighten me. Their tactics are just another challenge to work through."

"How are you working through this one?"

She didn't love the answer she was about to give, but because it was the honest one, she gave it anyway. "I've been so busy with the new product that I haven't given it much attention yet."

"And now that the product launch is rolling along?"

"If it becomes a bigger problem, I'll make it a priority."

"How big a problem does it need to become to get on your priority list, Suzanne?"

His words were deceptively calm and soft-spoken. But she knew better, had learned a long time ago, while growing up as the only female in a house full of males, how to read between a man's lines.

"I know your job is to look around every corner for the worst," she said in just as deceptively placid a voice, when in truth she was bristling, "but until I find some evidence that I'm in personal danger, I'm going to keep my priorities where they are."

"What if the evidence of a problem comes in the form of a knife or a bullet?"

She couldn't contain her shock. "You're kidding, right?"

"I wish I was."

"My servers and phone are the only things that have been attacked. Why on earth do you think someone would come after me personally when that's not how these guys work?"

"You tell me. After all, you're the one who is building one of the world's best digital security companies. I'm just doing the same thing here from my end. Doing whatever I can to make sure you stay physically safe and sound, no matter what."

It was way too early in the morning for this conversation, especially when she hadn't had nearly enough sleep last night. Because she'd been having sexy and romantic dreams about Roman. Thankfully, the taxi pulled up to her office building a moment later.

Still, as they walked inside in silence, she couldn't deny that his pointed questioning had gotten under her skin in a way her brothers' constant nagging over the issue hadn't. With Alec, Harry, and Drake, she'd been able to reason that they were being hypersensitive because they felt they needed to look after her.

But though they'd filled Roman's head with their worries, he did protect people for a living. And did it well, if Alec had been willing to trust him with her. Which meant that Roman must have a finely tuned radar for danger.

Danger that he seemed to think was real.

She shook her head, forcing the annoying thoughts away. She didn't have time for this today. Or any day, frankly. Thank God for her six thirty meeting and all the other work she had to do until that evening, so that she couldn't stew.

One thing was for sure, she couldn't pull off the whole be-sexy-to-tempt-Roman-into-resigning act right now. Nope, today it was going to take all of her energy to ignore the doubts he'd planted in her head.

And to forget the feelings about Roman she had begun to have, whether she wanted to or not, especially while he was standing guard over her not ten feet away all day long.

* * *

Roman knew Suzanne was upset with him for making her look at the hard truth of her situation. She was one of the most innately positive people he'd ever met. He hated to chip away at her faith in human nature. But he also couldn't let her keep her head in the sand. Not if it meant she might end up getting hurt.

Her morning was a repeat of the day before, with one meeting bleeding into the next. The only difference was the way her phone continued to buzz. She gave it to her assistant and asked Jeannie to monitor the calls in case something important came up amid the junk calls.

Five hours later, her phone finally stopped ringing. And that was right when his started—with a string of text messages from one of the underground personal investigators he'd contacted last night.

Instead of going to bed after taking Suzanne home the previous evening, Roman had put out feelers to get backgrounds on the people he'd met at the Sullivan Security offices and at Rosa and Drake's place. He'd also looked up Suzanne's top competitors and had sent their names to his contacts, as well.

Pulling out his phone, he read the texts not once, but twice.

Damn it. Why hadn't Suzanne told him about this?

He knew she didn't want him there, but she'd seemed so genuine. He understood that women lied, but after spending time with her, he'd wanted to believe she was different.

His jaw clenched tighter and tighter as he waited for her to conclude her current meeting. As soon as she was off the conference call and Jeannie popped in to let her know that she was going to hold any further calls until mid-afternoon so that Suzanne could get some lunch, Roman moved out of his position in the back corner of her office.

"I'd like to speak with you about something I just

learned."

Her hand was on the back of her neck, working to rub out the kinks from doing so many back-to-back meetings. He had to shove away the urge to rub it for her as she said, "What now?"

For the past five hours, she'd been unfailingly polite to everyone she worked with, even when a few people weren't delivering the results she was looking for. She had a knack for being encouraging, yet firm, without the temper tantrums some CEOs were famous for. But he knew he was pushing all her buttons simply by being here.

Too bad for her that he was going to be pushing those buttons even harder after what he'd found out.

"Seems you left out an important piece of information this morning when we were talking about why someone might go after you personally."

She looked so confused it was almost comical. Except that nothing about her situation was funny. Not if she was in danger.

"Left something out?" She spun her chair around so that she was facing him. "What are you talking about?"

"Craig Boylan."

Her eyes grew big, a beat before her face colored slightly. Obviously, she knew why he was asking her about that guy specifically. A beat behind surprise came anger. "You're snooping into my personal life now?"

"I'm not snooping," he clarified. "Doing backgrounds on the people you work with is part of my job."

"A job I never asked you to do."

Though he couldn't argue that point, he still needed to know more. "Tell me about your association with Mr. Boylan."

"Craig is harmless," she said with a wave of her hand.

Roman moved another step closer. "Craig is the co-founder of CP Systems, one of Sullivan Security's top competitors." He paused to make sure she understood just how bad it was that she had deliberately kept this information from him. "And an ex."

But she didn't look even the slightest bit guilty. In fact, all he got from her was another eye roll. "I wouldn't call someone I only slept with a couple of times an ex."

Jealousy slapped him upside the head before he was prepared to slap it back. "He might not agree."

"Of course he does. It didn't mean any more to him than it did to me. We were at a conference. We had a little too much to drink. One thing led to another. In the morning, we went our separate ways."

She was so off the cuff about it, as if she hadn't given the interlude another thought since it happened. Whereas Roman knew the guy had to be still pining for her. Who wouldn't be?

"You were together more than once."

Finally, she got up out of her chair to come at him. Close enough for him to see that her pupils had dilated slightly. "I can't believe you're grilling me for the details," she shot at him. "If I didn't know better, I'd think you were jealous."

She was wearing another outfit today that should be illegal—a sexy dress that cupped her breasts and waist and fluttered around her thighs, with fire-red heels that were the cherry on top of the sexy outfit. She was always breathtakingly beautiful, but when her eyes were spitting fire like this, he was hard-pressed not to give in to the answering fire leaping inside him.

Nonetheless, he couldn't let her know that she was dead on the money about jealousy eating away at him. He had no right to care that she'd slept with someone else. He wasn't her boyfriend. Wasn't anything but the paid help. Unfortunately, those hard, cold facts weren't doing a damned thing to douse his feelings.

Deliberately ignoring her comment, in as measured a voice as he could manage with her scent drawing him in even deeper, he said, "You wouldn't impede anyone else here in doing their job." From her reaction to hearing the guy's name, he now realized she truly didn't think she had been keeping anything from him in the taxi that morning when he'd asked about who might be a personal threat. She truly thought this guy she'd had a two-night stand with was harmless. If there was any chance at all that he wasn't, Roman needed to know. "Help me do mine."

"I can already tell you that you're barking up the wrong tree, but so you don't feel like I've left one single thing out, the second—and last—time Craig and I had sex, we were at SecureCon." He could feel the bravado behind her words, the way she was trying to act so tough about sleeping with some guy she had no emotional connection with. But Roman knew firsthand how empty that could leave you. "Since he hadn't made a big deal about the first time we hooked up, I decided to give him another whirl."

In her fury, she'd moved close enough that her chest was now pressed against his. He could feel how soft she was, how perfect. Sweet Lord, he'd known this job was going to be hard, but he'd had no idea how difficult things could get.

"Is that enough detail for you," she said, "or do you need positions too?"

Visions hit him—hard—of Suzanne naked and entwined with some other guy. Those pictures in his head twisted his gut into knots, even as he could barely look away from her full, red lips. Lips he was barely holding himself back from tasting.

Devouring.

"I've got what I need now," he gritted out past a jaw clenched brutally tight. Roman couldn't believe he had spent twenty years honing his control, only to have one beautiful, brilliant woman unravel it as easily as she would a ball of yarn.

"Well, that's good to hear," she said with no small measure of sarcasm. "Let me know if you change your mind, and I'll be happy to walk you through every single thing we did during our two nights together."

As far as Roman could see, Suzanne didn't believe much in fighting—she usually leaned toward calm and rational to make her point when she was working. But when she finally decided to get into the ring, she was scrappy. His respect for her rose another notch even as jealousy continued to hit him low and hard in the gut from her well-aimed jab.

Right now, however, he needed to clear the red haze from his brain so that he could make a plan to keep Suzanne safe for a couple of hours while he went to put the fear of God into Craig.

And yet, in the moment, he didn't see how he could possibly do anything but erase that final inch between them, how he could stop himself from dragging her all the way into his arms and crushing her mouth beneath his.

He almost had his hands on her—was *this close* to kissing her—when a knock sounded at the door. She bounded out of his almost-embrace at the same moment he forced himself to take a step back.

They were both surprised to hear Harry's voice. "Hey, Suz. Can I come in?"

He watched as Suzanne worked to pull herself together so that she could open the door for her brother without looking as if she'd been on the verge of making out with her bodyguard.

"Of course you can." She pasted on a smile and opened her arms. "What a nice surprise."

Harry returned her hug, but frowned as he pulled away and took a closer look at her outfit. He seemed to be especially surprised by her shoes. "You look..." He shook his head as if he couldn't quite believe his eyes. "I've never seen you wearing such..."

"These clothes have been hanging in my closet forever!"

"Sorry." Harry seemed to realize that he'd upset her. "You look really nice, sis. Just a little fancier than usual." When her expression barely softened, he wisely stopped digging himself deeper. "I was hoping you might be able to squeeze me in for lunch. Any chance of that?"

Finally, she gave him a smile. "I'd love it." Her smile faded again as she turned back to Roman. "You can trust me to have a meal alone with my brother, right?"

"You bet. I'm going to step out while you two eat." He looked at Harry. "It would be great if you'd stay with Suzanne until I return."

Her mouth set into a hard—but still gorgeous—line. "I don't need a constant babysitter."

"I didn't only come to eat," Harry said, obviously working to smooth things over with the sister he adored. "I also wanted to get your thoughts on some new research I've been trying to figure out how to best present to my students. You always seem to have a knack for getting inside their heads."

Looking slightly appeased by the fact that her brother was looking for her advice, she put her arm through Harry's and walked away from Roman without a second glance.

CHAPTER NINE

"I was going to ask how things are going with Roman," Harry said as they headed for her company's dining hall, "but from that exchange I just witnessed, it seems I've already got my answer."

Still fuming, Suzanne replied, "It's bad enough that he thinks he's in charge of my safety, as if I can't take care of myself, but now he's digging into—"

She bit back the rest of her sentence when several of her employees came over to Harry to say hello. Her brothers were always a hit around the office, partly because they were so nice to everyone at her company parties—but mostly, she suspected, because they were so good looking. Thankfully, her brothers knew better than to date anyone on her staff. Few things would need more damage control than if Alec or Harry broke one of her engineers' hearts.

Bypassing the sushi and salad bars, she headed straight for the burger and fries station. Normally, she ate healthier food, but after her showdown with Roman—a showdown she was all but certain she had lost—she needed to drown her irritation in a big plate of grease.

After she and Harry had their food on trays, she suggested they head back to her office. They usually ate in here with everyone else, but she was afraid she was going to have a hard time keeping her voice down while talking about Roman.

No one had ever torn at her self-control the way he did. Right from the first night she'd met him, he'd driven her absolutely bonkers. The only silver lining, she thought with a slightly evil upturn of her lips, was that she was certain she was driving him equally nuts.

Back in her office, Suzanne and Harry sat at the glass café table in the corner by the window…after she cleaned off the stack of computers, tablets, and phones that had taken up residence there.

Harry, who could eat pretty much anyone under the table and never gain an ounce due to the jousting and fencing he loved so much, immediately dug into his food. Suzanne, on the other hand, couldn't eat anything just yet. Not when her stomach was still so twisted up over Roman's behavior.

Not when she was still so twisted up over her *own* behavior.

Because even when she'd been furious with him for accusing her of keeping her fling with Craig from him, she had wanted to kiss him.

"What exactly is Roman digging into?" Harry asked.

She stood up and started pacing. "My personal life."

She hadn't meant to spit the words at her brother. Although it *was* his fault that Roman was around in the first place.

When a pang hit her in the middle of the chest at the thought of Roman *not* being around, she got even angrier. It wasn't like her to waffle like this or to be wishy-washy over a guy. And it definitely wasn't like her to break her own hard-and-fast rules about men. Rules she'd vowed to keep as soon as she'd been old enough to understand how destructive her parents' marriage had been.

She had always made sure that the men she dated fell into a specific category. Good looking and fun and intelligent, of course, but also careful not to push her too far or too fast. The men she'd been with had been respectful of her wanting to move their relationship forward at a safe, careful, civilized speed.

Whereas the sparks that kept shooting between her and Roman felt almost primitive. Reckless. Wild. All the out-of-control emotions that had torn her parents to shreds.

"What parts of your personal life is he digging into?" In typical Harry style, his tone was gentle.

She hadn't told any of her brothers about sleeping

with one of the founders of CP Systems. It wasn't something they or anyone else needed to know. Now, however, she hated feeling as though she had deliberately hidden it from them. Because wasn't that what Roman had been insinuating earlier? That she should have divulged this information to him when they were talking about anyone who might have it in for her? He'd seemed so angry. So distrustful.

It had hurt to have him look at her like that. More than it should have, when all they were supposed to be to each other was bodyguard and client. Definitely more than it should have when she was currently supposed to be implementing a plan to get him to resign and leave her to go back to the way her life had been before him. Before everything had felt so electric and heated and—

She was doing it again, letting herself spin off on conflicted thoughts and feelings about Roman. She forced her attention back to answering her brother's question. "He's been doing background checks on everyone I come into contact with. And he's got a crazy idea that one of the guys I've"—she paused to search for the right word—"dated could have done this."

"Someone you've dated?" Harry mulled that over. "What makes Roman think it might be personal?"

She looked out her windows over the park. It was a

great day outside. The sky was bright blue, the trees were leafy and green, and flowers were blooming everywhere. If only she could be out there running instead of trapped in her office with Harry having the most mortifying conversation of her life.

"I was—" Darn it, how could she possibly find the right words? Although Harry tended to be the most reasonable of her three brothers, he was protective enough that she was wary of oversharing. But since there was no way around this now, she made herself say, "Intimate." They both grimaced, and she wanted to drop her face into her hands and hide as she finished, "With one of the founders of CP Systems."

Harry dropped his fork onto his plate with a clang. "What the hell, Suz?" He looked nearly as upset as Roman. "How could you just mention this now?"

"Because," she said, unable to hold back a scowl, "like I told Roman, Craig would never hurt me. Trust me, even if he cared that I ended things after we got together those couple of times—which he didn't—he doesn't have it in him."

Harry pushed away from the table and moved to where she was standing at the window. "I do trust you, Suz. We all do. But even nice people can do crazy stuff when their egos are crushed."

"I didn't crush his ego. It wasn't even anything serious."

"Maybe it wasn't serious to you, but what if it was to him?"

Suzanne knew she could be stubborn, but she always tried to make sure that stubbornness didn't edge over into stupid just so she could win her point. When Roman had suggested that Craig might have been more upset than he'd seemed over "losing" her, she'd outright rejected it. But now that Harry was saying the same thing...

She finally accepted that she needed to make herself take a closer look at whether she was wearing rose-colored glasses where Craig was concerned. Maybe she should reach out to him to make sure everything was as okay between them as she'd thought.

Yes, she decided, that approach made the most sense. And then once she confirmed that Craig wasn't an issue, she'd make sure Roman understood that the rest of her personal life was off-limits.

"Okay," she said as she turned to Harry, "I'll admit that you've made me think. I promise I'll look more closely at this possibility."

But instead of looking happy about it, Harry said, "Maybe you should let Roman look into it, Suz."

"No." She wouldn't bend on this. "I'm not going to tiptoe around anyone. If I hurt someone's feelings, I'm going to be the one to ask if that's what I've done. And then I'm going to fix it."

Harry looked as though he wanted to give her more unwanted advice. Wisely, all he said was, "Just be careful, okay? We love you too much to let anything happen to you."

"I love you too. I love all of you, even if you need to stop poking your noses into my life."

"Drake and Alec will be glad to hear that you've forgiven us."

"You and Drake, maybe. But Alec…" She scowled. "You don't have to tell me that he's the one who steamrolled this whole bodyguard thing. I can guess. And I'll tell you what, I *really* don't appreciate the way it's tumbled my life upside down."

"Is it really that bad having Roman around?" Harry held up a hand before she could shout *yes* at him. "Let me ask that another way. From the time I've spent with him, he seems to have a solid head on his shoulders. And Alec wouldn't vouch for someone he doesn't respect the hell out of. Are we both wrong?"

Sometimes she hated being fair. But no matter how annoyed she was with Roman right now—no matter how annoyed she was for the totally unacceptable *feelings* she was having for Roman—she couldn't live with herself if she told her brother lies about him.

"I suppose *solid* is a good word." She crossed her arms over her chest. "Like a big block of cement who is always there whether I'm working or running or with family."

"Doing his job, in other words."

"I suppose so. It's just that…" She tried to put her conflicted emotions into words. "I can never quite focus when he's around."

"You?" Harry looked extremely surprised. "Lose focus?"

"You have no idea how much of a struggle it's been to get things done since Roman's been following me around. He always finds a way to rile me up."

"That's interesting."

Realizing far too late that she'd said far too much, she quickly changed the subject. "Any word from Dad?"

Instead of answering, her brother gently put his hands on her shoulders and moved her back toward the table. "I know how busy your days are here. Sit and eat before someone comes knocking on the door needing you to solve all their problems." After she'd sat and picked up her burger, he said, "It sounds like Dad's been really busy lately on a last-second project that popped up."

"A new house for someone on the lake?" She took a bite of her burger, and it was so delicious she immediately took another bite before even finishing the first.

"He said he'd be able to tell us more about it soon."

"Sounds mysterious."

"Dad always is."

When Suzanne's mother took her own life three decades ago, William Sullivan had pulled back from his four children. Very recently, Suzanne and her brothers had learned that lingering grief over losing his beloved wife wasn't the only reason their father had become so remote. It turned out that he blamed himself—and his obsessive love that had manifested itself as hundreds of paintings of her—for Lynn Sullivan's death.

Suzanne had made sure to tell him that she would never in a million years blame him for her mother's suicide. But while she wasn't sure he believed she meant it, or if he would ever be able to absolve himself of the guilt he felt, at least they were slowly inching closer to the father-daughter relationship she had always longed for.

"What about you?" Since she had just divulged the most embarrassing thing in the world to her brother, she wanted something from him too. "Seeing anyone lately?" Women threw themselves at her good-looking academic brother, but none of them had ever managed to make inroads into Harry's heart.

When he shook his head, she asked, "Surely there's someone you've got your eye on?"

"No, there isn't."

She would have taken his denial at face value had it not been for how fast and how firm it was. As if he wasn't only trying to convince her that he wasn't interested in a specific person—he was trying to convince himself too.

Lord knew she understood that situation all too well right about now...

Harry was saved by a knock at her door. "Come in," Suzanne called. She'd just have to keep working to get the dirt on whatever her brother was hiding from her.

"I'm sorry to disturb the two of you," Jeannie said, "but I've got Cinthia from Brazil on line one. I know you've been trying to reach her for a while."

Harry sat on the couch and reached for one of the pads of paper on the table in front of him. "Go ahead and take the call, Suz. I want to write down some thoughts I've just had about an upcoming talk I'm giving. And then once you're off, I'd still like your feedback about how to best approach that new research I mentioned earlier."

She had a feeling there wasn't really any big problem he needed her help with—and they both knew he could make his notes anywhere else than her office couch. But since he'd given his word to Roman to keep watch over her until he returned, Harry wasn't going anywhere for the time being.

"Sure," she said, eating one last French fry before she picked up the phone and pushed Roman into the very back of her brain.

Unfortunately, even without him standing in the corner of her office taking everything in with his dark, intense eyes—and even while dealing with business matters that demanded every ounce of her focus—she still couldn't stop thinking about him.

No matter how hard she tried.

CHAPTER TEN

Roman covered the handful of city blocks to Craig Boylan's corporate headquarters in record time. He knew better than to let emotion get the best of him. Battles were always better fought with cool and calm.

But just thinking about Suzanne sleeping with this guy made Roman's blood boil. It had been a long time since he had used his fists for sport, but his hands were clenched tight as he shoved through the glossy black doors of the CP Systems building.

Where Suzanne's lobby was bright and welcoming in its simplicity, this one was trying too hard to impress, with dark marble everywhere. Clearly, this guy was making up for deficiencies elsewhere.

And yet, Suzanne had still slept with him.

She wasn't Roman's. She would never be his. But that didn't make the thought of her sleeping with someone else sting any less.

"I need to see Craig Boylan," he told the woman behind the reception desk. "Now."

Flustered by his curt demand, the young woman

opened and closed her mouth a couple of times before any sound came out. "I'm sorry, could you please tell me your name?"

"Roman Huson. I work for Suzanne Sullivan. Which floor is Mr. Boylan on?"

"If you will give me a moment to call his assistant—"

But Roman was already pushing past the security gate and walking into the elevator. The receptionist came running up right as the door closed in her face. Roman figured Craig would be on the top floor. Ornate headquarters and penthouse offices went hand in hand. Along with being bitter enough over losing Suzanne to attack her, tech style. To begin with, at least.

The main-floor receptionist had obviously put a call through to Craig's office by the time the elevator door opened on the top floor. But Roman wasn't about to be stopped by a man wearing a black security guard's uniform who said, "I'm going to have to escort you back downstairs, Mr. Huson."

One quick glance told Roman that the guy wasn't private security. He was strictly a nine-to-fiver who had the easy and likely extremely boring job of making sure that none of the employees stole anything.

Roman walked past the guy and headed for a stern middle-aged woman who he guessed was Craig's personal assistant. "Mr. Boylan is not expecting me, but I work for Suzanne Sullivan, and I need to discuss her safety with him."

"Has something happened to Miss Sullivan?" She sounded genuinely concerned. "Is she all right?"

"She is, and as her personal security detail, I plan to make sure she stays that way." Deciding he'd given Craig's assistant enough time to alert her boss to his presence, he headed toward the closed double doors a short distance from her desk.

"Craig." There were three men in the office, but Roman instantly deduced who his target was. Unfortunately, it wasn't the skinny guy or the short guy. It was the one most women would have referred to as *tall, dark and handsome.* "I'm here for our meeting."

Boylan barely hesitated before saying to the other men with a faint Irish accent, "If you'll excuse me, I'd appreciate it if we could continue our meeting later this afternoon."

Soon they were alone, the double doors closed behind them. "I understand you work for Suzanne Sullivan." He actually had the nerve to look as if he didn't know why Roman was there. "Is there a reason she didn't come to me personally to discuss whatever the problem might be?"

Roman took a deliberately menacing step closer. "I'm here to give you a warning, one I hope you're smart enough to heed." There was a time when he'd regularly used his size and strength to bully people. To hurt them. But though he'd worked like hell to be a different and better person who fought only when necessary—at times like this, he was more than happy to physically intimidate. And he wouldn't hesitate to beat the hell out of this guy, if it came to that.

"A warning?" Craig's frown deepened even as he had the presence of mind to look a little scared.

"Keep your distance from Suzanne. Don't call her. Don't even think about her. And keep your dirty hands off her company."

Craig stared at him in shock. "I can see that you're angry. I just don't know why." He shook his head. "I haven't done anything to Suzanne."

Roman got in the guy's face so quick he didn't have any choice but to stare up at him as Roman growled, "We both know what you did to her. You don't deserve to touch a hair on her head. She might have made the mistake of sleeping with you, but I won't let you keep making her pay for cutting you loose."

The guy's face went ruddy under his perfectly clipped beard. "You're here because we had sex a couple of times? I thought you said you're her new security detail—not her new boyfriend."

Roman's blood was pumping so fast with jealousy—and he was so invested in shutting down any and all threats to Suzanne—that he had the guy up against the wall in a heartbeat. "You're going to promise me right now that you'll leave her alone."

"I have," Craig choked out. "I am."

"Damn right you are. She's wasted enough time and energy on your attacks."

"Attacks?" The other man coughed the word out. "What attacks?"

When Roman was growing up, he'd been taught by his father to throw punches first and not stop until his opponent was completely out of commission. Over the past two decades, he'd always made sure to stop and think clearly before using his fists, especially while on the job. But he was so invested in Suzanne that he hadn't been thinking clearly at all. Hadn't wanted to see that throughout his entire interrogation, Craig had looked more bewildered and confused than like he was trying to hide something.

Abruptly lowering his hands, Roman moved back. "You really don't know anything about what's been happening to her, do you?"

Putting a hand over his throat, Craig shook his head. "I really don't. But I can see it must be pretty serious stuff if you thought you needed to attack me in my own office. What's going on?"

"I can't tell you that. But I will apologize for my behavior. I see now that I made the wrong assumption based on your previous relationship with Suzanne."

"I'm not going to lie to you—there was a time when I did want something more from her than just a couple of nights together. A hell of a lot more. So I get why you're here." The other man walked behind his desk and sat down, impressively composed and in control again. "But whatever's happening to her, I'm not behind it." He pointed to the framed pictures of himself with his arm around a pretty blonde, pictures Roman should have noticed before now.

Jesus. He'd really screwed this one up. Suzanne had already been furious with him before he'd left her office. When he went back and told her where he'd been, she was going to be absolutely livid. So much for convincing her that having him work as her bodyguard wouldn't interfere with her life.

He pulled out a card and laid it on Craig's desk. "If you can think of anyone who might not have her best interests at heart, I'd appreciate the name."

Right then, another man pushed through the door. Where Craig had a slightly rugged look to him, this man was polished, from the top of his head to the tips of his shiny thousand-dollar shoes. "Craig, is there a problem? Eloise said you had an unexpected visitor."

Roman could hear the hint of an Irish accent in this man's voice as well. From the backgrounds he'd done on Suzanne's competitors, he recalled that the men had met at school in Ireland before coming to America to make their fortunes in high tech. Not only did they make digital security software, but they had also ventured very successfully into home automation systems. Their units were in most of the high end homes in the city.

"Roman," Craig said, "this is my partner, Patrick O'Conner. Patrick, Roman works for Suzanne Sullivan. He had some questions for me about a couple of conferences Suzanne and I both attended last year."

Patrick looked at Roman suspiciously, obviously wanting to ask more questions. But when his cell rang, whoever was calling was obviously important enough for him to leave to take the call.

As Roman turned to see himself out, he was surprised to hear Craig say, "Hey, Roman. If I ever find myself needing someone to watch out for my soon-to-be wife, I'm going to give you a call. Despite the bruises I'm bound to have tomorrow, I appreciate the fact that you'll do whatever it takes to protect your client."

Craig was right. Roman would do whatever it took to protect Suzanne. And not just because she was his client.

But because, despite knowing better, he had started to *care*.

CHAPTER ELEVEN

Suzanne knew it must be Roman knocking on her office door by the sound of it—solid, steady, firm, sexy. Okay, so maybe a knock couldn't sound sexy, but somehow he managed the impossible.

A part of her wanted to tell him to go away. The other part wanted to fling open the door and kiss him with all the pent-up passion she'd been trying so ineffectively to shove away.

God. For the first time in her life, she was an utter mess over a guy.

She took a deep breath to try to ground herself, but it was no use. And she couldn't leave him standing outside for much longer, or Harry would wonder what was going on between the two of them. As it was, she was afraid she had already said too much over lunch.

"Come in."

Her office was large and spacious. But the moment Roman stepped inside and closed the door behind him, he dominated the room. And all of her attention.

"I apologize for needing to step out," Roman said

to both of them before turning to Harry. "Thank you for staying with Suzanne until I returned."

"My pleasure." Harry immediately rose from the couch. "Thanks for lunch, sis." After she stood too, he hugged her good-bye. "Your ideas on how to approach my new research were excellent, just like I knew they would be. I swear, you could almost guest teach my classes at this point."

"I'd be happy to take you up on that sometime." She always liked a new challenge, and after reading so many of Harry's books and papers about medieval history over the years, she was nearly as fascinated by the subject as he was. Though she knew Roman was listening, she refused to monitor what she said because of it. "Remember when I was a little girl, how I used to want to do whatever you and Alec did?"

He smiled at her exactly the way he used to when she was constantly trailing behind them with her hair bursting out of pigtails and dirt beneath her fingernails. "You were our little shadow."

"Just imagine if I'd stuck with that plan. I'd either be sending people off on fancy planes like Alec or teaching them medieval battle plans like you." She grinned. "Actually, both of those things sound like fun."

"Alec's clients would drive you crazy," Harry pointed out, "and my students probably would too."

He was right. She had little patience for the filthy rich men and women who used Alec's private planes. So many of them thought the world should be handed to them on a diamond-encrusted platter. And she would have been a terrible professor. Teaching had never been her gift. She was so impatient to see results that she had a bad habit of accidentally steamrolling past people who didn't understand what she was talking about.

"Call me if you need anything," Harry said, and then with a nod to Roman, he was gone, leaving the two of them alone in her office.

There were a dozen things she needed to work on this afternoon, but as she looked up and found Roman staring at her with his dark, intense gaze, she honestly couldn't remember a single item on her to-do list. All she could do was heat up, inside and out.

And *want*.

"I just spoke with Craig."

Roman's unexpected statement jarred her brain out of its blank state. Her body, however, stayed stubbornly in *want*, even as she said, "You called him while Harry and I were having lunch?"

"I went to his office and confronted him, face-to-face."

"You went to see him?" Shock that he'd acted so quickly after their conversation made her brain feel rusty, as if the gears inside her head needed to be oiled. "Why would you do that?"

"After what you told me about your previous relationship with him, it seemed obvious to me that he must be involved in the attacks on your servers and your phone."

She didn't realize she was moving toward Roman until she was standing chest to chest with him. "Are you *crazy?*" She didn't normally get this emotional in her office. Yes, she was passionate about what she did, but she knew better than to let anger take over on the job. Only, when Roman pushed her buttons over and over again, in a way no one else ever had, all those lessons kept falling away. "I told you he wouldn't do something like that just because we slept together a couple of times. Why wouldn't you listen to me?"

"Do you have any idea what sleeping with a woman like you does to a guy?" Roman's words were low. Raw. "Do you have any idea what your beauty does to a man? The way your laughter reaches all the way inside his chest? The way he can't stop breathing in your scent? How he's constantly marveling at how damned smart you are and just wants for one second to be able to see the world the way you see it? Because you're the brightest, most beautiful woman he's ever known." He erased the distance between them as he moved forward to close the final gap. "Any guy who's lucky enough to be with you isn't going to want to lose you. Unless he's a complete fool, he's going to do whatever he can to convince you to come back. And to stay."

She opened her mouth to respond, but no words came. Not when every one of Roman's passionate words were reverberating through her.

No one had ever told her that her laughter, her scent, or her brain affected them this way. And no one had ever looked at her this way either. As though he wanted to kiss her more than he wanted to take his next breath.

When Roman's gaze dropped from her eyes to her mouth, she could almost taste his kiss from that look alone. Could almost feel the heated sizzle of his skin against hers.

She had never wanted anything more than she wanted to feel his arms around her, the tangle of his hands in her hair, the press of his muscles all along hers as he finally—

"*Damn it.*"

His curse came a beat before he stepped back from her. Coolness from the air conditioning rushed to fill the space between them...but it wasn't nearly enough to douse the flames inside her.

"I overstepped, Suzanne." Each word sounded as if it came from between clenched teeth. "I shouldn't have said that. Any of that."

She wanted to move closer again, wanted to tell him she was glad he'd said it. That he'd made her feel special in a way no man ever had before. Because no one had ever noticed her the way he did. Not only as a brain. Not only as a woman.

But as both.

Instead, she said, "Never apologize for being honest with me." Her words were soft, but serious. "If that's what you feel, if that's what you think, I want to hear it."

"You didn't want to hear it before." He wasn't accusing now, simply pointing out the facts.

She let out a long, hard breath. "I know I can be stubborn." By the look in his eyes, it was obvious that she needn't have bothered telling him that, since he'd already figured it out. "But I usually come around when something makes sense."

"So you agree that talking with Craig made sense?"

She nodded. "I was going to speak to him tonight."

"With me there?" She couldn't read Roman's expression. Not when his man-of-stone mask was back in place. "Or without?"

She'd asked him to be honest with her, which meant he deserved the same from her. "Without. Which I now see might also have been the stubborn route. But now you've beat me to it." Her anger mostly gone now, she asked, "What did he say?"

"He isn't behind any of it."

She couldn't stop "I told you!" from bursting out.

"I now believe that he's not the one causing you problems," Roman said again, "but you were wrong that you didn't mean anything to him. He wanted you back, Suzanne. More than he ever let on."

That gave her pause. "How do you know?"

"He told me."

She hadn't seen that coming, hadn't guessed that Craig's feelings for her might have gone beyond a few hours of letting off steam together in the dark. "What did you tell him about the"—she paused to search for the right word—"problems I've been having?"

"I didn't give him any details. But he was concerned enough to offer to help if we need it."

We.

The tiny word leaped out at her. Her brothers, her friends, had always been there for her. But she'd never been a *we* with a man. The thought of being a *we* with Roman filled her with crazy longing. Even though it was the very last thing she should want.

"Next time," she made herself say in the midst of her rampantly conflicted thoughts, "I'd like you to tell me what you're planning so that I can either talk you out of it or go with you. I guess your talk with Craig wasn't that big a deal."

Roman looked uncomfortable. "I was pretty rough with him."

"Define *rough*."

"I shoved him up against the wall." He paused a beat before adding, "By his neck."

"Why?" She couldn't understand what would have driven Roman to such lengths. "Why would you do that?"

"I need to protect you."

"You've got to see by now that I'm not fragile."

"I know you're not. You're anything but fragile, Suzanne."

"Then…" It felt like she was trying to pick her way through a minefield to get to the other side. And yet she couldn't stay where she was. Not if there was a chance that reaching the other side would be worth the risk. "Why are you so hellbent on protecting me?"

Her phone rang in the space where his answer might have come. Standing closest to where the device lay on the corner of her desk, he looked at the screen, likely to assess whether it was another one of the junk calls.

"It's Smith," he said as he handed it to her.

Though she was always happy to hear from her cousin—he was so busy with his film projects that she didn't see him nearly often enough—she couldn't help but wish he'd waited another five minutes to call today.

"Smith, how are you?"

"Couldn't be better, Suz. Any chance you can come to Summer Lake for a couple of days?"

Joy jumped inside her as she instantly guessed why he must be calling to ask that question out of the blue like this. "Is Valentina finally going to take you off the market for good?"

"I've been off the market since the first time I laid eyes on her." Suzanne could hear the love in Smith's voice for his bride-to-be. "And yes, we've finally picked a date. How does Friday at noon sound to you?"

As it was already Wednesday afternoon, she would have to wrap up anything pressing at the office, pack her bags, and head to the Adirondacks first thing the next morning. She had a multinational corporation to run. She had a massive task list ahead of her for Rosa's foundation. And she was just beginning to accept that the server and phone attacks deserved more of her attention.

But none of those things was anywhere near as important as celebrating with Smith and Valentina as they made their vows of forever to each other.

"It sounds absolutely perfect. And I won't tell a soul. Well," she amended so that Smith would know she'd be bringing a hired plus-one, "no one except for my bodyguard, Roman."

She could easily imagine Smith's eyebrows rising. "I don't like the sound of that. Why do you have a bodyguard?"

"I'll explain everything when I see you. But until then, don't worry, I promise you I'm safe and sound." Roman, she was starting to understand, wouldn't allow anything else.

"I've got to tell you," Smith said, "you've got me worried. If you need help with anything—"

"I swear, I'm *fine*." Her cousins were as overprotective as her brothers. She loved them all, but sometimes it wasn't easy to be part of such a big family with so many alpha males surrounding her at every turn.

"We'll talk more when you get to the lake," Smith said, making it clear that they weren't done with this conversation, even if he was dropping it for now. "I've got most of Alec's planes on call to get everyone here on such short notice, so let him know what time you can be ready to head out."

"Thanks, but I'll probably drive." Her brother's planes were a really nice ride, but she wanted the flexibility to be able to come and go as she pleased for the next few days. "Give Valentina my love and let her know I can't wait to see her dress."

"You and me both," Smith replied. "I hope I can still form a coherent sentence when I finally see her in it. I've waited so long to make her mine..."

Suzanne sighed. Smith and Valentina were so sweet together. As one of the biggest movie stars in the world, it might have been difficult to see Smith falling this hard for anyone. But Valentina was special—the perfect woman for him. Not at all interested in the spotlight, but willing to brave it for the man she adored.

For a few moments after they hung up, she savored the sweetness of knowing Smith and Valentina were finally tying the knot. There was nothing more wonderful than true love turning to forever love. One day, she wanted the same thing for herself.

Despite the way her parents' marriage had turned out, Suzanne still believed in love, still held out hope that she'd find a man who cherished her, who appreciated her. That future love had always been nameless, faceless. Until today, when for some crazy reason, Roman's face—and all those breathtaking things he'd said to her in the heat of the moment—were suddenly filling in the blank spaces.

"Change of plans," she told Roman. "My cousin Smith is getting married on Friday. Since he's super famous, it's super secret and totally spur of the moment."

"I figured, based on your side of the call."

She appreciated that Roman wasn't freaking out over the fact that he was going to be attending Smith

Sullivan's wedding with her in a couple of days. So many other people had such stars in their eyes when it came to her family. Sometimes it felt as if she was nothing more than a stepping stone for people who were hoping for a piece of her family's money and fame.

"Wherever you go," he added in his deep voice, "I'll be there."

Perhaps she should have been irritated by this reminder that his job was to keep watch over her at all times, but the truth was that right this very second, she was more reassured than anything. Although maybe *reassured* wasn't exactly the right word for what she was feeling.

The simple comfort of knowing no one would harm her while Roman was there was one thing. But the butterflies in her stomach at the thought of attending a family wedding with him at her side—and the anticipation of sharing a dance with the most attractive, intriguing man she'd ever known—were something else entirely.

CHAPTER TWELVE

The six-hour drive to Summer Lake the next morning—with Suzanne close enough to drag onto his lap and kiss senseless—was a lesson in restraint for Roman. Restraint he'd already proved he sorely lacked.

What the hell had he been thinking saying, *Do you have any idea what your beauty does to a man?* and *Any guy who's lucky enough to get to be with you isn't going to want to lose you.*

He hadn't been thinking, that was the problem. Not when he'd grabbed Craig by the throat and shoved him up against the wall. And not when he'd nearly pulled Suzanne against him in her office and kissed her until she forgot all the reasons they couldn't be together.

She'd asked him if he was crazy, and the truth was that around Suzanne, he felt that way. One smile from her, one saucy word from her smart mouth, and all his hard-won control disappeared as if it had never been there at all.

And yet, after getting off the phone with Smith,

instead of spending any more time confronting him about his unacceptable behavior—which he definitely deserved—she'd been pulled into several overseas calls that went late. He understood that she needed to get as much done as possible before she left town for the wedding. But he also wondered if, perhaps, she was using work to avoid him.

Not that he blamed her for it. Ignoring the attraction between them was the smart thing to do. And Suzanne Sullivan was the smartest woman he'd ever met.

What's more, the stakes were higher than ever now. Not only did he need to figure out how to stuff away his attraction to Suzanne while they were alone together in this car for hours on end—but when they got to the wedding, he needed to make absolutely sure that he didn't give away even one ounce of what he was feeling for her.

If Alec so much as caught a whiff of the thoughts Roman was having about Suzanne, he'd be a dead man. And rightly so. No bodyguard should ever step over the line he'd been on the verge of leaping over outright in her office the previous afternoon.

Being the best bodyguard in the world was what he needed to focus on. Not the fact that she was drop-dead gorgeous, sitting beside him in her formfitting silk shirt and slim black pants, with her dark hair cascading down her back. Not all the places, all the ways, he wanted to kiss her. Not how much he wished he could see her smile again, hear her laugh, if only to know that the day was off to the right kind of start. The best start to any day he'd ever had.

Focus, Roman. Focus.

Roman had already let his investigators know that Craig was a dead end and to dig deeper, and faster, into who might be responsible for harassing Suzanne. Hopefully, he'd get more solid leads while they were in the remote Adirondack Mountains, a place that was as off the grid as you could get these days.

He was used to driving, but since Suzanne had immediately slid behind the wheel of her car and kicked off her heels, Roman did his best to relax and take in the scenery.

Growing up in the city, there hadn't been much green space apart from the city parks. For his entire adult life, he'd worked and lived in cities—New York, Los Angeles, Chicago, Miami. The closer they got to Summer Lake, however, the greener it got. So green that soon only the blue sky and the ponds and lakes they passed provided contrast. When Suzanne rolled down her window, the air was the freshest Roman had ever smelled.

"Pretty, isn't it?" For the first time since the day before, she smiled. "Summer Lake has always been one of my favorite places in the whole world."

She was in her element in her office, and had been pure strength and energy as she ran through Central Park. But as she took a deep breath of the pine-scented air and looked up at the fluffy white clouds in the blue sky above the two-lane road, he watched her finally relax. Almost as though she'd just let the weighty responsibility of being the owner of a game-changing digital security company fall from her shoulders.

Though he knew she'd only be able to take a small break for this wedding, considering how hard she ran herself, every break she could get mattered, no matter how small.

"How long have you been coming here?" The more Roman knew about his clients, the better he could protect them. He swore to himself that he was asking because she was his job, rather than because everything about her intrigued him.

"As long as I can remember. After my mom died—" She paused for long enough that he knew she still grieved the loss. The same way he missed his mother every day, even when he tried to tell himself that he didn't. "Once she was gone, Summer Lake was where my dad wanted to be, so this is where we spent most of our school vacations. When we were in school in the city, he'd come here whenever he could find someone to take us to our music lessons and after-school games, so that he could work on the house he was building. Pretty early on, he connected with a small home building company and began to help out with their projects. And as soon as Drake went to college, he moved full time to the lake. I think coming back to the city haunts him to this day, because all of his worst memories of losing my mother are there. Anyway," she said as she obviously tried to pull herself out of the dark places her story had taken her, "we'll be staying at the home he built. It's really nice, all done in knotty pine with views out across the lake from every window."

While doing his research into Suzanne and her past, Roman had been surprised to learn that when her father had stopped painting at the height of his international fame, he'd become a home builder instead. "It sounds like your father is as talented with a hammer as he was with a paintbrush."

"He is, although most people think it's really sad that he never painted again."

"Do you?" This was exactly the kind of question that he didn't need to know the answer to in order to do his job. But he had to ask it anyway, if only to get a deeper glimpse into what made Suzanne tick.

"I understand passion. I know how deep it can go. How it can drive you."

"It's how you feel about what you do."

"Yes."

She kept her eyes on the road, which let him drink in her every expression as she drove. He relished the chance to learn the curve of her dark eyelashes, how they rested for the briefest instant on her high cheek-bones when she blinked. He let himself take in the slight flush that had begun to brush over her skin as she answered his questions. He was mesmerized by the pulse point at her neck, a gorgeous inch of skin that he was desperate to taste.

"But," she continued, "if my passion ever became obsession—if it ever started to destroy me or the people I love—I would walk away from it. In a heart-beat." She sighed. "My father feels his passion for painting my mother is what destroyed both their relationship and her, so I understand why he moved on to something completely new. Besides, there are so many amazing things out there to focus on. Why do we have to choose only one?"

With every word she spoke, he was more and more drawn to her, despite knowing better. Roman's father had taught him that women couldn't be trusted, that one was as good as the next. But Roman was positive his father had never met a woman like Su-zanne.

"I've seen passion destroy people before," he found himself saying.

When she briefly took her eyes off the road to look at him, he could read the unspoken questions in her gaze. He'd never shared details of his past with other clients, but any way he tried to spin it to himself, it was impossible to deny that Suzanne would ever be just another client.

"My mother left us when I was ten." It wasn't just clients to whom he hadn't divulged his past. He'd never shared this with another woman either. But if anyone would understand, it was Suzanne. "My father was as passionate about claiming he'd never loved my mother as it sounds like your father was passionate in his love for yours. He nursed that hatred for her until it began to destroy him in a worse way than her leaving ever had. Everything you're saying about shifting gears when you've taken something too far makes sense. My dad should have shifted gears a hell of a long time ago."

The pity he expected to see on Suzanne's face never materialized. Instead, she said, "Our childhoods sound pretty similar. My dad and your dad came at things from opposite directions, but it still meant neither of them were really there for us, were they?" She was silent for a moment before adding, "Although we had a pretty big family breakthrough a few weeks ago, so now my dad is finally trying, at least."

"That's good." He was happy for her. At the same time, however, he hoped her father wouldn't end up disappointing her more than he already had. Roman hated the thought of anyone hurting Suzanne for any reason, family or otherwise.

She shot him a questioning glance. "What about your dad? Do you have a better relationship now than you did when you were a kid?"

"No." The word came out curt. Hard. The only way it could.

"Do you see him anymore?"

He could have shut her down the way he had when they'd been running and she'd suggested that they should get to know each other better since they were going to be spending so much time together. But that had been before he'd really begun to understand her.

Roman had never wanted to dwell on his childhood by spending hours in a psychologist's office rewinding through it. Nor had he been tempted to get drunk with the guys and joke about the shitty way his life used to be. Now, he found himself wondering if he'd been waiting for Suzanne to understand everything in an instant—because she'd been in similar situations with her parents.

"He pops up from out of the blue from time to time." Roman left out that it was always when his father needed money to bet on boxing matches.

"What about your mom?" When he didn't answer right away, she said, "Sorry. I didn't mean for this to turn into twenty questions. I know how you feel about personal boundaries with your clients, and you've already told me so much."

She was right—this conversation had already gone way past professional lines. But wasn't crossing the line into becoming friends better than crossing any other lines with her? Maybe, he told himself, being friends with Suzanne would be his best shot at fulfilling a need for her that was growing by the minute.

"I haven't seen her since I was ten. She jumped around the country for a few years, chasing whatever guy she decided she was in love with and sending me postcards, but the postcards stopped coming when I was eighteen."

"I'm sorry, Roman."

He was too, more than he'd ever wanted to admit to himself.

"I used to wonder," she said softly, "what it would be like to grow up in a normal family. Used to yearn for a mom who was waiting after school with a snack, and for a dad who didn't always look at his kids as a reminder of the woman he'd lost."

He felt every painful word Suzanne spoke like a punch to his gut. He wished he could rewind time to give her what she'd so badly wanted. What they'd both wanted. Because she wasn't the only one with unanswered questions. For the past twenty-six years, he'd wanted to know—had his mother regretted leaving? Had she missed her son when she'd gone off to chase after "love"?

Then again, he already knew the answers, didn't he? If she had missed him, if she had loved him, she would have come back to see him again. She hadn't.

"But maybe," Suzanne continued, "having to learn resilience from all the craziness around us as kids is what made us strong enough to go out there and fight for the lives we wanted as adults."

Roman didn't believe in feeling sorry for himself. He wasn't surprised that Suzanne hadn't wasted any time on self-pity either. She'd yearned, but she hadn't let unfulfilled yearning hold her back.

"If she were here now, your mother would be proud of you," he had to tell her. Because for all the professional boundaries this conversation was smashing to smithereens, it was the truth. A truth he needed to make sure she knew. "Damned proud."

"I hope your dad is proud of you," she said in a heartfelt voice. "He should be."

Roman could have let it go there. Should have let it go. But he couldn't stand feeling as though he was lying to her by leaving out the reality of his past. "When I was younger, I did a lot of things I'm not proud of." Even now, he didn't exactly treat the women he dated like a prince—at least, not the ones who wanted more than he did. Which was all of them.

At a stop sign, she turned to look him in the eye. "Who didn't do stupid stuff as a kid? I didn't know you back then, but Jerry from the pizza place did, and I see how much you mean to him. And we both know my brothers don't trust me with *anyone*, so if they're willing to trust me with you, you must be a pretty great guy."

He raised an eyebrow. "Are you saying your opinion of me has changed since Monday night?"

"Maybe a little." It was obvious that she was trying not to smile, but the way her lips twitched at the corners gave her away. "Although, I really didn't like you forty-eight hours ago, so the only way to go was up."

Her honesty surprised a laugh out of him, which in turn made her laugh too. He truly had never met another woman like her, who laid everything out on the line with no pretense.

Between the sweet sound of her laughter and her excitement at seeing Summer Lake suddenly appearing through the trees, the tightness inside his chest that he had come to believe would always be a part of him suddenly began to loosen.

Until he remembered they were going to be seeing her brothers and father soon—which made everything inside of him tighten right back up. The Sullivans trusted him to take care of Suzanne, not to use her the way he'd used every other woman in his life.

Just friends with Suzanne sounded good on paper, and her brothers wouldn't be angry with him for being her friend. But he knew damn well that he was walking a slippery slope.

One where wanting to be friends with Suzanne could all too easily turn into wanting *everything*.

CHAPTER THIRTEEN

"Dad, isn't this surprise wedding wonderful?" As soon as William Sullivan opened the front door, Suzanne threw her arms around her father, who had already been reaching for her too.

"It is," he agreed, holding her tightly. "Even better because you're back at the lake again so soon."

In the car, she'd said that her father was working toward a better relationship with her than they'd had when she was growing up. Roman was really glad to see evidence of how much her father loved her simply from the way he held her—as if he wished he didn't ever have to let go.

When it came to Suzanne, it was a feeling Roman understood all too well...

"I wanted to tell you as soon as Smith asked me to help him put the wedding together a couple of weeks ago," her father explained. "But with the paparazzi always barking at his heels, I understood the risks of spreading the word at all."

"If anyone could understand the downside of

fame," she murmured, "it's you." A flicker of deep-seated grief moved across her father's face before she added, "Don't worry about not telling me—I'm just glad to be here to celebrate with them. And, of course, to help with the wedding in any way I can."

"I'm happy to help too," Roman offered. And while he certainly was, a large part of his offer stemmed from wanting to make sure that Suzanne didn't take on yet another massive project at this wedding when she needed some downtime to relax and recharge.

As Suzanne's father turned to Roman, she finally stepped all the way out of his arms.

"Hello, I'm Roman Huson," he said, putting down their bags to shake her father's hand.

"I'm Suzanne's father, William."

Roman was impressed with William's firm grip. Building houses had kept him strong. This was a father a guy didn't want to mess with.

"Come on in," William said as he stepped aside to let them into the house that was far more impressively built than Suzanne had let on. The knotty pine rafters rose at least thirty feet in the living and dining rooms, and the large windows had a direct sight line to the sun setting over the lake, with rolling green mountains beyond the blue waters. "You're both probably hungry and thirsty after your long drive. What can I get you?" Without missing a beat, he added, "And then you can tell me how you met." *So that I can determine if you're good enough for my daughter* was the clear subtext.

Suzanne put a hand on her father's arm. "I didn't want to try to explain over the phone, but you should know that Roman is here because he's working. As my bodyguard."

"Your bodyguard?" Her father instantly looked alarmed. "What's going on, honey? Why didn't you tell me you were dealing with trouble and needed a bodyguard?"

"I'm not in trouble," she said, her automatic reply. But then, after a pause, she added, "Not much, anyway. Just some weird technical stuff going on at work and with my cell phone."

"So then why did you need to hire Roman?"

"I didn't." Her full mouth set into the irritated line Roman had become rather familiar with over the past two days. And that he found far too sexy. "Alec, Harry, and Drake hired him behind my back. I found out Monday night at Drake's gallery show."

"The whole situation should have been handled much better," Roman agreed.

William hadn't stopped frowning since the moment his daughter had said the word *bodyguard*. And no wonder—what parent wanted to think their child might be in danger?

Roman instantly ricocheted to a memory of being

fourteen years old and in the boxing ring with a guy who was five years older and fifty pounds heavier. A boxing ring his father had put him in to win a bet. Funny how Roman being in danger never seemed to bother his dad at all.

"Even though your daughter didn't hire me herself," Roman said as he grounded himself back in the present, "I want you to know that if anything should escalate, I'll make sure she remains safe and sound."

"Safe and sound." Suzanne repeated his words in an irritated voice. "Of course I'm going to remain safe and sound, just the way I always have. Because I can take care of myself."

The look her father shot him was almost a mirror image of Alec's. One that said, *Suzanne means the world to us. If I'm going to trust you with her safety, you'd better be sure to earn that trust every goddamned second.*

"Of course you can," her father said in a gentle voice, "but someone still should have told me what was going on." It didn't escape Roman's notice that William seemed more than a little hurt to be left out of the family loop.

"I didn't want to worry you. I'm sure the boys didn't either."

"I'm your father. Worrying is my job. If you need my help, I want to know."

While a part of Roman was impressed by how William was trying to step up after not being there for Suzanne and her brothers when she was a kid, another part of him was wary. Roman wanted to protect Suzanne from everything, including the possibility that her father might hurt her more than he already had.

Just then, Alec, Harry, Drake, and Rosa came in through the front door, likely having been on the same plane. "Let's get this party started," Alec said by way of greeting as he dropped a leather travel bag by the door.

As Suzanne and her father went to greet the new arrivals, Roman had a minute to take in the family as a whole. They were a great-looking—and obviously successful—bunch, but far more impressive was how close they all seemed to be. Even with William slightly on the fringes, Roman could see that they had a real bond. A strong bond. The kind of bond he and his own father had never forged, no matter how many beers they drank together, or how many boxing matches they won.

"Perfect timing," William said. "Smith and Valentina are hosting cocktails and dinner at the inn for whoever can make it tonight. They said to come by as soon as we're ready."

"I've got to change out of my jeans," Suzanne said, "and then I'll be ready to go."

As if her brother had finally noticed what she was wearing, Alec did a double take at her curve-skimming silk shirt, sleek black jeans, and heels. "Why are you wearing something so revealing in the first place?"

She scowled at her brother. "Everyone dresses like this."

He scowled back. "Not you."

"Well, I do now. So you'd better get used to it."

With that parting shot, she grabbed her bag and headed for the stairs. Something told Roman that if any of them thought her outfits had been revealing so far, they hadn't seen anything yet. If only so that she could turn the screws as tightly as possible on the brothers she was already furious with for hiring Roman behind her back.

Alec turned to Roman. "What's gotten into her? Harry told me she'd forgiven us for hiring you."

"You know Suzanne better than I do," Roman said, "but I'm guessing she didn't care for the way you spoke to her about her outfit. I'd apologize, and soon, if I were you."

"What the hell, man?" Alec was known for his fierce look, which he now aimed at Roman. "Whose side are you on?"

"Suzanne's." And not just because Alec and his brothers had hired Roman to protect her. But because he liked her.

Liked her more than any woman he'd ever known.

* * *

Maybe Suzanne should have been more intent than ever on getting Roman to resign after the way he'd gone rogue with Craig. When they'd first set out on the drive from the city earlier that day, that was what she'd been working to convince herself to do. Heck, all the previous afternoon and evening, she'd been trying to get herself to see sense. To remember all the reasons she couldn't fall for Roman.

But then, after their talk in the car and the way he'd opened up to her about his childhood, her hard-won resolution had simply disappeared. Right now, she didn't feel as if she needed to dress super sexy to tempt Roman into stepping over the line. But after the way Alec had spoken to her? She was angry enough to up the ante even over her previous outfits, if only to see how mad she could make him.

And if Roman happened to be wowed by the glimmering gold dress that skimmed so tightly over her curves it was almost as if she wasn't wearing anything at all—a dress so sexy even she couldn't quite believe she had the guts to wear it? Well, the truth was that Suzanne wasn't entirely sure she'd mind him noticing her. For real, this time, rather than because she was putting on a faux seductive act to get him to kiss her and then resign.

When he'd opened up to her about his past, she'd felt as if they'd started to become friends. Being able to share things with him—and having him share right back—had filled her with warmth. And tenderness. She'd forced herself to fight her intense attraction to him, but she didn't know how to fight against warmth and tenderness.

Granted, her brothers would freak if they thought Roman was looking at her with interest—and she was looking at him the same way. But she was beyond done with their trying to control her life in any way, shape, or form, all under the guise of protecting her. When would all of them see that she could protect herself just fine?

Head held high, she left the bedroom to make her way down the stairs to the living room. She wasn't surprised to find Roman waiting for her outside the bedroom door. What did surprise her, however, was when he stared at her in wonder.

"You're stunning."

She lost her breath at the heat beneath his words—and in his gaze. Actually had to work to get enough oxygen to say, "Thank you." She looked down at herself, then back up at him. "I was kind of angry at Alec when I headed up here. You don't think this dress is a bit much?"

"There's no denying how gorgeous you are in it,"

he said without pause. "But what's important isn't what I think. It isn't what your brother thinks. It's what *you* think. It's whether you like the dress."

After having so many men trying to tell her what to do her whole life, he couldn't know how much she appreciated his support for her decision—whatever it might be. They might just be talking about a dress, but it felt like the first step toward something bigger. Or, at least, something that might become bigger, if only the two of them decided to let it grow.

Looking down, she smoothed her hands over the pretty fabric. "I like it. And it's actually pretty comfortable," she noted with more than a little surprise.

Her jeans and T-shirts were easy to wear, but as they made their way down the stairs, for the first time she wondered if they were also a way to hide. She honestly didn't think that she harbored any issues about sex. She truly appreciated all the things her body was capable of—be it exercise, work, or pleasure.

But maybe one of the biggest reasons she'd never wanted to put her femininity on display was because her fears ran deeper than that. Though she swore she wanted to find love, she couldn't deny that any time things got semiserious or the slightest bit intense with a guy she was dating, she freaked out. Coming from a legacy of love-gone-wrong did that to a girl.

Other women might be looking for a whirlwind,

swept-off-her-feet romance, but Suzanne's dreams of finding "the one" had never looked like that. Not when her parents had lived that fantasy romance only to have it all come crashing down in the worst way possible.

Rosa, Drake, Harry, and her father were waiting at the bottom of the stairs, while Alec was out on the front porch making a call.

"What a fantastic dress!" Rosa said when she spotted Suzanne.

Suzanne appreciated the support from her brother's girlfriend. "I love yours too."

Rosa was one of the most drooled-over women on the planet, and anything she wore looked amazing. Though she was wearing a simple off-white linen dress tonight, she absolutely glowed in it. Love, Suzanne had often noted, did that to a person. All her cousins who had fallen head over heels in love now shone even brighter than before.

Alec walked back inside, and his eyes widened when he saw what she was wearing. Suzanne braced for the controlling comment that was sure to come out of his mouth. Instead, he said, "I was out of line earlier."

She couldn't believe her ears. "Are you apologizing to me?"

A muscle jumped in his jaw as if it pained him to admit it, but he nodded.

Of all her brothers, Alec was the worst at admitting he was wrong. Which made this a *really* big deal. She hugged him. "Thank you."

Her brother kissed the top of her head. "I just want you to be happy," he said in a low voice.

"I know you do," she said softly as she drew back. "But I'm not a little girl anymore. You've got to trust me to make the right decisions."

Though he didn't look entirely convinced, he nodded. "I'll try."

"Good," she said with a smile, "because I've just realized I like dressing up and looking pretty sometimes."

"You always look pretty, Suz. If you think you need to change out of jeans to try to impress a guy, he's the wrong guy."

She raised an eyebrow. "Is that your version of trying to trust me?"

He grimaced. "Sorry. Old habits die hard."

"Especially for an old man like you."

"Thirty-four isn't old."

She laughed as she walked away, throwing an, "If you say so," over her shoulder.

As the seven of them left the house to head to the Inn on Main Street for Smith and Valentina's cocktail party, Suzanne and Rosa walked side by side in front.

"Alec was so upset with me before I went upstairs,"

Suzanne mused quietly enough that her brother wouldn't be able to hear. "I wonder what turned him around?"

"Your bodyguard," Rosa informed her in a low-pitched voice.

"Roman? He's the one who got Alec to see the light about laying off on the whole overbearing big brother thing?"

"He flat-out told Alex to apologize to you for acting like an ass."

"Wow."

"I know you didn't want a bodyguard, but if you're going to be stuck with one for a little while, Roman doesn't seem half bad."

Suzanne laughed. "I agree that he isn't hard to look at."

"Not only that," Rosa said, "but he really seems to care about you. As more than just his client, I mean."

Hope fluttered in Suzanne's belly. Trying to act casual, she asked, "Why do you say that?"

"The security details I've worked with before have always kept to themselves. They did their jobs, but there was no connection on either side. Whereas the two of you not only seem like friends, it's also clear that *lots* of chemistry is there if you ever wanted to become more in the future." When Suzanne didn't reply right away, Rosa bit her lip. "I'm probably totally overstepping. I know we haven't known each other that long, but I feel so close to you already."

"You haven't overstepped at all," Suzanne assured her. "And we are close. It's just that I've been trying to get my head around how I feel about Roman. I keep thinking I should be keeping my distance, but then I want to get closer too—which doesn't make any sense. And I *hate* it when things don't make sense!" She looked at Rosa. "Please don't say anything to Drake about any of this. Especially since I'm sure it will all come to nothing."

"Of course I won't say anything. I'm always faithful to the girl code," Rosa said with a smile. "And trust me, if anyone gets what it's like to have nothing feel like it's making sense, I do. The last thing I thought I'd find when I did my runner from Miami was your brother. It wasn't even that I wasn't looking for love. I didn't believe anyone *could* love me the way he does." She looked over her shoulder again at Drake. "I constantly feel like I need to pinch myself to make sure this is really my life now. I honestly can't imagine life without him. He's my everything, Suz. My whole heart and soul wrapped into one handsome, brilliantly talented, funny package."

Suzanne smiled at the woman she hoped would be her sister-in-law one day soon. "My brother would do anything for you, Rosa. I know you would do the same for him."

"Anything," Rosa vowed in a fervent voice.

Weddings, Suzanne knew, brought out the romantic in everyone. Especially people like Rosa and Drake, who were still in that first sweet flush of falling for each other.

And as she snuck another look at Roman from over her shoulder—only to find him looking at her too—Suzanne couldn't help but wonder what the wedding might bring out in the two of them.

CHAPTER FOURTEEN

Roman was one of a dozen security guards working the wedding. Smith Sullivan and his fiancée, Valentina, had *a lot* of famous friends, more marquee names and faces than Roman had seen together in one place since he'd gone to see the last Marvel superhero movie. Four of the five Maverick billionaires were here as well, with their kids, wives, and fiancées. Roman couldn't even begin to imagine the net worth of this crowd. More than some countries, probably.

Summer Lake was a small town with everything people needed to be happy—water, sun, sand, and mountains. Nonetheless, Roman's previous clients who weren't half as rich or famous as Smith Sullivan would have sneered down their noses at the idea of having their wedding here. Interestingly, though, no one in the Sullivan family seemed at all out of place at Summer Lake.

Smith Sullivan was clearly as happy as a guy could get—all because he was head over heels in love with Valentina. Hell, all the Sullivans from San Francisco

and Seattle and Maine to whom Suzanne had introduced him so far tonight looked absolutely smitten
with their partners.

Were they for real? How could so many Sullivans
have managed to find true, lasting love when everyone
else was a total mess? Especially Roman's parents. It
was small comfort to know that out of all the families
here, Suzanne's parents had been a mess too. He
wished yet again that she could have known nothing
but happiness growing up.

Speaking of happiness—while he'd worked for
enough A-list stars to know egos often reigned supreme, everyone in this crowd simply seemed intent
on relaxing.

And hitting on Suzanne.

For the past several hours, Roman had employed
great self-control in order to keep his hands from
fisting—and messing up the pretty faces of the movie
stars who had been chatting her up one after the other.
He belonged over in the corner of the Inn's main room
watching over his client like the other bodyguards. He
should stay out of the way and unobtrusive. But she'd
insisted he remain in the middle of it all with her.

"This is my family," she'd said before they'd
walked inside the Inn. "I'm safe here, which means you
can relax. And since Alex, Harry, and Drake are your
friends, they won't expect you to be on every single

second while everyone else is having a good time."

"Of course they do," he'd replied. "Regardless of the event, I've still got to do my job. I've still got to protect you."

She'd dug her heels in, like he'd known she would. "How can I have fun with you scowling at everyone? If I promise that I won't sneak away and get myself into any trouble during the wedding, will you at least try to enjoy yourself?"

How could he say no to that? How could he say no to her about anything, when all he wanted was to see her smile, hear her laugh?

Damn it. He needed to get a grip on himself. Suzanne Sullivan was meant for a movie star like Buck Elroy, who was currently flirting with her.

Unfortunately, Roman couldn't figure out how to take that much-needed step back as the guy said, "I hope you'll save me a dance tomorrow."

She cocked her head in surprise, as if she'd only just realized she was being flirted with. "You want to dance with me?"

God, she really didn't have a clue, did she? She still saw herself as a nerd girl, rather than an exceptionally lovely, intriguing, enticing woman who had the eye of every unattached man in the room.

"Of course I want to dance with the most exquisite woman here," Buck replied.

Her laughter rang out, attracting even more male attention. Despite the fact that Roman didn't want anyone to guess that his feelings ran deeper than merely a bodyguard's looking out for his client, he couldn't keep himself from scowling at them all.

"That's nice of you to say," she said, as if she didn't believe a word out of Buck's mouth. "I'm sure I'll have plenty of open dance slots tomorrow if you want one, and it's been really nice talking with you. I should go check with Christie, who runs the Inn, to see if she needs help with anything."

Though the movie star looked a little flummoxed at Suzanne not falling all over herself to spend more time with him, he played it smooth. "The pleasure's been all mine."

A woman with long, golden-brown hair waved at Suzanne from the door to what looked like the kitchen. "There's Christie," Suzanne said. "Roman, did you mean it when you offered to help earlier? I'm sure there are a million last-second details to take care of."

"Of course I did," he said, working not to feel too smug at the way Suzanne had already forgotten Buck was there.

The smile she gave him could have lit up the darkening sky outside. They left the main room and headed into the Inn's kitchen, where the two women hugged. "Christie, it's so good to see you again. This is Roman.

Roman, Christie runs the Inn along with her fiancé, Wes." After they shook hands, Suzanne said, "I haven't seen Wes yet. Is he busy setting up for tomorrow?"

"Unfortunately, he had out-of-town plans he wasn't able to change. He's really sorry to miss this wedding. He'd be here if he could."

"Which is where I come in to save the day," a man with dark hair and broad shoulders joked as he walked into the kitchen from the door on the other side of the room.

Suzanne went in for another hug, one that twisted Roman's gut up even tighter than it had been out in the main room when the movie star had been trying to make his moves on her. Because she was clearly close to this guy. And he wasn't wearing a ring, which meant he could very well have his eye on Suzanne.

"Roman, this is Calvin, Summer Lake's esteemed mayor. Saving people in town is what he does."

Suzanne grinned at Calvin as she made the introduction, treating him like nothing more than a buddy. By now, however, Roman knew better than to think any of the guys she spent time with felt the same way. Just because she was blind to her own irresistible beauty didn't mean anyone else was. Roman silently told himself to prepare for Buck Elroy, part two.

Strangely, though, the smile Calvin gave her didn't have any more heat in it, any more longing, any more sparks than hers did for him. And he definitely wasn't looking at Roman as if he were a potential rival.

"It's great to meet you, Roman. I always wondered when Suzanne would find a guy who could keep up with her."

"Oh no," Suzanne said, her flushed face only making her prettier. "We're not dating." When both Christie and Calvin looked confused, she clarified, "He's my bodyguard."

All night long they'd been having this conversation, one that was always awkward for Suzanne, while also being extremely worrying for the people who loved her. Smith had grilled her for a good thirty minutes before accepting that Suzanne and Roman had things taken care of.

"Tell us what we can do," Christie said.

"How can we help?" Calvin asked at the same time.

"Please, don't worry." Suzanne held out her hands to touch each of theirs. "Everything's fine."

"We've got everything under control." Roman put in to further reassure her friends. "Suzanne is perfectly safe." He wanted to reach for her, wanted to put his arm around her and pull her closer. Instead, he stuffed his hands into his pockets while working to divert any further discussion of Suzanne's problems. "We'd like to help with the wedding preparations. Please tell us what we can do."

Though both Christie and Calvin still looked worried, thankfully they took Suzanne's and Roman's reassurances at face value, at least for the time being. "The flowers just came in for the gazebo," Christie said. "The florist guaranteed that they'll look good for the next thirty-six hours, so I was trying to figure out if I could sneak away tonight at some point to begin decorating the gazebo."

"I took a flower-arranging course a few years ago," Suzanne said.

Calvin looked shocked. "How could we have been friends all these years and I never knew that you were a closet flower devotee?"

Laughing, she shot back, "It's a good thing your job is running the town, because that way it's okay when you think you know everything. Which, to be fair, you usually do. So I'm extra excited that I've managed to surprise you with my secret flower arranging skills."

Yet again, Roman was struck by the fact that while Suzanne and Calvin were obviously longtime friends, neither of them seemed to want more. Roman didn't understand why Calvin hadn't made a move on Suzanne, but he couldn't deny that he was glad the other man was happy with just being friends.

"Anyway," she continued, "I read somewhere that creative work like flower arranging can help you tap into solutions for analytical problems. It actually does help me when I'm having problems with my code."

"Great, then I know Smith and Valentina will be in good hands," Christie said with a smile.

"Any hands but mine would be good ones when it comes to flowers," Calvin noted. "Thanks for taking this off our to-do list, guys. Speaking of," he said with a nod down to the tablet in his hand, "I've got to have a word with the bartending staff about focusing on their jobs instead of spending all their time flirting with the guests." He shook his head at Suzanne. "You Sullivans are a distracting bunch."

"Why do I have a feeling Alec is causing half the problems with your female wait staff?" Suzanne asked.

Christie, who looked to be a very nice, mild-mannered woman, practically growled at the sound of Alec's name. "I love your brother, I really do. But at times like this, when I'm trying to get things done, I'm tempted to lock him up in the cellar until everything is over."

"Knowing him, he'd probably have a woman stashed in there, just in case," Suzanne commiserated, making all of them laugh.

Christie reached under a stainless-steel countertop and pulled out a couple of large lanterns. "We're keeping the outdoor lighting off while we make the finishing touches so that everyone will *ooh* and *aah* tomorrow. Which means you're going to need to take these out with you to see what you're doing. The buckets of flowers we're using for the gazebo are along that wall. The florist did a quick sketch of how they could be arranged." She scrolled down the screen on her tablet. "Darn it, where is that picture?"

"Don't worry, Christie." Suzanne was already heading for the buckets of flowers. "We'll do you proud."

After Suzanne and Roman loaded up with several buckets of flowers, the two of them were on their way outside when Christie called out again, "Great dress, by the way, Suz. If I were ten inches taller with mile-long legs, I'd ask where you got it."

Suzanne blushed the way she had all night when people complimented her. "One of my cousins sent it to me, but you can borrow it anytime."

Yet again, he could see that she not only had no idea how beautiful she was, but it also seemed that the way she was dressing lately was way out of the norm. Almost as if she were dressing to attract a lover.

Surely she couldn't be trying to catch *his* eye, could she? Because she damn well didn't need sequins or skin-tight dresses to do that. All it had taken was one look. One smile. One day spent listening to her be both brilliant and kind in meeting after meeting.

No, it didn't make any sense that she would want to make him take a second look when all she'd wanted from the start was for him to leave.

Then again…maybe that was what made the whole approach so brilliant. Because if he couldn't stop looking at her, it wasn't too big a leap for his lack of control to extend to kissing her. And if that happened, he'd have no choice but to—

"Have you ever worked with flowers before?"

Her question yanked him out of the questions spinning around inside his head. "I've got a black thumb, so I'm going to need you to tell me exactly what to do."

"*You're* asking *me* what to do? Music to my ears."

"Don't get used to it."

She laughed, making everything inside his chest go even warmer than it already was just from being near her.

As they began work on decorating the gazebo, it didn't take long for Roman to see that Suzanne not only had an innate sense of flower placement, but she also knew exactly how to combine the colors and sizes of the flowers.

"You didn't only take the flower-arranging class because you thought it would help you code, did you?"

She paused midway through winding a long-stemmed rose around a pillar. "Why do you say that?"

"Anyone else with your eye for this would have become a florist." He held her gaze in the faint light of the lanterns. "Or a painter."

"I'm terrible with a paintbrush."

"I'll bet you're not."

He knew he should back off. Knew with every word out of his mouth that he was getting closer to the red flashing lights of the danger zone. Knew he should revert to being strictly professional and apologize for speaking about any of these things with her. But, damn it, he wanted to know the answers.

He wanted to know *her*, plain and simple.

"Though only Drake made painting his career, something tells me that you, Harry, and Alec could have been artists, couldn't you?"

"Drake didn't know our mother. He didn't see the two of them together. He was just a baby when she left."

"So were you."

"I was old enough to remember." Though she was still looking at him, her eyes unfocused slightly as she fell into memories. "There was so much passion. So much emotion. So much angst. And so much sadness after she was gone." She swallowed hard. "Painting meant all those things to me. Whereas computers were safe." As soon as the words fell from her lips, she stilled. She looked stunned as she repeated, "Computers are safe."

"They're not just safe—you also clearly love everything about technology. I don't know computer code, but I'm going to go out on a limb and guess that yours probably could go up in a museum somewhere."

That surprised a shaky laugh out of her. "I'm pretty sure my *if:then:else* clauses aren't going to be framed and put on display anytime soon."

"Other people with your talents can't wait to spread the word about how great they are, any way they can. But the Sullivans I've met so far are damned modest. Especially you, Suzanne. Take how Buck Elroy was falling all over himself flirting with you. You honestly had no idea he was interested, did you?"

Fireflies had begun to dance in the darkness around them. A breeze blew in off the lake. Laughter and conversation drifted toward them from the Inn. But all Roman was aware of was the woman standing with him beneath the gazebo.

"It doesn't make sense," Suzanne replied. "He could have anyone. And that's not false modesty. I know my face, my body—they're not bad. But I'll never be the kind of beauty my mother was, or that my cousins Lori or Sophie or Mia, or my Aunt Mary are. I've seen it happen so many times, how when they walk into a room, everyone stops. Stares. And because they're such sweet people, it makes them even more interesting to look at." She grinned crookedly. "But no one looks at me like that. No one stops. No one gasps.

And, honestly, I'm glad they don't." Her smile faltered. "My cousins and aunts are all strong enough souls to let their looks roll off them, but my mother wasn't. She couldn't bear the weight of it. And..." She let out a breath. "I'm not sure my father could see past her beauty. Not completely, anyway. It's almost like he was so mesmerized by her face and form that he was never quite able to tap into what was beneath her skin."

Roman wanted to put his hands on her and shake in the truth that she was precisely as attractive as her mother and cousins and aunt. Even more so when a guy spent any time whatsoever plumbing that intense and brilliant brain of hers.

But that wasn't the full truth. He wanted to put his hands on her, period. Anywhere on her. *Everywhere* on her. Suzanne was no longer merely an attraction.

She was rapidly becoming an obsession.

CHAPTER FIFTEEN

"I didn't know your mother, and though I only just met your father, I'm sorry for what happened to them. I'm sorry for what you lost." He should shut the hell up right now. But for the first time in his life, he couldn't keep his feelings locked inside the way he always had before. "I can see why you might want to believe you're not as beautiful as your mother when her beauty seemed to be her downfall. But the fact is, people stop, people gasp when you walk into a room. No matter how much you want to believe you're an invisible geek girl—it's all there, Suzanne. Your beauty, your sweetness, your brain. You're right that Buck Elroy could have anyone. But he's smart enough to want you."

She licked her lips, seemingly as lost for words as he was filled to the brim with them tonight. "The women you've dated, they were lucky."

It was the last thing he'd expected her to say, and so off base that he barked, "You're wrong."

Shaking her head, she ticked off her fingers. "First,

you defended me and my clothing choices to Alec. Second, you got him to apologize, which is nearly impossible. Third, you just told me all the reasons you believe a movie star would want to be with me. I'm just your client, so if you were anything at all like this with your girlfriends—"

"I wasn't." He bit out each word. "I'm not." And she was nowhere near being *just* a client.

She made a face, one that was far too adorable for his peace of mind. "I find that hard to believe."

He could have told her any number of stories about the women he'd dated and dropped over the years. The way each woman went in—then out—a revolving door, one after the other. But he didn't want to tell her those stories, because he didn't want to dim the light in her eyes when she looked at him. As though he might be a good guy after all.

He yanked another rose from the bucket so hard that the petals snapped from the stem. "We should get back to work before Christie starts to worry that we aren't up to the task of decorating this thing."

Suzanne stared at him for a few moments before picking up another couple of blooms and getting back to work. As they continued in silence, voices and laughter drifted up on the breeze from the beach that had been empty earlier. A couple was walking in the moonlight, their arms around each other. When they stopped to kiss, something throbbed deep inside Roman's chest, right in the place that had always remained so numb and unaffected.

Suzanne deserved a man who worshipped her the way the man on the beach obviously adored the woman he was with. And yet, the thought of her with anyone else ate him up.

"I wonder what that's like," she said in a soft voice. "To be with someone you can share all your fears with. Someone you can trust with your darkest secrets. Someone who always makes you laugh. Someone you can't wait to wake up and see every single morning. Someone who will hold your hand on the beach at night and kiss you like they can't live without you."

Roman had shared more with Suzanne than he ever had with anyone else.

He'd trusted her with darkness that he'd never before revealed.

She'd made him laugh from the start.

He looked forward to seeing her first thing every morning.

And he was dying to take her hand, out there on the beach, and kiss her.

Roman had always assumed the biggest mistake he could make would be sleeping with one of his clients. But now he knew better. While crossing those physical lines was undoubtedly bad, losing his heart to Suzanne was what would ultimately break him.

"Have you ever fallen in love, Roman? Been so head over heels that you couldn't think about anything but her?"

Yes. The word burned a hole in his tongue. *With you.*

But he couldn't say that. Couldn't admit that he was committing the cardinal sin of falling for his client. This wedding, all her cousins who were so deliriously happy with their mates, knowing she was off-limits, being too close to her for too many hours—all these things had to be playing into the crazy thoughts he was having.

Roman didn't love. Hell, he hadn't been anywhere close to feeling this way before. So to think that it could happen this fast? And with a woman who was the polar opposite of every other one he'd been with?

No. He couldn't go there.

He wouldn't let himself go there.

And yet, as he stared into Suzanne's eyes, he knew all this lying to himself wouldn't make a damned bit of difference. Because she meant something to him. Something big that wasn't going to go away like the other women who had passed through his revolving door.

When he didn't answer her question, and she didn't push him on it, he should have been relieved.

Should have been glad that the next words out of her mouth were, "Can you come wind the other side of this stem for me to the ceiling beams? I thought I was tall enough to do it, but I miscalculated."

The space was so tight that in order to reach the long stem, he had to wedge in against her, his chest to hers, their hips and thighs flush. He nearly groaned at being so close to her, at getting to feel the press of her taut muscles and soft curves.

As he reached for the stem of the flower she'd already partially attached to the ceiling, his hands were shaking with barely repressed need, and his heart was pounding with emotion he had no idea how to deal with.

"If you wind the stem around the beam and then tuck it into the joint," she said in a slightly breathless voice, "I'm hoping it will stay."

Not trusting himself to speak again when it was taking every ounce of his control not to lower his hands to her curves—and his mouth to hers—he did as she directed. Quickly, so that he could get out of there as fast as humanly possible.

But just as he finished tucking the end of the stem between the beams and thought he was home free, she held up a handful of flowers. "Can you do these too?"

Who would have thought that one totally innocuous question in the moonlight was what would finally make him lose hold of everything? His role as her bodyguard. The fact that her brothers were friends—friends who trusted him with their sister. Even that he wasn't anywhere near good enough for her and didn't have what it took to give her what she deserved.

One kiss.

He needed one kiss.

He needed to know her taste.

He needed to hear the sounds she made when she was falling into pleasure.

He needed *her.*

"Roman."

His name was the barest whisper on her lips. One that had him drawing even closer in the darkness, aware of nothing but the two of them and the kiss that they were finally about to—

"Suzanne? Roman?"

Christie's voice had them jumping away from each other like two guilty teenagers who had been caught making out...even though they hadn't gotten to the making out part.

Roman slammed his head and shoulders on the gazebo's lowest beams, but he deserved a hell of a lot more pain than that for what he had almost done.

What was he thinking, making a move on Suzanne out here? A handful of seconds more and he would have been all over her. As it was, anyone could have seen them pressed close like that. Not only her brothers and father, but also her cousins and friends from Summer Lake.

"We're almost done with the flowers," Suzanne called to her friend. "Do you need help with something else?"

"Yes, if you don't mind." Though she was obviously trying to downplay it, Christie sounded more than a little stressed out. "And it's kind of urgent."

"We'll be right there."

Instead of leaving the gazebo right away, however, Suzanne turned to look back at Roman. And when she did, he could see on her face all the desire—and the conflicted emotions—that he felt himself. He wished he knew what to say to change things so that she was just his client and he was just her bodyguard. He wished he knew how to stop wanting her.

But he was coming up empty on both counts.

"We should go help," he finally said.

"We should," she agreed.

And still, neither of them moved, staying right where they were in the middle of the gazebo, staring at each other. Until the slam of a car door abruptly broke the spell that the lake, the night, the upcoming wedding had woven around them.

But Roman knew that it was more than just being here, away from the city, away from real life, that had changed things. It was their connection, one that was already so much deeper than he'd ever known with another woman.

Silently picking up the empty flower buckets and the lanterns, they headed back into the Inn's kitchen to find Christie on her hands and knees on the floor. She looked up at them, nearly in tears. "I accidentally knocked the bite-sized cupcakes the baker delivered for tomorrow off the counter. *All* of the cupcakes."

Looking closer, Roman realized there must be three hundred tiny little cupcakes smashed onto the wood planked floor.

"We can make enough cupcakes tonight to replace all of these," Suzanne said. "Right, Roman?"

Suzanne needed a break. She needed to relax. She had spent more than enough time this week going a thousand miles an hour. But her friends, her family, meant everything to her. She'd rather bake three hundred cupcakes in a hot kitchen until midnight than be out in the main room sipping cocktails with movie stars. And she obviously didn't care that she was in a fancy dress and heels either, as she was already winding her long hair up into a knot on the top of her head.

He reached for Christie's hand and pulled her to her feet. "Let me finish cleaning the floor while you two find recipes and gather ingredients."

"Thank you, thank you, thank you!"

Christie threw her arms around both of them so that the three of them were in a group hug. He tried not to notice how soft, how warm, how perfect, Suzanne's curves felt against him, but it was a losing battle.

From the moment he'd set eyes on her, he'd been floored by her beauty. The first day he'd gone with her to work, he'd been stunned by her brilliance. And on the drive to the lake, he'd realized that she still ached from losing her mother, the way he still did. Those were some of the reasons he'd been so drawn to kiss her in the gazebo. But those reasons only scratched the surface.

Because while everyone else was enjoying the party, she was poring over cupcake recipes to help a friend, her lower lip held between her teeth in concentration. She accepted an ex reality TV star like Rosalind Bouchard into her family with wide open arms and no judgment. Not only that, but she was willing to give her father another chance to be the parent he should have been all along.

Suzanne Sullivan had the biggest heart of anyone Roman had ever known.

CHAPTER SIXTEEN

Even when Roman was dressed in a finely tailored dark suit that was perfectly appropriate for a wedding, he didn't quite look civilized. It was as if he were a lion trapped in a cage, pacing behind the bars, ready to break free at the first possible chance.

This morning, she felt exactly the same way. As if the attraction to Roman that she'd tried so hard to keep leashed, to keep contained, was about to burst free in front of her entire extended family.

She wanted to eat him up. Wanted to leap onto his lap and tear off his suit to finally feel his muscles, his skin, finally feel his lips pressing against hers. Against *all* of her.

Last night, after Suzanne, Roman, and Christie had finally finished with hours of baking and frosting cupcakes, she'd been so tired she'd been tempted to curl up on one of the Inn's couches. But after Christie had dropped them back off at her father's house, she'd barely been able to sleep knowing Roman was only one wall away. Were it not for her brothers and father sleeping down the hall, she likely would have found herself standing outside Roman's door in her PJs, begging him to let her inside so that they could finish what they'd almost started in the gazebo.

For today's wedding, she'd chosen a teal silk dress that was both elegant and sexy. All morning she'd been drowning in compliments from family and friends. During the past week, she'd been surprised to realize that she had begun to grow comfortable wearing something pretty and feminine. Comfortable enough that, for the first time, she wasn't instinctively brushing off their compliments.

But right now, only the appreciation—and the heat—in Roman's eyes mattered. Appreciation and heat that he kept shuttering so quickly, she was left wondering if they had ever been there at all.

Yesterday, he'd told her she was stunning in the gold dress. Today, they'd barely said a private word to each other. Yes, they'd been surrounded by her family since earlier that morning. But it was almost as if both of them knew how close they were to the edge. So close that even a few simple words might be too much for them to handle, to resist.

Somewhere along the way, her intention to seduce him into making a move on her so that he would resign had shifted. She'd been attracted to him from the first moment—a white-hot attraction unlike anything she'd ever felt before. But even bigger than that was how much she'd begun to like him. She desperately wanted to get beneath the bodyguard shield he wore, and everything he'd told her about his past, his hopes, his fears, felt like golden nuggets.

She still didn't want or need a bodyguard, but if that was the only way she could get him to stay...

God, she could hardly believe she was thinking this, but the truth was she'd take it. Take whatever part of Roman he was willing to give her. If only for the possibility of one day getting to have that kiss—and then finding out if there was more, if there could actually be something real between them.

Suzanne couldn't deny that a part of her longed for that to be the case. After all, in addition to the inescapable heat between them, there were so many places where they connected. Neither of them had grown up with a mom. They both loved the outdoors and being active. She felt safe with him—and not just because keeping her safe was his job.

He made her feel special time and time again, with nothing but a few sweet, heartfelt words.

Then again, given how stiffly he was sitting beside her right now, keeping a careful distance so that no part of him touched any part of her, maybe her mental gymnastics where he was concerned were a moot point.

Fact was, just because she was losing sleep over him didn't mean he was losing sleep over her. Maybe she was reading too much into a few looks, a few nice words, a few almost-kisses. Roman had obviously built a great career for himself by going for what he wanted. So if he *did* want to kiss her, wouldn't he have up and done it already, professional boundaries be damned?

Still, as the first bars of the *Wedding March* rippled out from the harp, she had no choice but to be swept away by Smith and Valentina's wonderful romance. Smith was standing in the center of the gazebo, with his mother and brothers and sisters fanned out to the sides of the structure. Clearly, he was on pins and needles waiting for Valentina to appear in her wedding dress.

When Valentina appeared at the very edge of the beach looking like the most beautiful bride in the entire world in a simple floor-length sheath with a ten foot long mist of a veil lifting in the breeze so that the sun shone through it, the gasp that left Suzanne's lips came at the same moment her first tear fell. And when she turned to see Smith's reaction, she saw that she wasn't the only one crying.

Smith was too. One of the world's hugest movie stars was utterly undone by the woman who had captured his heart.

"Suzanne." Roman's low voice sounded in her left

ear, his hand resting for the barest moment on her lower back. "Are you okay?"

More tears spilled down her cheeks as she looked up into his dark eyes. "I'm just so happy for them."

He looked momentarily confused, as if he couldn't reconcile the idea of tears ever going along with happiness, but then he nodded. "I am too. They're good people."

For a long moment, though Valentina was making her way up the grassy aisle that was strewn with rose petals of every color, Suzanne forgot to look back at the bride. All she could do was stare at Roman. And as he stared back at her, it was as though they were alone in the gazebo again, being drawn together by a force that was bigger and stronger than anything she'd ever known. It was only the *oohs* and *aahs* of the guests as Smith swept Valentina into his arms and kissed her that brought Suzanne back to reality.

A reality where she and Roman were anything but alone—and where she still had no idea how he really felt about her. To be fair, she wasn't completely sure where she stood on things either. After all, she'd spent her entire adult life trying to make sure that her relationships met a very specific list of neat and tidy parameters that were the opposite of the way things had gone for her mother and father. She never let emotions get out of control. No one on either side was

allowed to become obsessed with the other person.
And both parties had to remain rational at all times.

The way she felt about Roman broke all three
rules. Her emotions were a roller coaster. She was
more than a little obsessed. And she was very much
afraid that rational had gone out the window that first
night, when she'd practically been yelling at him on the
sidewalk.

She should know better.

She *did* know better, given that the horrible de-
struction of her parents' relationship—and their lives—
had remained big news in the art world for her entire
life.

But knowing intellectually what she should and
shouldn't be doing didn't make it any easier to get the
message through to her heart.

"We're all extremely happy and honored that all of
you came to Summer Lake today to be a part of Smith
and Valentina's wedding," Calvin said from beneath
the gazebo, where as mayor, he was now standing to
officiate. "Before they speak their vows to one another,
they would like to say a few words to everyone
gathered here today." Moving against the back wall of
the gazebo, Calvin gave the bride and groom the full
stage.

Smith and Valentina were holding hands as they
turned to face their family and friends. Both of them

were smiling, neither one looking at all anxious or nervous about the vows they were about to make.

Suzanne's heart fluttered in her chest, the way it always did when she was at a family wedding. What woman wouldn't dream about being in Valentina's shoes one day, standing hand in hand with the man she loved, ready to make promises of forever in front of the people who meant the most to her? Suzanne's family history had definitely made her wary about all the ways love could go wrong—yet here at Summer Lake, beneath a bright blue sky with the sun sparkling on the lake beyond the gazebo, emotion swelled within her chest from witnessing love gone oh-so-right.

Smith lifted Valentina's hand to his lips, their gazes holding as he kissed her skin. And when Valentina turned to speak to their guests a few moments later, Smith's awestruck gaze remained on her.

"Smith and I will never be able to thank all of you enough for dropping everything to come to our spur-of-the-moment wedding." Everyone laughed, including the bride and groom. "It truly means the world to us that you could be here with us today, to be a part of the most important day of our lives so fa—" When she choked up on the word *far*, Smith drew her closer and gave her a soft kiss on her lips.

"We hope you know how thankful we are that you've made this trek to the Adirondacks so that we could be with everyone we love and appreciate most," Smith said in his deep, mesmerizing voice. A voice most people would recognize with their eyes closed. "And now, I'm sure you'll all understand that we're going to keep our thank-yous short and sweet, because I've never wanted anything more than I want to marry Valentina." He turned to his bride. "Shall we?"

Glowing with happiness, Valentina smiled and nodded.

"They're so perfect together," Suzanne whispered, instinctively leaning into Roman's hard muscles. Though she hadn't meant to make physical contact, she also couldn't deny how right, how warm, how good it felt to be close with Roman—even if she only let herself stay that way for a second.

Calvin moved back into place as officiant. "Valentina, Smith, in honor of the commitment you are both about to make to one another, you have each written special vows. Smith, why don't you begin?"

Smith gazed in wonder at Valentina for several long moments before he finally spoke. "Four hundred years ago, Shakespeare wrote,

Hear my soul speak.
Of the very instant that I saw you,
Did my heart fly at your service.

"I spoke those words dozens of times from the stage before I ever truly understood them. Because the moment I first laid eyes on you, Valentina, my heart didn't just fly, it soared." When tears spilled down her cheeks, he reached up with their clasped hands to gently wipe them away. "I grew up with a mother and father who shared a love that was so strong, I thought I already understood big love. But the day you walked into my life, I instantly fell for your smart mouth, your brilliant mind, and your fierce passion for family. That was when I finally learned how deep, how true, love could be. There's nothing I wouldn't do to see you smile, to hear you laugh, to make you happy. And I've never wanted anything more than I want to be here with you now, knowing you'll soon be mine forever."

Valentina moved her hands from Smith's to cup his jaw, her cheeks wet with tears. She was so radiant with emotion that Suzanne's chest squeezed tight.

"I love you," Valentina whispered to Smith, before giving him a kiss so full of love that Suzanne felt it radiate from the gazebo to her seat.

When the couple finally drew back from each other, Valentina took Smith's hands again. She inhaled a long breath as if to ground herself. "I always swore I wasn't afraid of anything, that there was nothing I couldn't handle if I only put in enough hard work and effort. And then I met you." Her lips trembled with emotion. "Falling for you was the scariest thing in the entire world, and losing my heart to you was the most terrifying thing I could imagine. Until I finally realized why I was so afraid. I thought I was going to lose myself in you, when the truth is that with you is where I've finally found everything that truly matters. Because of your support, and your belief in me, and your unconditional, unwavering conviction that we are soul mates. Your love was, and is, the biggest, most beautiful thing I've ever known. And I promise to love you forever and ever and ever and ever and ever and ever and—"

Valentina's words were lost as Smith tangled his hands in her hair and kissed her so passionately that Suzanne had to fan herself so she didn't overheat. Even Roman seemed blown away, saying, "Hot damn," under his breath.

Everyone in the audience was on their feet cheering as the couple exchanged rings and Calvin said, "By the power vested in me by the State of New York, I now pronounce you husband and wife."

Suzanne had heard nearly a dozen touching wedding vows these past few years as her cousins from San Francisco and Seattle married off one by one, but they'd never meant as much to her as they did today. Everything Smith and Valentina had said to each other about fear and flying resonated deeply with Suzanne.

Because the very first moment she'd set eyes on Roman, something deep inside her had soared.

And nothing could possibly have scared her more.

CHAPTER SEVENTEEN

Roman stood on the edge of the dance floor as Suzanne danced to a slow song with her father. She'd been dancing nonstop with family and friends since the band had begun to play. Though he tried like hell not to let himself notice, he hadn't been able to look away as she swayed her hips like she'd been born to dance instead of program computers.

Seeing how innately sensual she had been during the previous songs had made his brain spin off in exactly the directions it shouldn't. Where he was the one holding her in his arms. Where they lived in a world in which he could have her. Where he was good enough for her. Where he deserved to know if she made love with as much passion as she approached everything else in her life.

He shoved the thoughts away for the millionth time to keep his focus where it should be—making sure none of the guests made any suspicious moves toward Suzanne. All while keeping an extra close eye on Buck.

For the past fifteen minutes, the movie star had

been watching her, and Roman didn't care for the look in the other man's eyes. He wanted her, that was abundantly clear. After calling his investigators for intel on Buck, Roman knew more than he'd ever wanted to about the guy's sexual proclivities. Nothing even remotely illegal, but also nothing Suzanne needed to get mixed up in.

Buck Elroy would hook up with Suzanne over Roman's dead body.

Christie looked a little harried as she moved across the crowded dance floor straight for Suzanne and her father. Roman had learned yesterday what a large role William Sullivan had played in putting on this wedding. He'd not only built several temporary structures for the beach and the lawn, he'd also put together the lighting and run electrical throughout the site. After putting her hand on William's arm to get his attention, Christine pointed at the string of lights up on the porch of the Inn. One of the cables was hanging halfway from the porch ceiling.

Roman could easily guess that while Suzanne was telling her father she'd help him fix it, he was encouraging her to keep dancing. At precisely the same time, Buck made a move toward them, obviously deciding this was the perfect chance to swoop in.

Like hell.

Before Roman could rethink what he was doing, he

was standing in front of Suzanne and her father. "Do you need someone to step in?"

"Yes, we do, Roman." William put a warning hand on his shoulder. "Take good care of my daughter." He gave Roman a borderline threatening smile. "I wouldn't want you to accidentally step on her toes."

That should have been enough to warn Roman away from Suzanne. He should take them off the dance floor and into a safer situation where there could be no touching, no close contact, nothing that would make the flames already burning inside him leap even higher.

Instead, he gave in to the need he couldn't keep at bay another second and pulled her into his arms.

Though he could feel her surprise at his impulsive action in the momentary tightness in her shoulders and upper back, she soon relaxed against him, putting her arms around his neck and resting her head against his shoulder.

How could he do anything but pull her closer? Her curves, her scent, were both intoxicating. And as they moved together, he knew no other woman would ever be such a perfect fit.

Roman would have given anything to stop time and make their dance last forever. But these few precious minutes with Suzanne in his arms were already more than he'd thought he could ever have.

When the song ended, letting her go was the very

last thing in the world he wanted to do. He nearly couldn't get his hands and arms to obey his silent orders to drop away from Suzanne's body, or his feet to take a step back.

"Stay." Her voice was low beneath the din of the other guests' conversations, but he was watching her so intently that he was easily able to read her lips. Her skin was flushed, her lips wet from where she must have licked them while they were dancing. "Dance with me again, Roman. *Please.*"

Everything in his life used to be clear-cut. Work was work, play was play—and his heart never got involved, never grew attached. But those clear-cut lines had begun to blur the second he'd met Suzanne. And now, though they stood in the middle of a crowded dance floor with her entire family surrounding them—with everyone counting on him to protect her—he could barely think straight enough to remember that not only could they not have one more dance…

…they couldn't have anything at all.

He needed to get them away from all these romantic couples, the sexy music, the breathtaking setting. He couldn't risk another dance with Suzanne. Not when the first had nearly broken his control to smithereens.

"You barely ate your meal, and you must be thirsty after all this dancing." He could hear how ridiculous he sounded, answering her request for another dance by telling her she looked parched. "Why don't we go grab something from one of the waiters?"

"Why do you keep doing this?" Her cheeks were even more flushed now, but not from exertion. Her voice rose slightly as she said, "Why do you keep pulling away every time we start to get close?"

One more dance, one more close moment together like the ones they'd shared beneath the gazebo, was all it would take for Roman to do more than just drag her into his arms.

He'd outright *devour* her.

He'd never been so close to losing hold of himself and the emotion he'd been careful to keep carefully leashed for his entire adult life. But Suzanne had pushed him right to the edge of reason.

The last thing he wanted to do was hurt her, but he needed to shut this attraction down and douse the sparks, once and for all. Through tightly clenched teeth, he made himself say in a low voice meant for her ears only, "Because I'm your bodyguard, not your boyfriend."

★ ★ ★

Ouch.

The last time Suzanne had been in anywhere near this much pain was when she'd accidentally run into a lamppost in the park. She had been thinking about a problem with her code instead of looking where she was going and hadn't even realized she had fallen until she found herself flat on her back on the concrete. She hadn't broken anything that day, but she'd been pretty bruised.

There weren't going to be any physical marks left on her body from what had just happened, but the wound Roman's words had made inside her felt deeper than the bruises she'd taken from her fall in the park.

She already knew she'd be hearing *I'm your bodyguard, not your boyfriend* on repeat every time she closed her eyes. He'd said it as though he couldn't imagine ever being with her. As though she were nothing more than an annoying client who refused to understand that he was off-limits.

When he'd swept her into his arms to dance so suddenly, it had felt like the most romantic thing ever to happen to her. He'd seemed overcome by passion, like a hero straight out of the romantic movies she streamed late at night after a hard day struggling with code.

Now, however, as she looked into his dark eyes and was unable to read even the slightest shred of emotion in them, she could see that he'd deliberately turned any warmth he might have felt for her to ice.

Like everyone, she'd had crushes over the years

where she'd liked a guy and he hadn't liked her back. But she'd always been able to brush off those rejections because they were from men who hadn't meant anything to her.

Where Roman was concerned, however, she couldn't figure out how to brush off rejection. Couldn't keep her stomach from hurting when she thought about the way he'd jumped away from her, literally leaping in the opposite direction, not once but several times since they'd met.

"Suzanne, I hope I'm not interrupting." She hadn't realized Buck had walked over to them. "You've been the most popular dancer out here, but now that there's a momentary break in your admirers, I was hoping I could steal you away from your bodyguard and convince you to dance with me."

The very last thing she wanted to do was keep dancing. She wanted to go back to her father's house and curl up in a little ball on her bed.

No. *No.* That wasn't who she was. She wasn't the kind of woman who fell apart over love. She wasn't her mother, damn it.

Forcing a smile for the movie star, Suzanne said, "I'd love to dance with you, Buck."

She hoped her words and her movements as she reached for Buck's outstretched hand didn't look as wooden as they felt. He was a nice guy, and he didn't deserve to be a pawn while she tried to regain some of her self-worth. But sometimes, no matter how much you wanted to be rational and fair and nice, you just couldn't pull it off.

She didn't look at Roman as she let Buck move them deeper onto the crowded dance floor, wouldn't give him the satisfaction of knowing how badly he'd hurt her.

CHAPTER EIGHTEEN

Suzanne didn't dance one song with Buck, she danced ten. Possibly more, since Roman lost count somewhere in the haze of jealousy that wrapped tighter and tighter around him every time Buck touched her or made her laugh. For well over an hour, Roman warred with himself over his urge to burst onto the dance floor and drag her away from the guy. But he couldn't do that. Not because he was afraid of what it would do to his career prospects with anyone else at the wedding, but because he'd already hurt Suzanne enough. He wouldn't embarrass her too.

As it was, he'd never forget the way she looked when he said, *I'm your bodyguard, not your boyfriend.* Every time he hurt her, it further reinforced how right he was to keep his distance. She deserved the true love Smith and Valentina had, not the emotional devastation that Roman had seen go down between his mother and father.

Over and over again, he reminded himself that Suzanne and Buck were just dancing. Since there was no way that Roman was going to let the movie star take things any further, for the rest of the evening he needed to shake off his irrational jealousy and focus on doing the job he'd been hired for.

At long last, Suzanne and Buck didn't dance straight through to the next song. Instead, she pointed off in the direction of the restrooms, while Buck gestured toward the bar, obviously hoping she'd join him for drinks. When she nodded her agreement, Roman growled—loudly enough that he startled one of the nearby guests.

"Is there a problem?" she asked, clearly concerned at seeing one of the security guards so visibly upset.

"No, ma'am." And there damn well wouldn't be a problem as long as Buck didn't try to ply Suzanne with alcohol so that he could make his move.

Roman kept a good dozen feet between himself and Suzanne as she headed off the dance floor, while making sure he never lost sight of her until she went into the ladies' room. Though she was probably dying to get away from him at this point, he knew she wouldn't go back on her promise not to sneak away during the wedding.

While he waited beneath a maple tree, several female guests sent smiles his way. But Suzanne was the only woman who got his engine running now.

Suzanne spotted him immediately when she left

the ladies' room. She hadn't looked his way since she'd accepted Buck's invitation to dance, giving Roman the cold shoulder he more than deserved. But instead of heading off to have a drink with the movie star, she made a beeline for Roman.

"Do you have to follow me *everywhere*?"

She already knew the answer, and he knew she was simply venting, which meant the professional response would be to let her question go. But she wasn't the only one who needed to vent.

Making sure no one was close enough to overhear, he said, "I do. Which is why you should tell me if you're planning to sleep with any movie stars tonight, so I can get my background checks done before your clothes come off."

Her eyes went big, as if she couldn't believe what he'd said. Hell, *he* could hardly believe it. He'd never spoken to a client this way before. Never come close.

"Did you really just ask me if I'm planning to sleep with Buck tonight?"

Her question was loud enough that Roman said, "Unless you want people to talk, we'd better finish this conversation in a more private location."

"I can't wait to *finish* it."

He followed her behind the building and off into a grove of birch trees. Soon, the branches around them were thick enough that the sound of the band and guests was only a low hum.

She spun around to face him. "I already told you, I'll sleep with whomever I want, whenever I want. And just so you know, I wasn't even the slightest bit interested in sleeping with Buck. But now that you've made me consider it..." She shrugged and bared her teeth at him in the faintest possible approximation of a smile. "Maybe it would be a good idea to let off some steam with someone who isn't always pushing me away and seems to want me."

He knew he should count to ten inside his head before replying. Knew he should get his goddamned heart rate down. Knew he should try to muster up even the barest shred of professionalism. But there was no way to hold back anymore.

Not when it felt like he'd been holding back with Suzanne for an eternity.

"How many times do I have to tell you, *every guy here wants you!*"

"You don't!"

Roman had never yelled at a client before. But Suzanne had stopped being *just* a client almost from the very start. And whether he wanted it to be true or not, he wasn't *just* her bodyguard either. He had always been way too close to the line with her. Closer now to falling over the edge than ever before.

He needed to back away. Needed to find another

bodyguard to take his place. Needed to turn around and never look back. Needed to shove thoughts of Suzanne out of his head—and desire out of his body—forever.

But he couldn't. Not when the most brilliant woman in the world seemed to believe something so stupid. So utterly idiotic.

"Are you kidding me? Of course I want you. I've wanted you from the first minute I set eyes on you. Your mouth, your brain, your body—all of you is irresistible." He couldn't stop the words from coming. "That's why I've been hellbent on staying your bodyguard. Because you need someone to watch over you, someone to make sure you don't end up with the wrong guy. A guy like me, who doesn't deserve you." His lungs were heaving as if he'd sprinted around a track. "But not kissing you is the hardest thing I've ever done."

He didn't realize how still she'd become until he finally shut up. Didn't realize until it was too late to take his confession back that the gleam in her eyes had shifted from anger to *desire.*

"Do it." Where he hadn't been able to modulate his voice down from a roar, hers was barely above a whisper. "Kiss me, Roman." She licked her lips, moving closer. "So I can know how you feel." She lowered her gaze to his mouth. "How you taste."

Every moment since the night at the gallery when he'd started working for her, he'd been fighting. Fighting his desire for her. Fighting to remember all the reasons he couldn't have her. Fighting to convince himself that they shouldn't cross any client/bodyguard boundaries.

But tonight, after a wedding steeped in the kind of romance he'd never believed was true, after seeing Suzanne with her close-knit family, after being eaten up with jealousy while watching her dance with another man—he couldn't fight it a second longer.

Still, as one hand moved to tangle in her hair and the other curved around her hip, he made himself give it one last shot. "You're going to regret it."

"No, I won't." Her words were breathless. Excited. "All I want is for you to kiss me."

Lord, did he ever want that too. And yet, now that she was finally in his arms and he was letting himself touch her, he had to stroke her jaw with his thumb. Had to memorize the hitch in her breath as her breathing sped up.

"You're beautiful, Suzanne." He inhaled her sweet and spicy scent. "So beautiful I can't stop looking, can't stop wanting to touch, even when I know I shouldn't."

She reached for him too, putting her hands on his biceps, then running them up and over his shoulders and back, his muscles and tendons flexing at her touch.

"You're the beautiful one." She splayed her hand over his abs, which tightened beneath her fingertips. "A work of art." She licked her lips. "I've never wanted anyone the way I want you. I've never had the kind of dreams about anyone that I have about you. Wicked. Sexy. You have no idea how badly I ache when I see you in the morning and know I can't drag you inside to my bedroom and make those dreams real."

His groan at hearing she'd been having sexy dreams about him was muffled by her hair as he rubbed his cheek along hers. She was so soft. So warm. As if simply being in his arms like this was more than enough to heat her up all over.

He'd never been so enthralled by anyone, never been so attuned to every beat of a woman's heart, to every breath she inhaled and exhaled, to the way her strong, lithe body trembled against his as she pressed her luscious curves more completely against him.

Finally, he put his mouth on her, feathering the lightest of kisses against the curve of her ear. She made a purring sound and her hands came around his hips to grab the dark wool of his slacks so that his arousal throbbed hard and thick against her stomach.

Kindling turned into red-hot flames as he crushed her mouth beneath his and finally *devoured*. And she devoured him right back, two ravenous souls finally taking the kiss they'd both been starved for.

She tasted like sunshine.

She tasted like sin.

She tasted like the sweetest treat in the world.

Roman had never believed that time could stop, that the earth could fall off its axis, that his entire life could change in an instant. Not until this kiss, when the pleasure of being with Suzanne was the only thing that mattered. When it felt like he'd finally found the reason he was here. All the hurt, the worry, the boundary lines that had been between them slipped completely away as they moved as close as they could get to one another.

Roman couldn't think. Couldn't plan. Couldn't stop. Couldn't do anything but give in to the greatest pleasure he'd ever known, from nothing more than kissing the woman in his arms.

Her mouth was a gift, one he wanted to spend hours exploring. Days. Weeks. And yet, he couldn't keep his lips from roving across her jaw so that he could lick the sensitive skin of her neck.

Touching, tasting her like this was more than he'd ever thought he'd get to experience. But now that his pent-up need was finally starting to spill through the cracks in his control, the entire dam was about to break. A handful of perfect kisses wasn't enough to quench his thirst for her. He wanted more. *Needed* more.

So much more that when she said, "I can't get enough of you," he officially lost his mind and reached around to the back of her dress.

Easily finding the zipper, he felt her shiver as he slid it down her spine, his fingertips grazing her soft skin. Just like that, the dress fell, and she was bared to him. There was enough moonlight shining through the trees for him to see that she was wearing only a wisp of panties.

Heels.

And nothing else.

Suzanne wasn't shy as he took in her nearly nude body, nor did she start posing for him like other women had. She simply stood and let him look his fill.

Let him reach out like a man possessed to caress her breasts.

Let him cup the soft swells in his big hands.

Let him slide his callused fingertips over the tightening peaks.

Let him lower his mouth and run his tongue over her.

Let him rain endless kisses over one breast, and then the other, while she arched into his hands, his mouth, whispering his name and tangling her hands in his hair to bring him close and keep him there.

He wanted to drop to his knees before her. Wanted to worship every inch of her body. Wanted to take off the last inches of fabric that hid the rest of her from him. Wanted to press hot kisses between her thighs until she wasn't just whispering his name, but crying it out.

He was so far gone that he was already halfway there, was pressing kisses to the undersides of her breasts, to the top of her rib cage, to the delicious skin above her belly button, his knees almost on the ground, when a branch broke beneath his foot. Loud enough to break through the desire that had made him blind to all reason, to all sense.

What the hell was he doing?

The question whiplashed through his brain as he finally came back to his senses. Close enough to sanity to realize that not only was he kissing Suzanne, but he'd also stripped off her clothes outdoors, right outside a massive celebrity wedding where anyone could walk by and find them.

He'd told her brothers, *She's safe with me.* He'd said, *I won't let anything happen to her.* But he'd just made a complete mockery of those promises.

He'd vowed to protect her.

He'd nearly ruined her instead.

CHAPTER NINETEEN

Best. Kiss. Ever.

Suzanne had never felt so good. So alive. She almost pinched herself to make sure it wasn't just another sexy dream.

She'd thought kissing Roman would be good. But the reality was a whole lot closer to *mind-blowing*. Although even that wasn't strong enough for the way his kisses were making her feel.

It had all happened so fast. First they were yelling at each other. Then he was saying all those amazing things about how much he wanted her. Then one kiss was spinning out into a dozen across her face and neck and shoulders. Then her dress was off...and he was doing the most incredible things with his hands and mouth.

He kissed her, touched her, with pure, unadulterated desperation. She wanted him as badly. Craved him more with every touch, every kiss. She wanted Roman sweet. She wanted him rough. She wanted him slow. She wanted him fast.

She wanted him any and every way she could get him.

"Suzanne, we shouldn't be doing this here."

She wouldn't have been at all averse to making love right where they were, but he was right. It would be smarter to find somewhere more private. A room they wouldn't have to leave for hours and hours.

"I know a place," she told him. "There's a cabin near my father's house that no one ever uses."

She was about to take his hand and lead him there when she belatedly realized her dress was lying on the ground. That was how much his kisses had spun her out of the real world—she hadn't even realized she was wearing only her underwear.

"I should probably put this back on first," she said with a laugh as she bent to pick up the dress. She felt giddy, as though she would never be sad again, never stop smiling.

He silently helped her into the dress, holding the fabric out so that she didn't accidentally catch it with a heel. She loved how gentle his hands were as he slid the dress up over her naked skin, then zipped it into place.

Desperate to kiss him again, she wound her arms around his neck and was closing her eyes and leaning in when she felt his hands grip her forearms.

"Suzanne, stop."

Her mouth grazed his as the words came out. But it wasn't so much what he'd said that gave her pause—it was the way he was touching her. For the past few minutes, he'd been doing anything he could to pull her closer.

Suddenly, it felt as if he was trying to push her away instead.

"No." She wouldn't let him do this again. "You're not going to tell me this is all a big mistake." But by the set of his jaw, she could see that was *exactly* what he was about to say.

"I shouldn't have talked to you like that. Shouldn't have kissed you like that." His teeth clenched tightly before he unlocked them enough to grind out, "Shouldn't have unzipped your dress and touched you like that. Shouldn't have been about to get on my knees so that I could—" He cut himself off with a curse.

Earlier, when he'd pulled away on the dance floor, she'd assumed it must be because she wasn't pretty enough, wasn't sexy enough, wasn't feminine enough for him. But now she knew for sure that none of those were the true reasons.

Roman wanted her. Wanted her with a depth of passion that took her breath away. And not because she'd somehow managed to seduce him into crossing professional lines the way she'd originally planned.

The attraction, the heat between them was real. Unavoidable. Undeniable.

"I lost control with you," he said, guilt underpinning his every word.

"I *loved* it when you lost control." How could she get him to see that they were two adults who could break whatever rules they wanted to? That just because he'd come into her life as her bodyguard didn't mean they had to hold to any kind of professional relationship now. "I loved kissing you. I loved everything we were doing." She'd never been this bold with a lover before, but she needed him to know. "I want to do more." She wouldn't let herself back away now. "I want to do *everything*. With you. Tonight."

* * *

Roman battled viciously with the desire that was swamping every cell in his body. He needed to force himself to do the right thing, rather than wishing he could keep kissing Suzanne. He needed to stop fantasizing about stripping her dress away again so that they could finish what they'd started beneath a moonlit sky and a thousand silver branches.

But as she stood in front of him in her wrinkled dress, her hair tangled from his hands, her mouth swollen from his kisses, she was... God, she was stunning. Just looking at her made him ache. And now that he knew how she felt in his arms? Now that he knew her taste? Now that he'd heard her sounds of pleasure?

No. He couldn't let himself spin out on any of that. What he needed to do was keep his mouth and hands to himself from here on out, and then go confess everything to her brothers.

Pain speared him right in the center of his chest from the sure knowledge that tonight was going to be the last night he ever spent with her.

Ever since he'd become an adult, Roman had always done what needed to be done, no matter how difficult. But nothing in his life had ever felt as hard as saying, "I need to take you back to your house and confirm that your father can stay with you. And then I'm going to find your brothers."

She shook her head, hard enough that her long hair moved as if in a wild breeze over her shoulders. "Don't."

"I have to."

"They'll insist you quit."

The twisting in his gut tightened down. "They will."

"And you'll go, won't you? You'll just walk out of my life as fast as you walked in. Here one day, gone the next, as if nothing that happened between us mattered at all."

"*Suzanne.*" He couldn't hold back the emotion in his voice. Could barely keep himself from reaching for her as he said, "It mattered. *You* matter."

Renewed hope flashed in her eyes. "Then you'll stay."

Lord, how he wished he could. "We both know that's a bad idea."

"You want to hear about bad ideas? The clothes I've been wearing, the skin-tight dresses and heels? They aren't me. But I had a plan the first couple of days to try to *seduce*"—she put the word in air quotes—"you into kissing me so that you'd have to resign."

Before he could say anything in response to her admission—one that finally had everyone's reactions to her outfits making perfect sense—she said, "I know, it was stupid. And wearing heels this high and pointy all day sucks, by the way, although the dresses aren't so bad. But I was so frustrated by the way my brothers had forced a bodyguard on me, and by how stubborn you were about taking the job, that I couldn't see any other way out of it. Only, now that you've kissed me, I don't want out of it anymore. Even before you kissed me, I didn't want you to leave. And I don't think you do either, no matter how many times you've tried to act like you do whenever we start getting close."

"Suzanne—"

But she wouldn't let him get a word in. "Don't you

see, we don't know if we're a good idea or a bad one yet. And if we do things your way, if we do things my brothers' way, and you resign tonight just because we kissed, we're never going to have a chance to find out. I've spent nearly my entire life writing code, and you know what I've learned a million times over? That if I give up every time something doesn't work, it will *never* work. I've always fought like hell for the things that matter most." Her eyes flashed in the moonlight. "For the *people* who matter most."

The words had barely left her lips when she spun around and went flying through the forest in her dress and heels, back in the direction of the wedding reception.

CHAPTER TWENTY

With everything Suzanne had said spinning around inside his brain—inside his heart—Roman was slower than usual as he pursued her through the trees.

"Where are you going?" He knew, of course, but maybe a miracle would happen and she'd give him a different answer than the one he was expecting.

"To talk with my brothers before you do." She whipped him a warning look over her shoulder. "And don't try to stop me. This is *my* life, not theirs, and it's long past time the three of them understood that."

Roman saw where she was coming from, and he couldn't say he didn't agree. At the same time, Suzanne's standing up for herself with her family didn't change what he had to do. She needed another bodyguard, someone one hundred percent professional who wouldn't constantly be distracted by attraction and jealousy. Someone who would do his job, rather than spend all his time trying to learn the inner workings of her heart.

She knew exactly where to find her brothers—two

of them, at least. Alec and Harry were sitting on the end of a boat dock halfway between the Inn downtown and their father's home, beers in hand. Roman could easily imagine the four Sullivan siblings together on this dock over the years.

"You're lucky to have them, you know."

That stopped Suzanne at the edge of the dock. "I know I am." She turned to him, and the moonlight illuminated the beauty and fierce intelligence that rocked his world every time he looked at her. "They've always taken care of me, the same way I've taken care of them. But being loved by someone doesn't give them license to walk all over you."

Her words hit home in a big way. Roman's father had always said he was pushing Roman to fight more, to win more, to play for the bigger purses, because he loved him. Because he was looking out for his son. Because he wanted Roman to have a better future than he did working at the factory. It had taken Roman a lot of years to understand that his father hadn't been lying—it was the best way Tommy Huson could parent after being raised by a father who had always spoken with his fists. Unfortunately, it had turned out that what Tommy thought was best for his son was the worst. Spending every night as a teenager in the boxing ring hadn't made Roman happy. Especially when he could never make up for the damage he'd done to some of the other guys he'd fought.

Alec heard them first, turning with a smile. "We were wondering where you and Roman were." His grin fell away damned quick, however, as he took in Suzanne's wrinkled dress, messy hair, and fierce expression.

"Something happened." Alec jumped up from his perch at the end of the dock, Harry springing up beside him. "Are you okay, Suz?"

"I'm fine." When one of her heels caught between two planks of wood, she kicked them off. Being barefoot and at least half a foot shorter than her brothers didn't make her any less impressive, however, as she walked up to them. "I asked Roman to kiss me." She paused as if for impact. "He did. And I kissed him back."

A feral growl emerged from Alec's throat as he leaped past Suzanne to get to Roman. He wouldn't normally have let the other man's hands grip his neck, but it was no less than he deserved for doing exactly what he shouldn't have with the one woman on the planet who was completely off-limits.

Harry and Suzanne were both working to pull Alec off as he roared, "We hired you to protect our sister." His fury reverberated through the night sky. "Not to take advantage of her!"

"He didn't take advantage of me," Suzanne said as

she finally pushed between them, making Alec's fingers slide from Roman's neck. "I already told you, *I'm* the one who asked him to kiss me."

If anything, Alec grew angrier. "He's your god-damned bodyguard, Suz! Not some guy we set you up with on a blind date."

"Roman is a great bodyguard. I don't want one, and I still have to admit that. But he isn't just a great bodyguard. He's intelligent. And sweet. And easy to talk to. And—" She shook her head. "I don't have to explain anything to you. Neither of us do. If we want to kiss again, then we'll kiss again whether you like it or not."

Jesus, she was a fireball. A gorgeous fireball whom Roman hadn't been able to figure out how to keep his mouth—or hands—away from.

"Like hell you will." Alec shot Roman another furious look. "You're fired, you bastard. And if you come anywhere near my sister again, I'm going to absolutely destroy you."

"Alec." Harrison's voice was loud. Firm. As firm as the push he gave his brother in the opposite direction of Roman and Suzanne. "Tempers are too high right now. We should let everything settle and come back to discuss things later when everyone is feeling more rational."

"I'm feeling *perfectly* rational," Suzanne insisted.

Roman wished he could say the same thing. But the truth was that he hadn't felt rational since the second he'd set eyes on Suzanne.

She turned away from her brother to face him. "I know you came here to resign, and I know that's what I've said I wanted all along, but now I want you to stay."

"You've changed your mind about wanting a bodyguard?"

"You make me feel safe. And like I said before, I have more thinking to do about things before I can make any definite decisions." She held his gaze in the moonlight. "But I don't want you to go. Not yet."

"If you think I'm going to let this guy work for you anymore—"

She spun back to Alec. "I didn't come here so that you could tell me what to do! I came here because I love you enough to tell you I've made up my mind, and you're not going to change it." Again, she turned to Roman. "Stay."

He'd never wanted anything more. But just because he wanted it didn't mean it was right. "You need someone who can be totally professional."

"Someone who doesn't care about me as anything but a job, you mean?"

Damn it, when she put it like that...

Still, he made himself say, in as gentle a voice as

possible, "I'll make some calls first thing tomorrow and find you—"

"No. It's you or no one. And you know I'm not bluffing. I'll chew up and spit out any other bodyguard you assign to me."

"What's going on?" None of them had noticed Drake walking up the dock. "I came to let you guys know Smith and Valentina are heading out soon, so you can say good-bye. You guys look like you're about to throw punches at each other."

"Roman and I kissed," Suzanne informed her youngest brother. "And now he thinks he needs to resign, even though us kissing in no way diminishes how good he is at his job. Even if I'm still not sure I need a bodyguard, he's the best. And if we want to kiss, we're going to kiss, no matter what you or Harry or Alec think, or say, or do."

Drake looked from Suzanne to Roman to his brothers, then back at his sister. "I'll admit we were pretty heavy-handed about hiring Roman, but if you two have crossed a line—"

"Crossed a line?" She poked Drake's chest. "I've supported you every step of the way with Rosa. I freaking *love* that woman, but even if I didn't, I would have sucked it up and gotten behind you both. How dare you even think about questioning what I'm feeling for Roman?"

She felt something for him.

Roman's heart swelled. It didn't matter that he knew better, knew she was completely off-limits, knew he could never be with her in a million years. It still meant something hearing that his feelings weren't one-way. Meant something big. Because a woman like Suzanne wouldn't feel something for a guy who was completely worthless, would she?

No one had ever stepped up for him the way she was tonight. No one had faced down a firing squad for him. No one had put her relationship with her family on the line for him. Roman wished she could know how much it meant to him. But at the same time, he'd never forgive himself if he put a wedge between her and her family.

"I'm not worth it, Suzanne. Not worth fighting over."

"Maybe you are, maybe you aren't," she retorted. "But I'm not letting you walk out of my life until I know for sure one way or the other. And," she said as she glared at each of her brothers, "I'm not letting any of you force Roman out of my life either."

"Suz," Harry said, "this isn't like you."

Though tensions were about as high as they could get, Harry wasn't yelling. Roman had noticed over the past couple of years that when the academic spoke, people always listened. Likely because he never raised his voice. And also because he was a good guy on every level. Someone who would never cross the kind of line Roman had tonight.

"There's no question that Alec needs to cool down before he opens his mouth again, and Drake probably should too." Harry shot serious looks at both his brothers to make sure they understood. "But in the morning, Suz, I'm sure you'll understand why Roman needs to resign and find you a new bodyguard."

"No, *you* need to understand something. All of you need to understand it. I'm done being the peacekeeper. I'm done being the one to make nice between everyone and keep my own thoughts and hopes and desires at bay to try to make sure everyone else gets what they want and stays happy. *I'm* finally going to be the one making some waves. And all of you are going to have to deal with it." She glared at her brothers. "I forgave you for going behind my back and hiring Roman in the first place. But don't test me on this one." She ran her hands over her hair and then her dress. "And now that I've finally said what's needed to be said for a very long time, I'm going back to the wedding so that I can say good-bye to Smith and Valentina. If Roman wants to follow me back, fine. But the rest of you had better keep your distance right now." With that, she stalked back down the dock, only slowing to pick up her shoes.

Of course Roman was going to follow her. And not

only because it was his job. Inside of a week, she'd become the most important person in the world to him. But first he needed to say a few things to her brothers.

"I owe all of you an apology for what I've done," he said in a grave tone, "and I want you to know I won't be taking any money from you. I never intended for this to happen."

"Damn straight kissing our sister shouldn't have happened," Alec snarled, his rage not having lessened. "We hired you to protect Suzanne, not take advantage of her."

Roman knew he was in the wrong—he shouldn't have touched Suzanne, plain and simple. But that didn't mean he could let her brother get away with being an idiot where she was concerned. "If you actually think someone could trick your sister into kissing him, then you don't know her as well as you think you do. Suzanne is too smart and too tough to be taken advantage of by anyone, no matter how beautiful she is."

Alec advanced on him again. "Of course I know Suzanne is smart, tough, and beautiful. She's too good for you in every way."

"She is."

Roman's quick agreement made Alec pause. A couple of beats later, however, he let his anger loose again. "I know what you're like with women. I know how you treat them."

"I'm making a vow to you right now that I will never treat Suzanne like that."

"Are you asking us to believe you're going to change your stripes now?"

"No."

"Then what the hell are you going to do?"

"I'm going to do whatever I can to convince her that she needs another bodyguard, and then I'm going to get out of her life. And stay out."

Roman had turned to track down Suzanne at the party, when Drake asked, "What if she won't let you go?"

Roman's gut twisted tighter than ever before as he shook his head, letting Drake know that wasn't an option. If push came to shove and he had to tell Suzanne the full truth about his past, once she heard it all she'd understand why he could never be her dream man. No matter how hot their kisses were, she'd want to run from him and never look back.

"Don't worry," he promised her brothers, "she will."

* * *

"Something's gotten into Suzanne." Alec was still fuming. "She's never acted like that. Never talked to us like that."

"No, she hasn't, but that doesn't mean she isn't right." Harry looked pensive. "She's always been the peacekeeper. She's always put herself last if it meant making sure everyone else was happy."

"Face it, guys," Drake said, "from what I've seen so far, Roman seems to make her pretty happy. Happy enough that she's not about to let him quit until they figure out if they can make things work." None of them wanted to hear it, but that didn't change the facts. "I'm worried about her too, but you both know I never liked this plan to hire a bodyguard behind her back."

"It was the only way we could make sure she was protected." Alec's hands fisted again. "At least, she *should* have been."

"Looks to me like he's doing a good job of protecting her," Drake pointed out. "All they did was kiss."

"He's her goddamned bodyguard!" Alec's frustration bubbled over again. "I can't believe I handpicked him for the job. What the hell was I thinking?"

Harry rubbed a hand over his head, leaving his dark hair standing on end. "Two things are clear right now. She won't stand for letting Roman resign—or be fired. And, whether this was the plan or not, she likes him. More than she's liked any guy in a very long time."

"I wouldn't have let any of you stand in my way

with Rosa," Drake said. "If Suz is serious about Roman, she's not going to be any different."

"Jesus." Alec looked like his whole world was turning inside out. "You really think she's *serious* about that bastard?"

"That bastard was your friend ten minutes ago," Drake pointed out.

"I'm itching to rip into someone," Alec growled. "Don't push me right now, little brother."

"If you need a sparring session to let off some steam, old man"—Drake took a step forward—"I'm up for it."

Just as he had dozens of times before, Harry got between them. "Beating the crap out of each other tonight isn't going to help Suzanne."

Alec's fists opened and closed several times before he finally backed away from Drake. "Swear to God, if he hurts her…"

"If he hurts her, we'll all make him pay," Harry agreed. "But right now the three of us need to do exactly what she said—take a step back and let her live her own life without us always butting in."

"I can never forget the way she looked when Mom left and we found out she wasn't coming back." Alec's eyes were bleak as he remembered the past. "She cried so long, so hard, that her eyes swelled completely shut. Our nanny took her to the doctor, and I insisted on

going with them. The doctor said nothing was wrong
with her, that the swelling would go down by the next
day. But he didn't know what he was talking about—
everything was wrong. From that day forward, I vowed
never to let anything happen to make her cry like that
again." He looked at his brothers. "If Roman makes her
cry, I won't be able to control myself."

Harry picked up Alec's beer and brought it to him.
"You've done a hell of a job taking care of Suz. Seems
to me that the beatdown she gave us proves that she
learned plenty from you about how to take care of
herself."

"She did a great job of nailing us to the wall, didn't
she?" Alec grudgingly admitted.

"She sure did," Drake agreed. "I kind of wish I'd
seen the first part of the fireworks out here."

"Something tells me you're going to have another
chance, because if she and Roman do end up working
things out, we're all going to have to figure out a way
to deal with the two of them being a couple." Harry
nudged Alec. "Especially you."

"Roman said he's going to do whatever it takes to
make her forget about him." Alec sounded so hopeful
that Drake felt a little sorry for his brother.

"I never thought Roman was a fool," Harry said.
"But if he believes that she'll let him walk out of her
life, then he's just proved me wrong. And you

shouldn't make the mistake of believing that's going to happen, either."

Alec's jaw tightened. "Just the thought of them as a couple makes me want to go ballistic."

"I feel sorry for your future daughters." Only his siblings could have gotten away with talking to Alec like this. No one else in his world would have the guts. "If you're this protective of your sister connecting with someone you like," Drake continued, "you're never going to let your own kid out of her tower on high."

Alec shuddered at the thought. "Yet another good reason never to get married or have kids. I'll leave that to the two of you. And to Suz." He scowled again, obviously thinking of Roman kissing his sister.

Alec talked a big game about staying solo forever, but when it came right down to it, he was utterly committed to family. And one day, Drake had no doubt, a woman would come along who would change Alec's mind about absolutely everything, exactly the way Rosa had come along and changed his.

CHAPTER TWENTY-ONE

By the time Roman caught up to Suzanne at the wedding reception, he was clearly dead set on reverting to the no-emotions bodyguard, trying to act as if they'd never kissed. He kept her in sight, but kept his distance at the same time.

She'd always prided herself on being the kind of woman who talked things through with people in a reasonable manner rather than stomping away. But if she went up to Roman now, she was either going to punch him or kiss him. Or both! She wouldn't regret another kiss…but she might regret knocking him to the ground in front of everyone.

A group of her cousins from the West Coast were all chatting by the rose arbor. They were always fun to be with and made her feel loved. Lord knew she needed that even more than usual tonight. She was heading over to them when Buck Elroy intercepted her.

"I've been looking for you. Any chance you'd still like to have that drink?"

She'd forgotten all about him. Hadn't given him one single thought since she and Roman had went off into the woods together.

Feeling awful about the way she'd treated Buck, she said, "I'm glad we've gotten to know each other, and I had a lot of fun dancing with you, but I didn't mean to give you the wrong impression. Not," she added, "that I would assume you're interested in me in that way."

"I am."

"Oh." That stopped her for long enough to realize that Roman had been right. If she'd been up for a wedding fling, Buck would be more than willing to join her. "Well, the thing is—" She couldn't keep from looking over at Roman, who was standing by the fountain glowering at everyone. Especially Buck. "I'm not actually on the market." Because even though she and Roman were at a heck of a crossroads, she couldn't turn away from her feelings for him.

"I'd like to try to change your mind, Suzanne."

Buck was sweet. She knew how hard Hollywood relationships could be, but one day she hoped he'd find a wonderful woman to be with, the way Smith had with Valentina. "Sorry, Buck."

She didn't get the sense that he let much defeat him, but tonight he simply leaned closer to give her a peck on the cheek. "He's a lucky guy."

Buck had barely walked away when her eagle-eyed female relatives waved her over.

"Spill," her cousin Lori said the second Suzanne sat down. The women had kicked off their heels and were relaxing on outdoor couches with cups of hot tea as the night wound down. Lori's skin glowed from the pregnancy she was wearing as well as she wore absolutely everything.

Lori's twin Sophie nodded. They were both very pretty, but as different as could be. Lori was loud and always moving, whereas Sophie carefully considered every word before it came out of her mouth and was happy to spend hours curled up with a book. Their nicknames—Naughty and Nice—fit them perfectly. Sophie's husband Jake had taken their three-year-old twins to put them to bed a while ago.

"Normally," Sophie said, "you know I'd tell Lori to butt out, but I'm dying to know what's going on with you and Buck Elroy and your bodyguard. Even Mom is utterly intrigued by your love triangle—aren't you?"

Mary Sullivan looked a little guilty. "Sorry, honey."

Mia walked up, curiosity gleaming in her eyes. "Are you grilling Suz about all the men who want her?" When Lori nodded, she turned to Suzanne and said, "I haven't missed the good stuff, have I? Tell us *everything*. Seriously, don't leave anything out."

Suzanne nearly groaned out loud. "First of all,

there's absolutely nothing going on with Buck. He's nice, but I'm not interested."

"Of course you're not," Mia said. "I mean, Buck Elroy is a good-looking guy and all, but I swear, I could kill Ford for not letting on that he even *knew* a body-guard this exceptionally gorgeous, let alone that Roman was working for you. So...what's going on with the two of you?"

"All I know," Suzanne said, "is that I didn't want him around, but then I kind of did, and then I thought we were getting closer, but he kept pulling back, and then tonight we kissed, and it was the best kiss of my entire life, and—"

"The best kiss of your life?" Lori fanned herself. "I knew it. Look at him." She wasn't the slightest bit subtle as she ogled him. But Suzanne figured married, pregnant women could get away with it. "How could he kiss any other way? Which begs the question, what are you doing here with us right now when you could be doing more super-crazy-hot kissing with your super-crazy-hot bodyguard?"

"Because right after we kissed, he apologized for stepping over a line and tried to resign." Suzanne tried to keep her lips from pulling up into a snarl. "I wouldn't let him. And I wouldn't let my brothers fire him either."

"*Brothers.*" Lori, Sophie, and Mia sighed the word

in unison.

"Don't even get me started," Suzanne said, losing the battle to hold back a snarl.

"When you were a little girl," Mary said, "Alec wouldn't let you out of his sight. Not to play with his friends or to let you play with yours. He even insisted on being there to drop you off at school and pick you up every day." She put her hand over Suzanne's, her fingers still elegant and strong though she was in her seventies. "He wants so badly for you to be happy."

"I know he does." Suzanne squeezed her beloved aunt's hand. If only she could have had a mother like Mary. But she couldn't go back and change time. No one could. All she could do was keep moving forward, the best way she knew how. "Alec has been the most terrific brother anyone could have. So have Harry and Drake. But what if Roman makes me happy and they refuse to see it?"

Mary pulled her in close, as if she were one of her own daughters. "As long as I've known you, you've never let anyone stand in your way. Whatever you decide about Roman, I guarantee all of us are going to be behind you one hundred percent. Even your brothers. And if Roman's kisses are as great as you're saying..."

Suzanne lifted her fingers to her mouth, which tingled just from the memory of Roman's kisses. "They are."

"Good," Mary said with a wide grin. "As far as I'm concerned, every woman deserves a man who knows his way around a kiss."

"Amen to that, Aunt Mary," Mia said as she raised her glass.

And as the other women all joined in the toast, Suzanne gave silent thanks, yet again, that she had the best family in the world.

* * *

Suzanne's cousins walked back with her and Roman to her father's house so that she could give Lori a Wild Child rattle toy and Sophie the LEGO Duplo building kits she'd brought for her twins. Lori, predictably, pestered Roman the entire way with invasive questions about his other clients. He was polite, but didn't divulge anything.

By the time her cousins left, Suzanne realized she was absolutely exhausted. Too tired to keep trying to work out exactly what was going on between her and Roman—and what she wanted to do about it. Yes, she wanted him to be her lover. But even if he could forget his rules about client/bodyguard relations long enough to make love to her, would one sinfully hot night with Roman come anywhere close to being enough?

By the time he walked her up to her bedroom, the

only thing she knew for sure was that she wanted him to wrap his arms around her and hold her. She'd known how to ask for a kiss, but she didn't know how to ask for that. But when they stopped in front of her door and she turned to look up into his dark, serious eyes, he somehow knew. He'd barely opened his arms for her when she barreled into them.

Being close to him, touching him, was electric as always, but as he stroked her hair, there was comfort there too. So much warmth and relief that she swore she could almost fall asleep standing up, if he kept holding her like this.

"Get some rest, Suzanne." His low voice caressed her the way she wished his hands would. "I'll be right here in the morning."

Despite the way her brothers had always watched over her—or maybe partly because of how they'd hovered so close—she'd spent her entire life proving to everyone that she was tough. Bulletproof. But tonight, it seemed, Roman saw the truth. That she was only human, after all. And sometimes she needed someone else to lean on.

Only the knowledge that he wasn't going to disappear on her in the middle of the night could have made her let him go. Taking one last deep breath of his clean, masculine scent, she forced herself to draw away from his arms. But instead of letting her go completely, he slid his hands up from her waist to cup her face.

"No one has ever stood up for me the way you did tonight. I would never want to come between you and your brothers, but you need to know how much it meant that you'd face them down for me."

God, she loved it when he touched her like this. When he looked at her like she amazed him. Couldn't he see that he amazed her too?

"They tend to forget how to be rational when they go into overprotective mode." She wanted to say so much more. She wanted to invite him into her bedroom to continue what they'd started in the forest with the kiss of a lifetime. But Roman would never forgive himself for sleeping with her in her father's house, with her brothers down the hall.

Roman was one of the most respectful, honorable people she'd ever met. Regardless of how badly she wanted him—*needed* him—it wouldn't be fair to ask him to cross any more boundaries tonight. Or to break any more of his rules. Especially when she still hadn't completely figured out her own boundaries, her own rules, where he was concerned.

Her heart had never been at risk like this before. And the truth was that for all she claimed not to be afraid of anything, right now she was downright terrified.

His lips brushed her forehead as he lowered his

hands from her face. "Good night, Suzanne."

"Good night, Roman."

When she stepped inside her bedroom and turned on the light, she almost didn't recognize the woman who stared back at her from the mirror over the dresser. Had her eyes ever been that bright? Her skin that flushed? Her expression so full of longing?

Turning away from the mirror, she unzipped her dress and forced herself to hang it up instead of leaving it lying in a heap on the shiny pine floorboards. By the time she'd finished brushing her teeth, her eyes were nearly shut. Wearing only her underwear, she crawled beneath the sheets. But the sleep she so desperately needed wouldn't come.

By three a.m., Suzanne was so tired of tossing and turning that she put on the sweatshirt and sweatpants she kept in her old bedroom's dresser and went downstairs to scrounge up a snack, then settle in with some new code on her laptop in the kitchen. If she couldn't sleep, she might as well work.

After putting together a sandwich on Summer Lake Bakery's delicious bread, she headed for the front porch that looked out over the lake. She was settling down on a double rocker under a blanket when she saw a shadow moving on the sand just beyond the porch.

She froze, her heart pounding like crazy and her

breath stilling in her chest. Were her brothers right? Was someone truly after her? Someone who had tracked her down to her cousin's wedding, news of which had finally leaked out to the entire world?

Damn it, no. She wasn't going to sit here and be a victim. She was going to fight like hell.

But before she could scream or spring up out of the rocker to throw any punches, moonlight illuminated her father's face. "Dad, it's you." She sat back hard, her hand over her chest as if that would help slow her heart rate.

"Honey, I didn't mean to scare you." He moved quickly up to the porch and scooted in next to her on the rocker. "I couldn't sleep, so I took a walk along the shore." He looked down at the sandwich she'd yet to take a bite of. "Couldn't sleep either, I take it?"

She shook her head. She gestured to her food. "Want half?"

"Sure." He took it, then said, "Want to talk about what's wrong?"

Normally, she'd say everything was fine, that she was up because of a problem she was having with her code. Anything to make sure that her father never had to worry about her. But she couldn't tonight. Not after that *kiss*.

And not when she'd longed for a moment like this with her father her entire life.

She put the sandwich on a side table. "I'm confused."

"About Roman?"

It shouldn't surprise her that he'd figured it out so fast when pretty much everyone she'd spoken to tonight had commented on the sparks between them. Even Buck, with whom she'd danced half the night, had immediately accepted that he couldn't compete with her feelings for Roman.

When she nodded, her father put his sandwich on the other side table. "What happened?"

He had never asked her such a direct personal question. She hoped this meant things really were starting to change between them.

"I didn't want Roman around at first, at least, not as my bodyguard. But I've come to really like and respect him. And—" This was kind of weird to talk about with her dad, but she didn't want to hold back now that he finally seemed ready to connect. "Well, there's an attraction between us that just won't quit, even though he's hellbent on keeping our client/bodyguard relationship strictly professional. But though he's one of the most honorable men I've ever met, something happened between us tonight."

Her father tensed up beside her as she ventured into TMI territory, but he didn't immediately flip out and start raging the way Alec had. Instead he remained silent, letting her process her thoughts. It reminded her of Harry, who never stomped over the silence the way she and Alec so often did.

"I stopped Roman from resigning after he kissed me. And I stopped the boys from firing him too." Her heart was in her throat as she said, "I can't stand the thought of his leaving. Of never seeing him again." Again her father remained quiet as she tried to make sense of all the thoughts, the feelings spinning around inside. "All my life I've been so rational, especially about the men I date. But with Roman, I've never felt *less* rational. I almost wonder if the wedding is messing with my mind. Because even though I love these family weddings, every time I go to one, I can't help but wish for someone special for myself. Someone to say all those lovely vows to. Someone who wants to say them to me too." She would have laughed at herself if she could have. "What if that's all this is? Just post-wedding longings?"

As if he understood that she'd gotten everything out, her father finally spoke. "Do you really think that's all this is?"

"I don't know."

"I'm sorry that I wasn't always around when you were a kid—"

"Dad, you don't have to keep apologizing."

"I do. And I will. But right now I'm trying to be the

father I should have been a long time ago by reminding you that the words *I don't know* aren't in your vocabulary. More than any of the other kids—heck, more than anyone else I've ever known—you don't stop until you get exactly what you want."

That gave her pause. "I wish I could be clear-headed and rational about Roman the way I am with everything else."

"Love doesn't work like that, honey."

She turned so quickly to see if he was serious that she nearly gave herself whiplash. *"Love."* The word croaked out of her throat. "You think I'm in *love* with Roman?"

"Back when you were in high school, you were the only girl who was more passionate about computers than boys. I expected that to change, but it never really did. Not until Roman came into your life. Because I never saw you look like this with any of the guys you've dated. I've never heard you sound like this when you talk about any of them. And I've definitely never seen any of them look at you the way Roman does."

Maybe it would make her father uncomfortable if she asked him this, but she needed to know. "How does he look at me?"

"Like he'd do absolutely anything for you. Like the moon and the sun both revolve around you." Her father's lips curved up at the corners. "Like he loves you too."

Longing and panic battled within Suzanne as her father reached for her hands and gripped them tightly. "I wish things had been different for you and your brothers. I wish your mother and I hadn't made such a mess of things. I wish we'd showed you what healthy, sweet, good love looks like so that you'd recognize it when you found it yourself."

"I see it with my cousins. With Drake and Rosa."

"I'm glad you see that love can work. That you believe it's possible."

"I've always believed love could work. That's why I've been so careful about making sure to take things slow and think things through carefully with everyone I've dated. Because I want to make absolutely sure that nothing goes wrong for me like it did with you and Mom. But with Roman...that's not how it's been. Nothing's been slow. And I can barely think straight when he's around." There was no way to hold back the truth any longer. "I'm scared, Dad. Absolutely freaking terrified about what I'm feeling for him—and how fast it hit me."

Her father squeezed her hands tightly. "I know how scary that can be, but it doesn't mean *fast* or *irrational* is bad."

"It was for you and Mom." She felt bleak as she

looked into his eyes. "It was horrible."

"It was. But you're not your mother. Yes, you have the same huge heart that she did, but where she was flyaway, you're grounded. Where she was anxious, you're confident. Where she was lost without someone to guide her every step of the way, you're a brilliant explorer, always braving new territory and conquering it." Emotion swamped his face, his voice. "If you love Roman, and he loves you, I sure as hell hope you won't let anyone, or anything, stand in the way of being together."

"Don't worry," she said with a slightly soggy laugh, "I won't let Alec run my life."

"I'm not just talking about Alec." Her father inhaled deeply, as if he was afraid he was about to say something she wouldn't want to hear. "I know you love your computers. But take it from someone who learned the pitfalls of obsession the hard way—enjoy your work. Take pride in being the best at what you do. But always remember that in the end, love and family are the only things that really matter."

CHAPTER TWENTY-TWO

There were a million things Suzanne wanted to say to Roman during their drive back to New York City the following day. She wanted to confess it all. Her feelings. Her confusion. The way her father had held up a mirror in front of her last night and made her see the truth that she had never been—and could never become—like her mother. He'd reminded Suzanne that she was strong. Courageous.

She had always been willing to take a risk with her software and her business. Now it was finally time to take an even bigger risk with her heart. But would Roman be willing to take as big a risk with his? Especially given that for all the times he'd come close, he'd always ended up pulling back.

Unfortunately, within minutes of waking up after the three hours of sleep she'd managed to get in, she was pulled into a call with her Information Systems team. Though it was a Saturday, they were working to decode a new bug in the MavG1 software. She'd promised the Mavericks they were going to get into beta testing right away and all of them intended to make good on that promise.

Within the hour, she was deep in work mode. Still, when Roman knocked on her bedroom door, her heart leaped. She'd already become addicted to seeing him first thing every morning.

As soon as he opened the door, he stepped inside and noted the two laptops she had open—along with the fact that she was wearing only a sweatshirt over her underwear. The thick duvet she was sitting on cross-legged covered her up pretty well, but she was still aware of how much skin she was showing.

He cleared his throat as he dragged his gaze away from her legs. "Problems?"

She put her call on mute. "There's a bug in the new code, which means I need to get back to the office right away. And I'll need to work in the car, if you don't mind driving." Her voice sounded as breathless as his did rough.

"I'll pack food and coffee for the road. Focus on what you need to do and I'll take care of everything else."

She already knew Roman was someone you want-ed with you in a crisis, but the way he quietly and efficiently moved through the bedroom and bathroom packing up her things almost made her want to cry with relief. "Thank you. I owe you big time."

"You don't owe me anything. I'm happy to help anytime you need it." He paused for a beat before adding, "And not because it's my job."

It was the perfect opening for the talk she so badly wanted to have. But her staff was waiting for her to weigh in on how to fix the code.

Reluctantly, she took her phone off mute. "I'm going to need fifteen minutes to get on the road, guys, and then you'll have my full attention again."

But though she managed to say a quick good-bye to her father, the only other person in her family who was awake, and then immediately got back onto the call with her team in the car, only part of her attention was on work.

She couldn't stop thinking about Roman. Couldn't help but be distracted by his nearness, his heat, his wickedly sexy good looks. Couldn't stop wishing he would put his arms around her the way he'd held her last night, when he'd made her feel so safe. So comforted.

Before this morning, she would have been horrified by anything less than one hundred percent focus on her job. But after staying up nearly the entire night mulling over what her father had said, she was no longer sure it was a bad thing.

Was her obsession with computers and code really all that different from her father's obsession with painting her mother?

And could she lose everything that truly mattered because of it?

The irony wasn't lost on her that she was asking herself this question while working in a car going seventy miles an hour on the freeway beside the man with whom she was desperate to have a heart-to-heart.

* * *

After five hours of intense work done via phone and computer, she finally pulled out her earbuds, closed her laptop, and dropped her head back against the head-rest. "We're pretty sure the problem is fixed, but I should probably go to the office for a little while, just in case." She could sleep for days. And maybe she did fall asleep for a few minutes, because when she opened her eyes again, Roman had already driven past her office building.

"Where are you going?"

"Home. You didn't get enough sleep last night and you've been working nonstop since you woke up." He frowned, and even that was so sexy she thought she might burst from wanting him. "You work too hard."

"Says the man who's outside my door early every morning and doesn't go to bed until I do."

He didn't argue with her. Rather, after a moment of silence, he nodded. "You're right. I need to make some changes too."

As hope swelled within her, she shoved her computer and phone off her lap. She'd given enough attention to those devices today. It was time to focus on the warm and wonderful human being sitting beside her now. Time to finally confess the depths of her feelings for him. But just as she reached for his hand, he swore.

Following the direction of his furious gaze, she realized they were stuck behind a half-dozen fire engines. And those engines were parked in front of her apartment building.

She reached blindly for the door handle so that she could get out and run over to one of the firemen to find out what had happened. Roman must have anticipated her reaction, because he reached for her hand and held it tightly.

"Wait. Let me pull over, and then we'll find out what's going on." He waited until she looked into his eyes. "Together."

Together. No word had ever sounded so sweet before.

"Okay." Her voice sounded funny. A little airy and squeaky.

Odds were low that this fire had anything to do with her...but what if it did?

It was that *what-if* that had her heart pounding too

fast.

"I'm not going to let anything happen to you." He lifted his hand from hers to stroke her cheek.

She leaned into his touch. "I know." She took another deep breath, and then she was ready to face what she needed to.

Once they got out of the car and had a better sight line to the action, she easily confirmed that it was, in fact, her apartment that had caught fire. Her windows were open and there was a ladder up to her kitchen window. When Roman reached for her hand again, she gripped it tightly. She couldn't imagine facing this without him.

She stopped the closest firefighter, who happened to be the fire chief. "That's my apartment. What happened?"

The man looked sympathetic. "You're Suzanne Sullivan?" When she nodded, he said, "I've been trying to call you for the past half hour."

"I'm sorry, I was on a conference call." Since she hadn't recognized the number as belonging to any of her family members, she had ignored it, figuring it was probably another junk caller.

"Do you have any pets? Any visitors or room-mates?"

"No. Just me. And I've been out of town since Thursday morning. Roman has the apartment next door, and he was with me the whole time."

The fire chief noted their linked hands. "Our investigators are working to figure out where the fire started, and why. I'm afraid we don't have any conclusive evidence yet."

Suzanne always had a solution for any problem that arose, or at the very least, was able to come up with good enough questions to figure out a solution. But all she could do right now was wonder in horror at what could have happened if she and Roman had been home—or if one of her relatives had been staying in her apartment while she was gone. She couldn't stand the thought that anyone else might have ended up hurt because someone wanted to hurt *her*.

As if he could read her mind and knew that her mouth had gone dry and her brain had seized up, Roman drew her into the shelter of his body. "When will Suzanne be able to get back inside?"

"Not tonight, that's for sure. We're doing our best to save your things, but it looks like the fire may have been smoking for a while before it lit. Fortunately, a neighbor downstairs smelled smoke and called 911." She could easily read the concern in the man's eyes. "I'm sorry this happened to you, Ms. Sullivan. Your entire floor is uninhabitable at present due to the smoke damage and ongoing investigation. Do you have somewhere to stay tonight?"

"She'll be staying with me," Roman answered before she could reply that she had three brothers nearby. Roman also gave the fire chief both his cell and landline numbers. "Please also call me with any updates, in case Suzanne is unavailable."

"Is that all right with you, Ms. Sullivan?"

"Yes." It was more than all right. "Roman will look out for me."

After the fire chief shook their hands, then moved away to talk with one of his crew, she looked up again at her windows. A shiver ran through her despite the warm city weather.

"I'll get over losing my clothes and furniture. Junk calls and attacks to my corporate servers are one thing, but if this fire isn't an accident, someone is deliberately trying to destroy the things that are important to me. My father's and brother's paintings. The blanket my Aunt Mary knitted for me. The sculpture my cousin Ryan's wife, Vicki, made me. The family reunion pictures that always make me smile when I'm sitting at my kitchen counter."

Roman pulled her closer, as if he wished he could use his body to shield her from the sight of the fire trucks and firemen working to put out the fire in her apartment.

"When this just seemed like it was about me and my work, I knew I could take care of myself, take care of my company. But the apartment isn't mine. It's my cousin Ian's. And family and friends often stay with me. What if someone I love had been staying in my apartment while we were gone? What if they'd been hurt because someone has it in for me and they got in the way?" Anger burst through her shock and exhaustion. "If it turns out that this fire wasn't an accident, I'm going to give one hundred percent of my focus to figuring out who's after me and nailing them to the wall. They've gone after the wrong woman."

"Yes," Roman agreed, "they most certainly have."

But even as determination solidified within her, the combined feelings of violation and fear hit her so hard that her legs started to feel shaky and the blood drained out of her face. The next thing she knew, Roman had gently moved them back toward his car and they were headed away from the fire trucks and police vehicles.

CHAPTER TWENTY-THREE

Roman had never seen Suzanne like this. Despite her fierce words—and his sure knowledge that she would prevail—she was clearly shell-shocked as they drove to his loft. He held her hand the entire time, never wanting to let her go.

He wanted to tear apart whoever was responsible for making her so pale and quiet, wanted to make that person pay for causing Suzanne even one moment of stress. She already had more than enough to deal with between her company, her pro bono work, and her big family. She didn't need anything else to add stress to her life. Especially not a bodyguard who had let himself get too close. Too attached.

He'd been planning to convince her to accept another bodyguard on their drive back, but she'd been working so hard there hadn't been any time to talk. And then when they'd seen the fire trucks outside her apartment, Roman accepted that there was no way he could leave her until they'd neutralized the threat.

He had just gotten her settled on his couch with a

large glass of wine when she said, "Don't tell my brothers or my father what happened yet."

"They need to know."

"Of course they do. I just need a little more time to process things before they come swarming in even more overprotective and domineering than ever. Plus, they'll insist I stay with one of them. I don't want to leave you, Roman. Not tonight."

Though his first instinct had been to call Alec with the news of the fire, Roman understood why Suzanne wanted a night to let what had happened settle. Not only would she be working full time to corral the four Sullivan men if they were here—but there was simply no way Roman was going to let her stay with anyone else tonight. And not only because his loft was as secure as a fortress.

He needed to be able to look at her, needed to be able to touch her, and know that she was safe.

Because she had come to mean everything to him.

"Tomorrow." Though it was against his better judgment, there was no other choice he could make. "We'll tell them tomorrow."

"Thank you for giving me refuge tonight," she said softly.

"No more thank-yous," he said in a gruff voice as he made himself put some distance between them instead of moving closer. "This is what friends do for each other."

The hopeful look on her face at the word *friends* nearly had him reaching for her. But he knew that if he did, it wouldn't end at a hug. Or even a kiss.

If he pulled her into his arms tonight, he'd never be able to let her go.

A previous client had said he was a superhero. But Roman had never felt superhuman until the moment he had to use every ounce of self-control he possessed to move away from Suzanne and walk into the kitchen.

They hadn't stopped to eat on the drive back and she'd been working too intently to eat any of the snacks he'd packed for her. She needed something to soak up the wine she was already sipping, but he wasn't going to ask her if she was hungry. After the shock she'd just had, she'd probably say no, but if he could get good food in front of her, he'd somehow persuade her to eat it.

Roman quickly sent several text messages to his investigators asking them to dig into the city's under-ground channels regarding the fire in Suzanne's apartment building, then got out flour and eggs for fresh pasta, tomatoes and herbs for the sauce. When he turned around, he was surprised to find her pulling out a cutting board.

"I've got dinner covered," he said. "Why don't you sit down and try to relax? Maybe even take a nap until the meal is ready."

The stubborn look on her face would have made him smile if he hadn't been so full of fury—and fear—on her behalf. If she'd been asleep in her apartment when that fire had smoked into flames...

No. He couldn't go there. Couldn't even begin to imagine a world without her laughter, her brilliance, her beauty.

"I've always dealt with things head on," she said as she grabbed a tomato and a serrated knife. "But after fighting with my brothers last night on the dock and then finding firefighters at my place today—" She stopped slicing. "I just need a few hours to try to be normal, you know? Make a meal with you. Maybe stream a movie on the couch with a bowl of popcorn. You do have popcorn, right? Or wait—chocolate ice cream would be even better."

He gripped the edge of the counter so tightly to keep from putting his arms around her that he was surprised it didn't crack. "I can get you ice cream *and* popcorn." He wouldn't leave her side for a second, of course. "A kid around the corner runs errands for me sometimes." Eddie was the fifteen-year-old son of one of the guys the teenage Roman had beaten to a pulp, so badly that he'd lost an eye. Roman had helped out the family any way he could since then, which included keeping an eye on Eddie and making sure the kid stayed out of trouble. "I'll send him a text to let him know we need microwave popcorn—"

"With extra butter."

"How else would you eat it?" He was glad to see her smile again. A little one, but a smile nonetheless. "What kind of ice cream?" he asked.

"As close as he can get to chocolate fudge super chunk."

"I hadn't noticed your sweet tooth."

Her small smile widened. "That's because I wasn't ready to divulge it to you yet."

She was so breathtaking as she stood in his kitchen smiling despite her crappy day that his fingers fumbled on his cell phone screen as he sent the message to Eddie. The kid texted back so quickly Roman didn't even have time to put the phone down.

"He's on it. He said he'll be here with the goods inside of ten minutes."

Looking relieved to know that junk food was on its way, she found his wooden salad bowl, tossed the tomato slices into it, then washed the celery and began to chop it. Not only was this the first time a woman had settled into his kitchen as if it were her own, it was also the only time he'd ever let a woman into his loft, period. Since he never planned on letting women stay, it was easier to keep them out entirely. Food and sex had always happened either out on the town or at their places.

But having Suzanne in his home felt completely right.

The realization made it hard to keep his hands steady while he rolled out the pasta dough.

"Tell me the funniest—or weirdest—thing you've ever had to deal with on the job," she said. Though she was doing her best to hide it, he could tell how shaky she still felt. "I promise the story won't go any further."

Any other client would have been in tears or getting smashed by now. But Suzanne wasn't like anyone else. She was stronger. More resilient. And yet, at the same time, she was also more emotional than anyone he'd ever known. Close enough to breaking down that she was deliberately hunting for something to laugh about instead.

Client privacy was sacrosanct to Roman, but Suzanne would never repeat anything he told her. And she needed to be taken away from everything for a little while.

"Early on, I worked for a prince."

"A real prince?" She looked impressed.

"Yes, a real prince. He was a friendly guy in his mid-twenties and his family told me there had been threats sent to him in the mail. It was my job not only to shadow him, but also to intercept any packages either sent or given to him, and then turn them over to the head of palace security for inspection. His parents, the king and queen, were very clear that no one else must be allowed to see what was in the packages. Not even him."

"Weird."

"Definitely weird." Fifteen years ago he'd been a total greenhorn. Green, but so happy to be carving out a new life for himself that he was willing to take on pretty much any job that came his way. The worst client was better than making a living with his fists in brutal underground fights where you either destroyed...or got destroyed. "His family was working really hard at that time to find him the right royal match."

"Can you imagine marrying into a monarchy? I mean, I know there are perks like jewels and fancy dresses, but I wouldn't like always having to be *on*."

Roman agreed. "Marriage is hard enough without all of those pressures. Jewels are a pretty big incentive for most people, though."

Suzanne stopped chopping, then splayed her fingers. "I've never been able to wear big rings or bracelets because they get in my way at the computer. Earrings, however, are a different matter." She grinned. "I've always been partial to rubies, if you're wondering."

Roman was hit with an image of Suzanne wearing

ruby earrings and nothing else. He could buy them for her easily—but money wasn't the issue. The fact that it would be utterly inappropriate for him to buy her jewelry was. Because he wasn't her boyfriend, damn it.

Her work crisis and then the apartment fire had forced him to put the promise he'd made to her brothers on the back burner for the time being. He wished he could put it on the back burner forever...

"Anyway," she said, "I didn't mean to interrupt your story."

What had they been talking about before he'd gotten lost in his erotic daydream of Suzanne naked in his bed, wearing only rubies? Oh right, the prince.

"I intercepted a good half-dozen packages and turned them over. No one would tell me what was in them, but they made it clear that the threat was at a higher level than ever. The prince had a different event each night and I watched him like a hawk. Nothing was going to happen on my watch."

"Of course it wouldn't," Suzanne said, as if the idea was preposterous.

"The final night I worked for him, one of his friends from university came to visit. I did a background on the guy and when it came up clean, I let them head to his private suite of rooms with his friend's suitcases." He shook his head at his own stupidity. "It didn't occur to me that a visitor's private bags would be an issue. Especially not a close friend."

"It's always the ones you least suspect, isn't it?"

"It often is," he agreed. "I can't remember exactly why I needed to interrupt them. One of the staff desperately needed an answer about something for the prince's mother, probably. But I'll never forget what I saw."

"I know you said this was going to be funny, but the way you're telling this story, I'm a little worried now."

"Glitter."

"Excuse me?" She was half-laughing already. "Did you just say you found *glitter* in his room?"

"Turns out the prince was crazy about glitter. He would have covered the family dog in it if he could have. Fortunately, Fido knew better than to be anywhere near that wing of the palace." They were both chuckling now. "He begged me not to tell anyone what I'd found. Evidently, the packages being confiscated were full of glitter. His family was terrified that if anyone found out about his glitter fetish before he made the right match, no one would agree to the union."

"Surely a little glitter between husband and wife could be fun, couldn't it? Although," she mused with a crooked little grin, "I suppose that would depend on where the glitter ended up…"

He grimaced. "I can tell you for a fact that there are *definitely* some places you don't want glitter stuck to."

When she burst into a fresh round of laughter, the sound was so sweet that he nearly kissed her across the kitchen island. Only the pasta dough in his hands and the knife in hers could have stopped him.

"Where?" Her laughter rounded out the word. "On your face?"

He shook his head.

"Your arms? Hands? Torso?"

Three more headshakes.

Her eyes grew big. "You didn't let him glitter you below the waist, did you?"

He'd sworn to go to his grave before ever admitting what had gone on in the palace that night. But he'd do anything to make her laugh again. "Did I mention how persuasive the prince was? And that I was a young, stupid bodyguard who didn't know any better, particularly when my client insisted it was the only way to cure his obsession? Turns out glitter is small enough to get in even the smallest gaps in fabric. Days later, I was still finding glitter on myself."

She was laughing even harder by the time a knock came at his door. If only Eddie had appeared a few minutes earlier, Roman might have been spared telling the glitter story. But Suzanne's happiness was worth any number of stupid stories. Anything to make sure she didn't become shell-shocked and scared again.

"Roman, here's the junk food you asked f—" The boy swallowed the rest of his sentence when he saw Suzanne in the kitchen. "Wow. You're hot."

"*Eddie.*" Roman had taught the kid better than that. Then again, Suzanne had made Roman's brain go off the rails the first time he'd seen her too, so he supposed he couldn't blame the teenage boy for forgetting his manners. "Her name is Suzanne, but you can call her Miss Sullivan. After you apologize."

"No need for an apology," she said with a wave of her hand. "Handing over your junk food haul will be more than enough."

Eddie practically tripped over himself to get to her. "Two bags of microwave popcorn with extra butter and the biggest container they had of Triple Chunk Brownie Hot Fudge Chocolate Supreme ice cream."

Suzanne hugged Eddie like he'd given her the moon and the stars in a brown paper bag. Roman was caught between laughing at the teenager's bug-eyed reaction...and the urge to rip the kid away from *his* woman.

Not even the slightest bit aware of how far she'd rocked Eddie's world—and that she'd likely be providing him with late-night fantasy material for the next decade—she stepped back, peeled off the top of the ice cream container, and handed out three spoons.

"I've always been a dessert-first kind of girl." Her first bite of the sugary dessert had her eyes closing and a moan of deep pleasure sounding from her throat. Lord, how he wanted to hear that sound again—only next time in his bed, while he was making love to her.

Eddie quickly shoveled in several large mouthfuls, and was gaping at Suzanne like a lovestruck puppy when Roman put down his own spoon to say, "I'm sure your mom's expecting you for dinner."

"She'd probably let me eat with you guys."

"Sorry, bud," Roman said, "not tonight." When the kid's shoulders slumped, he knew Suzanne was about to say a third would be fine. But Roman wanted her to relax tonight, not feel obliged to entertain a fifteen-year-old boy who had fallen in love with her at first sight. "Maybe next time."

"Next time? So that means you're coming back, right?" Eddie asked Suzanne. "Because I've never seen a girl here before."

She raised her eyebrows. "Never? Not even one?"

"Nope. Roman's got this thing about not having girls at his place. My mom says it's weird. She's going to be super happy to hear about you."

"Really?" She shot a speculative glance at Roman. "So I'm the first girl to *ever* set foot inside this loft?"

"Except for my ma," Eddie clarified, "but she doesn't count because she's married to my dad."

"I sure hope I'll be coming back." She looked straight into Roman's eyes. "Lots and lots and lots of times." She licked off her spoon—inadvertently making both Roman and Eddie go a little crazier—then covered up the ice cream carton and put it in the freezer. "Thanks for the junk food, Eddie. And for being an all-around cool guy."

"Anytime. See you around." Eddie gave Roman the same look Jerry had. One that said, *Don't blow it with her, dude.*

How anyone thought Roman was in Suzanne's league, he couldn't imagine. Her brother Alec was right—he wasn't anywhere near good enough for her. But given the circumstances that now had them sharing his loft, he was going to have to dig even deeper for the control to keep from kissing her the way he had by the lake. Every night since he'd started working for her, it had been hell knowing she was only a few walls away. But later tonight, when she was in his bed while he slept out on the couch...

He honestly wasn't sure how he was going to make it through until morning without touching her, kissing her, holding her.

"Sorry about Eddie's big mouth," Roman said after the door closed behind him. "I've been working on his manners, but sometimes fifteen wins out."

"I thought he was sweet. And I also think it's sweet

that you've taken him under your wing like this. You must be really close to his parents."

"I am," Roman said, hating himself for the things he wasn't telling her. Things that would douse the light in her eyes when she looked at him.

He was about to reach into a drawer beside her hip for the pasta cutter when he made the mistake of letting himself look into her eyes instead.

Their gazes caught. Held.

And then, before he knew it, she was brushing her fingertips over his lower lip. "You've got some chocolate right here."

That was all it took for the hungry male inside of him to finally win. He stopped holding himself in check for just long enough to lick the chocolate from her finger.

The instant his tongue made contact with her skin, everything stilled. The laughter, the funny stories—they were all gone in an instant.

The heated attraction that had been simmering beneath the surface since the first moment they'd met was the only thing that mattered now.

CHAPTER TWENTY-FOUR

"I shouldn't have done that." But Roman didn't step away from her touch, and she didn't take her hand from his face.

"Yes, you should," she said softly. "As soon as we got into the car at the lake to come home, I was planning to make you talk to me about what happened last night...and how I want it to happen again."

"*Suzanne.*" He needed to remain rational. Even if it was the last thing he wanted. "We can't. I can't."

"Why not? And you're going to have to come up with something beyond my brothers and being my bodyguard. Those stopped being good reasons a long time ago. Especially now that my brothers already know about us and I've told them to back off, or else. And don't try to blame this on the fire in my apartment either. I'm not going to deny that it got me feeling a little shaky and scared—but that doesn't have anything to do with what was already going on between us."

Us. He liked the sound of that way too much. Wanted it so badly that he could barely shove his longing away as he made himself move out of reach.

"The way I treat women I hook up with—I couldn't treat you like that."

"You mean in bed?" She bit her lip, then let the succulent flesh go. "Because I'm pretty sure I wouldn't object to anything you wanted to try. Even if it's kind of kink—"

"No," he got out past a strangled throat. "Not in bed." Jesus, he could barely think beyond the breath-stealing image of Suzanne being kinky in his bed, didn't know how he was going to string together a coherent sentence. "I'm talking about everything else I do to them."

"You would never physically hurt a woman unless she was a threat to your client's safety. And even then, I know you'd regret it. So what could you possibly do to the women you date that's so bad?"

He couldn't lie to her, even knowing she would be disgusted by him once she knew the truth. Especially when that was supposed to be his goal, wasn't it? To make sure she understood that being with him was bad news. He'd promised her brothers no less than that on the dock last night.

"I don't care."

"You don't care..." She cocked her head. "About what, exactly?"

"Them." The word fell like a stone between them.

"The women I date. The women I sleep with. I don't care about them. I don't care about any of them."

"Are you saying that you've never been in love with any of the women you've been with?"

"I haven't, but it's more than that. I've never even come close to having feelings about any of them. Ever since I was a teenager, one woman has been the same as the next to me. Like father, like son."

"I still don't understand. How are you like your father? And how does this play into the fact that you've never fallen for anyone you've dated?"

Suzanne deserved so much. Deserved everything he couldn't give her. Which was why he made himself push even deeper into the truth. "My childhood was a parade of interchangeable women. Once my mom left, my dad could never trust another woman. But just because he didn't trust them, that didn't stop him from sleeping with as many as possible. I learned a long time ago that he was never going to change his stripes. And neither will I." His gut twisted as he strove to make sure she understood exactly what he was telling her. "Women have always, and will always be, inter-changeable to me. I can't stand the thought of ever hurting you, Suzanne. Which is why you and I can never be anything more than friends."

The last thing he expected her to do after he laid out the awful truth was smile. Or to say, "You weren't friends with any of your previous lovers, were you?"

"No, I wasn't."

"So that's already something different, because you said it yourself. You and I are friends." She didn't give his brain time to catch up before adding, "And if you don't want to hurt me, that means you already care about me." She looked triumphant as she concluded, "Which means your reasons to keep your distance no longer apply."

He should have known this conversation wouldn't go the way he'd planned. He should have expected Suzanne's superpowered brain to leapfrog his. But that didn't mean he could give up on convincing her to find someone better.

"I'm trying to protect you." And he'd never forgive himself if he let something happen tonight and ended up breaking her heart. "You need to listen to me."

"No, you need to listen to *me*." He'd never known anyone so strong, so powerful—and yet so gentle and good—all in one devastatingly beautiful package. "I see the way your eyes soften when you look at me. And when you kiss me, it's magic. Sweet, sinful *magic*." He watched her skin flush at the memory of the sparks that had exploded between them, and felt his heat up too. "No matter how hard you try, you can't hide what you're feeling. Not from me." She took his hands in hers, the flour from the pasta he'd been making coating her skin as she ran her fingers along his with shocking sensuality. "It took me a long time to understand that the mistakes my father and mother made were theirs, not mine. I've only just realized that I don't have to repeat their broken love story." She interlaced her fingers with his, then took a step closer. "And neither do you."

All he wanted was to believe that what she was saying could be true. He was beyond desperate to drag her into his arms and crush her mouth beneath his. Every last need, every ounce of his passion, was wrapped up in having Suzanne naked and pliant and gasping with pleasure in his arms.

At this point, there was only one last-ditch way to save her from the relentless, unquenched desire that had turned them both inside out. He'd tried blunt. But he hadn't been crude. Hadn't fully shocked her into seeing exactly what being with him would be like when he wasn't capable of being the man she seemed to think he was.

"I want you. We both know how much I want you." He let her see the unguarded truth of his intense need for her. "But I damn well won't let myself touch you tonight unless you can honestly tell me that after we sleep together, and I don't call, your feelings won't be crushed." He hated himself a thousand times over for painting such a bleak and brutal picture for her, regardless of its honesty. "No matter how hard you try," he said in an echo of her words from moments before, "you can't hide how much you long for a love like your brother Drake has found with Rosa, like what Smith and Valentina have. I'm not going to deny that I want to touch you, kiss you in a thousand different ways. I'm not going to claim that I don't want to tear off your clothes and take you right here on the counter, and then again in my bed, my shower, up against the wall, any and every possible way I can have you. But just because I can't control my desire for you, that doesn't mean I'm going to be the happily-ever-after you've been looking for. I'll never be that man."

This was where she would finally break away from him. This was where she would tell him to go to hell for daring to speak to her this way. This was where she would look deep into his eyes and see the emptiness, the darkness inside his heart from all the past misdeeds he could never undo.

She slid her hands from his, cupped his jaw, and said, "I promise I won't be crushed."

"*Suzanne.*" Her name was a plea. "Don't lie to me."

"I'm not lying."

"Neither am I." His voice was tight with emotion...and unquenched need. "I don't want to hurt you, but if we do this tonight, I know I will."

"You won't." She feathered her fingertips over his

face and went up on her tippy toes so that they were face-to-face. "You might not have wanted this to happen, but you're falling in love with me. Just like I'm falling in love with the bodyguard I swore I didn't even want"—she slid her arms around his neck and pressed the length of her body against his—"but now don't think I can live without."

* * *

Suzanne's heart had never pounded this hard. This fast. But it wasn't because she was nervous. How could she be nervous when Roman was the one she'd been hoping for?

She'd almost been too frightened by the depth and speed of her feelings to see what was right in front ·of her. But after her father had helped remove her blinders—and after Roman had just admitted how much she meant to him, and that he never wanted to hurt her—she was one hundred percent positive that he was the true love she'd always believed she'd find one day.

She wished he could see it as clearly as she did. But if there was one thing she'd learned from her endless hours of reworking code, it was that it took time to see some things clearly. Time—and focused, determined, passionate effort.

Tonight, she was going to apply all those lessons

she'd learned from running her business to something infinitely more important than any code she had ever, or would ever, write.

Roman's love was worth every ounce of focus, every bit of determination, and every single moment of passion.

Passion she already knew was going to last a lifetime.

But first she needed to be as brave as he'd repeatedly said she was. Brave enough to stand firm and not let him push her away tonight, no matter how hard he tried, no matter what he said. She wouldn't let herself give in to fear, wouldn't let herself run, no matter how fast her heart was pounding as she opened herself up to Roman. Body, heart, and soul.

Sex had never been more than merely fulfilling physical urges for Suzanne. But she already knew that being with Roman tonight would change everything.

Because it would truly be making *love*.

"The counter, your bed, the shower, up against the wall—" She listed all the places he had sent whirring through her minutes before. "I want you to take me in all of them, Roman. I want you to *love* me in all of them."

Before she realized his intention, he was lifting her into his arms and heading toward the stairs. He didn't speak as he took them two at a time, and she didn't dare say more either. Not yet. Not until she was absolutely positive that he wouldn't turn back, certain that he wouldn't pull away from her again.

As a tall woman with curves, she rarely felt delicate. And as a software programmer, she rarely felt feminine. But he was so big, so strong, that she felt both sensations tonight. He carried her as though she weighed nothing at all. And as he held her, it seemed as if he never wanted to let her go.

Twining her arms even more tightly around his neck, she inhaled his clean, masculine scent. She nuzzled her nose against the rough, dark bristles on his face and neck that had grown since they'd left the lake earlier that day. It wasn't enough just to breathe him in, though. She needed to taste him too.

She was about to lick his skin when she was suddenly falling. Straight into the middle of his big bed.

As she looked up at Roman, his face was a mask she couldn't read. But the fact that he hadn't denied having feelings for her—that he hadn't laughed in the face of her saying, *You're falling in love with me*—already spoke volumes. And the way he was yanking open his button-down shirt and shoving off his boots said everything else she needed to hear.

Regardless of what he believed to be true about his capacity to love, he wasn't going to turn away from her tonight.

CHAPTER TWENTY-FIVE

Suzanne Sullivan was in his bed.

Roman was undone by the sight of her long, dark hair strewn across his pillows, her cheeks flushed with arousal, her eyes bright with anticipation. Still wearing the black T-shirt and jeans she'd put on that morning, she was utterly stunning. And sexy as hell, even with nearly every inch of skin covered up.

How could he not kiss the bravest, most extraordinary woman he'd ever known? And how could he not make love to her, when every moment between them had led them here, to this inevitable night together?

From the start, he'd thought she was an open book, especially about things she loved. And now, where other women might hide their feelings, she'd said that she loved him.

Suzanne loved him.

She'd said he was falling in love with her too. Said it so sweetly. So confidently. As though she wasn't the slightest bit afraid it might not be true. He'd never known anyone strong enough to open up her heart like that. Open it up to the potential pain of not having that happily ever after.

He wished like hell he could prevent that pain. But once he told her the full truth about his past...

One night. He desperately wanted this one precious night with her. One night where honor could finally take a backseat to desire. One night where he could love her with his body in all the ways he didn't deserve to love her with his heart. He would tell her everything in the morning, but for the next few hours, he couldn't waste the chance to love Suzanne Sullivan with everything he had.

He tossed his shirt into the corner of his bedroom before prowling toward her.

"Wow," she breathed. "You're amazing."

She stared at his bare chest as if in awe, and he couldn't help but be filled with pride that she liked what she saw. All those endless hours of push-ups, pull-ups, and sit-ups had been worth it, if for no other reason than to please her.

"I don't feel the least bit sorry for the women you've been with and dumped before me. Not now that I know what they got to see." She reached for him. "What they got to touch."

He grabbed her hand before she could make contact with his abs, gently but firmly. When she'd nuzzled his neck on the way up to his bedroom, he'd nearly taken her right then and there on the stairs. But he needed tonight to be good for her. Not just good— *mind-blowing*. Which meant he couldn't let her touch him, kiss him, yet. Not when he was poised to erupt at any second from the slightest provocation.

After capturing her other wrist as swiftly, he brought both of her hands to his lips. He kissed her pinkies first, then the tips of her ring fingers, then her middle fingers, then her pointer fingers. When he got to her thumbs, he swept his tongue against each pad.

"*Roman*." Her voice shook as she said his name. "You're not going to make this quick and dirty, are you?"

Dirty? Yes.

Quick? Not on her life.

In lieu of answering her with words, however, he traced the three lines inside her left palm with his tongue. Her whole body began to tremble, and the flush from her cheeks seemed to have spread everywhere.

"I never knew my hands were erogenous zones," she whispered as he turned his attention to her right palm.

"Every part of you is capable of feeling pleasure," he murmured before running kisses up the tender skin at the inside of her wrist. "And I'm not going to let either of us rest tonight until we've discovered all of them." He punctuated his promise with a swirl of his tongue inside her right elbow.

He'd never met anyone with as unwavering a focus as Suzanne. Right now, it was gratifying to have every ounce of it on what he was doing with his mouth. Especially when the gentle scrape of his teeth over her bicep brought a gasp.

"You've only kissed my hands and arms, and I'm already about to do something I never thought I would do in a million years."

He stopped his onslaught of kisses to ask, "What's that?"

She looked as though she couldn't believe what she was about to say. "Beg."

He didn't even try to hold back a wicked grin. "Oh, you'll definitely be begging before I'm done with you."

"I don't like that word. *Done.*"

He didn't either, regretting it the moment he said it. But he didn't have a better word to replace it, not when he refused to be a bastard who made promises he couldn't fulfill. The only way he could erase the reminder that this night wouldn't last forever was with pleasure, with arousing kisses and naughty nips at parts of her body she'd never even known were sexual.

He lifted both arms above her head and wrapped her fingers around the iron bars of his headboard. "Keep your hands here until I tell you to let go."

"What if I don't?"

He liked her challenge more than he should. Liked everything about her more than he should, damn it. "I'll tie you up if I have to."

It was a million miles from the romantic things he was sure she wanted to hear, but you wouldn't have known it from the spark that lit in her eyes. "So either way, I win?"

She'd done this from the start, made him laugh with her smart mouth. "Tonight," he promised, "we're both going to win."

The sound of her breath catching in her throat at his sexy vow was unbearably erotic. And the teasing smile she gave him as she made a show of letting her fingers go slack on the iron before gripping it even tighter a few seconds later, had his blood racing so hot in his veins he was surprised there wasn't steam coming off his skin.

With her arms lifted over her head, her T-shirt rode up so that a couple of inches of smooth skin were bared. Forcing himself to go slow, to tease and taste rather than immediately devour the way he so badly wanted to, he feathered his fingertips over her stomach. Firm muscles danced beneath his fingers as she worked for breath. But he didn't plan on letting her get it back anytime soon as he lowered his head and pressed a kiss to her belly button.

She was still holding on to the headboard as her body arched toward his, a little pleading sound coming from her throat. "You taste so sweet," he murmured against her belly, before reaching for the hem of her shirt and slowly sliding it up to uncover the lower edge of her rib cage. He nuzzled his bristly jaw over her. "You feel so soft." Taking the cotton fabric between his teeth, he dragged it up even higher to reveal a delicate, yellow lace bra.

Perhaps he should have been surprised by the feminine undergarments beneath the black T-shirt. But he wasn't, because Suzanne was the full package. Brains and beauty, serious and sensuous, all at the same time.

He'd spent the past two decades trying to make up for his behavior as a teen in the boxing ring by holding himself to perfect control everywhere else. But with Suzanne, his control wasn't just fraying—it had shattered into so many tiny pieces that he honestly didn't realize he'd ripped her T-shirt in two until it lay splayed open on either side of her.

If ever there was a cue that it was time to stop the madness, this should have been it. But instead of cringing away from him, Suzanne urged, *"More."* She licked her lips, leaving them glossy and extra kissable. "I want more of you. More of your passion. More of *everything.*"

Permission granted—demanded, even—he cupped

her lace-covered breasts, groaning at how perfectly they filled his large hands. His thumbs stroking her soft skin, he loved feeling the tips pucker tightly against the thin layer of yellow lace.

Bending his head, he covered the lace with his mouth, licking, sucking, biting at her flesh like a man possessed. In response, she arched her back up off the mattress, giving herself over to him completely.

He'd known all along that she would be like this in bed, utterly unashamed, totally unafraid to follow wherever passion led. The fact that she wouldn't balk at anything—and that she would find pleasure wherever he did—made him even crazier. So crazy that, yet again, he was barely aware of what he was doing as he caught his teeth on the thin lace threads that held her bra together at the center and tore them apart. All he knew was that there was no going back. Definitely not tonight. Maybe not ever.

Because once he had Suzanne—once he had *all* of her—nothing would ever be as good. He already craved the taste of her, was a slave to her scent, was addicted to her sounds of pleasure.

His hands and mouth vied for possession of her breasts as he moved over her to take everything he so badly wanted. But he couldn't get enough of her, no matter how much he stroked, caressed, kissed, nipped. Again and again he loved first one breast, then the other, then both together. Her hips rose up against his as she said his name in a voice that grew more hoarse by the second.

"Roman. *Please*." He'd never heard anything more beautiful than the sound of her begging him to help her find release. "I'm so close."

The thought of taking her over that first peak with nothing more than his hands and mouth at her breasts nearly took *him* over the edge.

It was pure male instinct to push the hard ridge of his still fully clothed erection into the heated vee between her legs at the same moment that he cupped both of her breasts and suckled hard. In the space between heartbeats, every muscle in her body tensed, then let go as she went pliant with pleasure, undulating her hips beneath his to catch the waves of bliss that washed over her, through her.

When her climax finally subsided, she lay back against the pillow looking at him with a lazy smile on her face. "That was *amazing*."

And it was only the beginning.

He'd kept her jeans on to force himself to go slowly, but he was going to lose it soon if he couldn't finally see, touch, taste every glorious inch of her. He had her sneakers off and the dark denim on the floor within seconds, leaving her clad only in yellow lace panties.

In an effort to regain even the tiniest bit of his self-control, he closed his eyes and took a deep breath. But the scent of her arousal only revved him higher, pushing him that much closer to the edge of madness.

Reverently, he knelt between her long, toned legs and reached to cup her lace-covered sex. Her eyelids fluttered closed as she rubbed herself against his hand. "Do it again, Roman. Make me come apart again. With your hands. With your mouth. Any way you want me, I want it too."

He was already more than halfway to doing everything she wanted, but he understood why she was saying the words aloud. Because after spending so long vowing to resist her and believing it was the only honorable path forward, she obviously wanted him to know that he wasn't doing anything she didn't want him to do.

He wanted to tell her that he was going to make her come at least a half-dozen different ways tonight, with each climax better than the one before, but he couldn't get the words out. Not when he was wholly focused on hooking his thumbs into the edge of her panties and slowly sliding them down. He barely had them off when he had to cup her again and stroke her wet, hot skin.

She was slippery with arousal, his fingers sliding back and forth over her until he couldn't stand not to go inside, first with one finger and then a second.

Looking at her face, he realized she was watching him touch her, watching herself lift into his hand so that she could take him deeper with each stroke.

She climbed higher and higher, her skin flushing an even deeper rose, her eyes dilating as another orgasm beckoned, her breath coming even faster now than when they'd been sprinting through the park.

Her head fell back and her eyes fluttered closed as she chased her next climax, his name falling from her lips again. He'd never been this hard, never been this close to losing it as he was when she pulsed and clenched over his fingers in release.

Sweet Lord, if it was this good to feel her come, how was he ever going to survive making love to her?

He'd deliberately saved kissing her mouth for last, because once they kissed again, he wouldn't be able to keep from making her entirely, completely his. And he wanted her to know how precious, how special, she was to him before that happened. Not just to have a quick roll in the hay that would be over far too soon.

He ran the flats of his hands up her naked curves—the sweet flare of her hips that flowed into her waist, the swell of her full breasts, her strong shoulders. Finally, he tangled his fingers in the dark silk of her hair.

"You make me happy, Roman." He felt her words as much as he heard them. Felt them all the way down in a part of his heart he hadn't ever let come alive. "So, so happy."

How could he do anything but tell her the truth? "You make me happy too."

And then, his mouth was on hers, and hers was on his.

Finally.

Every nerve in Roman's body came alive when Suzanne opened her lips so that he could slip his tongue in to taste her. Nothing had ever been as sweet. And nothing had ever felt as good as it did when she slid her tongue against his.

Slowly. Softly. That was how he wanted to kiss her. He wanted this to be a kiss for the ages. A kiss that neither of them would ever forget. But there was no way to hold back the fire raging inside them both. One that soon made their kisses heated, feverish, frenzied.

Everything he wished he could say to her, he said with his kiss instead. The way their tongues danced, their breath merged, their sighs and moans filled the room—all of it was filled with hope. Dreams. Wishes. And hunger.

So much hunger that the more he had of her, the more he needed.

Somewhere in the middle of their kiss, her hands left the bed frame to run over his shoulders and back.

"I need you." She fumbled for the button on his

pants. "Inside me." He lifted his hips so that she could yank the button open and the zipper down. *"Now."*

She was starting to shove off his pants when he distracted her with another kiss. He needed to lick her lips from corner to corner, top to bottom, needed to stroke her tongue with his, needed to kiss and kiss and kiss her until she was practically coming again from that alone.

But she was too focused on her goal of having him inside her—the best damned goal in the entire world as far as he was concerned—to let him distract her for long. Grasping the dark wool of his slacks with her hands, she tore through them just as he had her T-shirt.

He'd never been with a woman this fierce, this determined, this captivating, this *perfect* in every single way.

And then she was shoving off his boxers and wrapping her long fingers around him. It felt so good that he could barely force himself to pull away from her hand.

"I knew letting your hands go free was a bad idea," he growled against her mouth as he threaded his fingers through hers.

If she touched him again like that, he'd explode, but that wasn't the only reason he needed to hold her hands. Their lips were one point of deep connection—their palms pressing close, their fingers entwined, were another.

He'd never in his life held a woman's hands, not

when they were walking down the street, and especially not when they were in bed. You didn't hold hands with someone you were casually sleeping with, only with someone you cared about. And as he'd confessed earlier in the night, he'd never cared about a woman before.

But he *needed* to hold Suzanne's hands. Needed to be close to her in any and every possible way. Skin to skin. Mouth to mouth. Hand to hand. And now…

She lifted her hips against his and he slid his erection over her slick heat, making them both moan at how good it was. "Again," he urged her, pushing against her wetness, but not quite inside. "Yes," he murmured against her mouth as she circled her hips so that the thick, hard head of his shaft was rubbing over her liquid hot center. "Make yourself feel good, Suzanne." He loved saying her name, loved the way the curves and edges of it felt on his tongue. "Make yourself come on me." Sweat dripped from his chest to hers as he worked to hold back his own release so that she could find hers. "Just like this, with nothing between us, just the way I know you've wanted me. Just the way *I've* wanted *you*."

She moaned her pleasure at his filthy words into their next kiss, then gasped as he thrust his tongue deep and she launched into her next climax.

Roman wanted nothing more than to drive himself

into her, but somehow, he remembered to just keep rubbing and grazing and grinding against her until she finally stilled beneath him. The very last thing he wanted was to pull away from her now, but he hadn't been thinking clearly enough earlier to get a condom ready.

She made a sound of protest as he slid his hands from hers and leaped off the bed. He grabbed a handful of condoms from the box he kept in his closet, then jumped back over her, scattering all but one of the little packages across his bed.

Her laughter wound around his heart. "Great minds think alike," she said. "We're definitely going to need more than one."

Utterly captivated by her smile, he momentarily forgot to rip open the package. All he could do was stare down at the most beautiful woman in the world...and marvel that she was here, in his bed.

Reaching for the small square packet, she said, "I'll take care of that." A beat later she was tossing the wrapper to the side and reaching for him again. "And don't you dare try to take over for me. I'm dying to get my hands on you." She licked her lips. "To start, anyway."

He deserved a medal for not losing it as her fingers slid over his shaft while she painted mental pictures of her lips doing the same. Gritting his teeth, he somehow withstood her teasing touches until she finished rolling on the condom.

He took her hands again, crushed her mouth beneath his, then sank deep in one hard, desperate thrust. As she wrapped her long legs around him to take him even deeper, they rocked and kissed and whispered each other's names. Pleasure climbed, climbed, climbed. So high that Roman temporarily forgot that they could only have tonight as he lost himself completely to the woman who had turned his world upside down from the very first moment he'd set eyes on her.

Finally—*finally*—he was loving her the way he'd wanted to love her from the start. Not only with his body, but with every piece of his once-hardened heart as well...and a soul that had been lost in darkness for far too long.

Roman had always vowed not to make the mistake of dreaming about true, lasting love that could never be. But as Suzanne looked into his eyes with pure, sweet emotion and whispered, "I love you," at the same time that another climax began to take her over, he had no choice but to let the forbidden dream become real as he fell heart first into ecstasy, with Suzanne held tight in his arms.

CHAPTER TWENTY-SIX

Suzanne had always dreamed of finding love. But nothing could have prepared her for the passion, the pleasure, the joy, the breathless wonder of loving Roman.

She wanted to lie in his bed forever, naked, limbs entwined, their hearts beating like crazy as they worked to catch their breath. But her empty stomach, and its loud growl, had other plans.

Levering up on one muscular arm, he stared down at her. "Sounds like you need that pasta I was planning to make you." He dropped his gaze to her lips, still tingling from his wonderful kisses. "Before you distracted me."

"It was the best distraction *ever*, wasn't it?"

She loved the way his lips curved up in a smile. "It was."

He hadn't made her any promises tonight, hadn't told her he loved her back, but though she hoped both would be coming soon, his lovemaking had already told her everything she needed to know about how he felt.

He touched her like she was the most precious woman on earth.

He kissed her like he didn't ever want to stop.

And when he made love to her, her heart grew so full it nearly burst from her chest.

She was on the verge of doing her best to distract him again when her stomach rumbled even louder.

"You need to eat"—he stood and pulled her from the bed so that she was standing against his gloriously hard, naked body—"so that you have enough energy for what I'm going to do to you next."

Mmmm. Didn't he know that when he said things like that, the last thing she wanted to do was go downstairs to the kitchen to cook and eat?

But before she could protest that she already had plenty of energy to make love to him again, he was buttoning her into his long-sleeved shirt, his yummy scent all over it.

After he pulled on a pair of faded jeans—she'd been wrong when she'd thought there couldn't possibly be anything sexier than the way he looked in a dark suit— he slipped a condom into the back pocket, then took her hand and led them out of the bedroom and down the stairs to the kitchen.

She loved holding his hand. She felt so giddy that, even though she had the worst singing voice on the planet, she wanted to break out into song. Especially when she thought about the condom he was bringing downstairs, as if he knew they wouldn't be able to keep their hands off each other long enough to make it back upstairs.

"I've never made pasta from scratch before," she said when they got to the kitchen and he threw out the dough that had grown hard while he'd been making her come over and over again. "Show me how."

The look he gave her as he first put the water on to boil, then got more eggs from the fridge and flour from the pantry, told her he'd figured out that she was up to more of her distraction tricks, but she didn't care. Any excuse to have him wrap his arms around her while they broke the eggs and folded them into the flour they'd dusted over the marble countertop. With his hands over hers, they kneaded the dough. She'd never been much interested in cooking before, but now that she saw all the sexy possibilities...

Turning her face to his, she caught his lips in a kiss. The dough was momentarily forgotten as he cupped her jaw and deepened the kiss, his tongue finding every wonderfully sensitive spot on her mouth, her cheek, her jaw. Too bad her darned stomach kept rumbling like a truck barreling down the highway.

With a groan, Roman lifted his mouth from her skin. "The dough's ready for us to roll it out and cut it into ribbons."

He put the heavy wooden roller into her hands, but though she could easily do this herself, she was glad that he didn't move away as she began to roll out the dough. Instead, he stayed with his chest pressed to her back and lifted her hair to the side to nibble at the sensitive skin he'd just bared.

Suzanne had always been rock solid when she was on the job. Nothing fazed her. Nothing ruined her concentration. But there was no way she could stay focused on the job of rolling dough when all she wanted was to turn in Roman's arms, wrap her arms around his neck, and kiss him again. Especially now that she knew how good it was to be with him, to have his hard muscles against her, his hands and mouth all over her while he drove her from peak to peak.

And there was that condom in the back pocket of his jeans, after all...

"Love me again, Roman." She whispered the words against his lips. "Right here. Right now. On the island. I'm a million times hungrier for you than anything else."

The next thing she knew, his hands were on her waist and he was lifting her up onto the counter. Her bottom squished into the half-rolled dough, but she didn't care about having to wait even longer for dinner, no matter how much her stomach rumbled.

All she cared about was finally getting to be with the man she'd been afraid she might never be able to have.

"I can't get enough of you," Roman said as he put his big hands on either side of the shirt he'd buttoned her into upstairs and tore it open. He cupped her breasts, then lowered his head to tongue her nipples, one then the other. Though they'd only just made love, he seemed utterly starved for her. He ran kisses down over her stomach, toward the part of her that ached for his touch. "I'll never be able to get enough of you."

She put her hands on his jaw so that he had to look into her eyes. "You never have to."

His expression flashed dark and intense...and then he was putting his hands on her ankles, lifting her legs over his shoulders, and lowering his mouth to her sex.

"Roman." She fell back to brace herself on the counter with her forearms as he turned her entire world inside out. No one had ever made her feel like this.

Like she would willingly give herself over to him, without question, without pause.

Like she would trust him not only with her heart, but with her soul too.

Like she was finally exactly where she needed to be, with exactly the person she was meant to be with.

"*Suzanne.*" The way he rumbled her name against her aroused flesh sent her even higher. "You're so beautiful." He punctuated his words with a flick of his tongue and a slow slide of his fingers inside her clenching heat. "I need you." The French kiss he was giving her between her legs made every last rational thought slide out of her head. "*I need you.*"

Hearing the urgency in his words—and the plea in them that she wasn't sure he'd meant to be there, but obviously couldn't hold back—had her shattering against his tongue and hands.

And then, as suddenly as he'd put her on the counter so that he could devour her, he was carrying her into the nearby living room, and pulling her down over him on the leather couch.

She didn't know when he'd managed to take off his jeans or put on protection, but she didn't care. All she cared about was sinking down onto him so that she could ride every thick, hard, glorious inch of him.

"Oh God." She had her hands splayed on his chest for leverage, while his were on her hips to help lift her up, then bring her back down onto his erection again and again, until she was nearly delirious from the pleasure of it. "Nothing has ever felt this good." She had never been a talker during sex, but with Roman she couldn't hold in what she was feeling. Didn't want to hold it in. "I never want to stop loving you." He shifted her hips so that every time he thrust deep, new blazes of pleasure rocketed through her. "I never want you to stop loving me." More waves of bliss moved through her when he rolled their hips together. "Please don't stop, Roman. *Please.*"

"I won't ever stop." His hands tightened on her hips as emotion swamped his face. "I can't stop. Not with you."

He rolled them over on the couch so that she was beneath him, his mouth on hers in a deeply emotional kiss, his body taking hers—*loving* hers—without restraint.

She'd been stunned by how beautiful making love with him had been in his bedroom. Now she was stunned all over again by how raw, how animalistic their passion was.

Once upon a time, she would have been afraid of a love this wild, but now she relished every moment of it. She'd finally met her match in Roman, a man whose depth of desire was as boundless as hers.

Her body should have been replete from their earlier lovemaking, but she was starved for as much of Roman as she could possibly have. She'd never slept with anyone she was in love with. The whole act was so much bigger, so much better—nothing else could possibly compare to the way she felt when she was in Roman's arms.

Their kisses soon grew so wild that they fell off the couch onto the rug. Neither of them cared. All that mattered was trying to get as close as possible to each other. Every moment of bliss, every second of ecstasy he gave her as she climaxed, she not only took—she gave just as much.

"I had no idea." She could barely get the words out, as hard as her breath was coming in the aftermath of their fiery-hot lovemaking. Her voice was muffled by his broad shoulder, but she didn't want him to move away from her anytime soon. Ever, actually, given how much she loved the feel of his heavy weight over her.

Yes, she'd happily stay right here with Roman on his living room rug forever.

"About what?" Obviously not in any rush to move either, Roman's question rumbled over the top of her head.

"How amazing sex could be."

Still holding her close, he rolled them so that she was lying on his chest again. "I'm glad you didn't know. I'm glad I could be the one to show you."

She hated the flash of jealousy that shot through her. "But you knew?"

He moved a lock of damp hair away from her cheek. "I thought I did. But with you..." His thumb brushed her lower lip as if he couldn't keep from touching her and she instinctively licked out against

him, the same way he had when she'd been wiping
chocolate ice cream from his mouth. "You make me
want things, Suzanne."

"You make me want things too," she said, with a
naughty little wiggle of her breasts and hips.

"I've never wanted anyone the way I want you—
but I'm not just talking about sex." He ran one hand
down over her curves as he gathered his thoughts, and
she held her breath for whatever he was going to say
next. "I'm talking about—"

Horror suddenly took over his face. "I hurt you."
She followed his gaze to her hips. There were red
marks where his fingers had gripped her during their
lovemaking. "I knew I couldn't trust myself with you."

"No." She put her hands on his jaw and made him
look at her. "You took me without holding back. You
gave me everything you have. Everything you are."
Her body was still buzzing from how good it had been.
How good it felt to be as close to him as she could
possibly be. "And I *loved* it, Roman. You know I did."

"I should have been more gentle. I haven't been
gentle with you. I haven't been able to control myself
long enough to go slow."

"Next time you can be gentle, but only if it feels
right to go soft and slow. Because if we need to be wild
again…" She kissed him, openmouthed this time, and
he immediately brought his arms around her waist to

drag her close.

She was more than ready to find out what *next time* had in store for them when her stomach roared between them. And she was *beyond* ready for him to tell her what other things he wanted from her besides sex.

But instead of going back to that vulnerable place, he said, "You'd better get some clothes on." He gently ran his hands up her back from her waist before levering them both up from the floor and stepping away from her. "Otherwise, I'm never going to finish making you dinner."

The only reason she went to grab her last clean T-shirt and underwear from her suitcase was because she could see that he needed more time to wrap his head around what he was feeling. Hopefully by the time dinner was ready, he'd be ready to spill the rest of his feelings to her.

Feeling sated—temporarily, at least—and more than a little overwhelmed by all the delicious sensations still zinging around in her body, instead of trying to help cook again when she was dressed, she gladly sat on a bar stool behind a topped-off glass of red wine. She smiled when she saw the Sullivan Winery label on the bottle of Zinfandel.

"I'm glad you got a chance to meet Marcus and his wife, Nicola," she said after taking a sip of the delicious wine.

"They both seemed like nice people," he said as he stirred his homemade sauce, the pasta already rolled, cut, and in boiling water.

Sitting at his kitchen island, watching him put dinner together, she decided she could get used to this kind of treatment. Not only did everything smell amazing, but the truth was her legs were still kind of shaky after their last very acrobatic round of sex.

"They are really nice. No matter how rich or famous or successful my relatives are, they're all good people. I'm not saying they can't be cocky sometimes, or drive you up a wall, but I can't see any of them deliberately hurting anyone. Especially each other."

"How do you think that happened?" He looked up from the stove. "I've met a lot of families doing security, and they spend most of their time fighting and arguing."

"Well, for my eight cousins in San Francisco, their dad died when they were really young, so maybe that bonded them together. I know Marcus did a lot to help raise his siblings, since Lori and Sophie were barely older than babies when it happened. For my Seattle cousins, their parents have always had a great marriage, but as far as I understand, they ran into some pretty big problems when my Uncle Max lost his job a bunch of years back. He wouldn't take any money from his brothers, even though I know my dad kept offering. My cousin Ian—you know, the guy who owns the building I'm living in—gave up a lot to help out. They were always close, but I'm guessing what they went through together helped bring them even closer. And then for my cousins in Maine—" She laughed at herself when she realized she was rattling on endlessly about her big family. "I'm pretty sure you get the picture."

He smiled. "I do. When your family goes through tough times, you band together. Just the way you and your brothers did after your mother passed away." His smile fell. "Whereas most families just fall apart."

She hated seeing the pain on his face and so badly wished she could help make it go away. "Roman, maybe if you talked with your father—"

His face was a hard mask as he plated their food. "If you ever met him, you'd understand why there's no point in wasting my time."

Roman had told her when they were making love that he wouldn't stop loving her. She wanted to believe he'd meant it—that it wasn't simply the orgasms talking. So if he did mean it, wouldn't that also mean she'd meet his father one day?

Considering they'd just made love for the first time tonight, and that only one of them had said *I love you*, she shouldn't get too far ahead of herself. But it was difficult not to when she'd always gone after what she wanted without second-guessing herself or letting fear impede her determination and focus.

After putting a loaded plate of pasta and sauce in front of her, he brought over his wine glass and plate, then pulled up the bar stool beside her.

"It smells incredible." She took a bite and made an embarrassing sound of culinary bliss.

"I take it that means you like it."

She would have answered him if she could have stopped stuffing her mouth long enough to speak. But between how badly she needed food and what a fabulous cook he was, all she could do was nod while she kept eating. And eating. And eating. Until her fork scraped against her plate and she realized she'd mowed through her meal in record time.

Grinning, Roman didn't miss a beat as he slid his still half-full plate over so that they could both eat. It wasn't just delicious, wasn't just romantic, it was also fun to sit in Roman's kitchen in his loft talking and loving and eating. And it felt right.

So perfectly right.

"I can't remember the last time I ate anything that good." She leaned over to kiss him. "Thank you for making me dinner."

"Thank you for being a woman who eats. I can't remember the last time I met one."

She looked down at the two plates she'd cleared. "If I weren't so stuffed from eating half your dinner in addition to my own, I would be licking the plates right now. So, yeah, I'd say I'm a woman who eats. And now that my energy has been restored, what do you say we leave these dishes in the sink for now so that we can—"

The door buzzer cut off the rest of her sexy proposition. "Roman, it's Dad. You home?"

CHAPTER TWENTY-SEVEN

Damn it.

Of all the nights for Roman's father to drop by, he had to pick tonight.

All Roman wanted to do was take Suzanne back upstairs and make love to her. The last thing he wanted to do tonight was face reality. Unfortunately, nothing got him closer to reality than Tommy Huson—a man who had loved too deeply and had never been able to recover when it all went wrong.

Roman knew better than to let himself love like that. And yet, when he'd vowed to keep his heart locked in a cage forever, he hadn't expected to meet a woman like Suzanne Sullivan.

"Roman," his father said again, obviously getting impatient, "some kid told me you're here. Buzz me up."

Suzanne put her hand over Roman's. "You're not alone anymore. You helped me with my family at the lake. What do you need me to do to help you deal with your father?"

A part of him wanted her to leave so that she didn't have to see what a train wreck the elder Mr. Huson was. Where Roman had come from. What Roman could have become if he hadn't fought so hard to get the hell away from that world.

But a bigger part of him wanted backup. Backup he'd never had before.

"Just be yourself. And don't take anything he says personally. He's not the most tactful, not the most polite guy on the planet."

"Don't worry about me. I grew up around my brothers and their friends. Not to mention all the strangers who have always pried into my family's private business because of how famous my parents were. No matter what your father says, I'll be fine." She squared her shoulders as if she was preparing for battle. One she would fight for him. "I'll buzz him up if you want to go grab a shirt."

She was right about putting on more clothes. He could only imagine the crude comments his dad would make if he knew they'd been having sex. If his father said one inappropriate thing to Suzanne...

Roman sprinted up the stairs, grabbed a dark T-shirt from his closet, and got back down to the main level just in time to hear the knock on the door.

Suzanne didn't look at all nervous. Instead, she seemed curious about the man who had raised him.

Curious and protective. Roman had always had to protect himself. His chest squeezed tight as he realized she'd really meant it when she said he wasn't alone anymore.

Knowing he couldn't put off the inevitable any longer, he opened the door.

"Son." His father clapped him on the back. "Looks like you've been keeping up the workouts." Suzanne moved forward to say hello and his father's eyebrows lifted practically up into his hairline. "I didn't expect to find a pretty woman here." He moved closer and grabbed the hand she'd extended. "Tommy Huson, at your service."

"Suzanne Sullivan." She smiled warmly. "You have a wonderful son."

"Sure do," his father said, nodding. "Couldn't be prouder of him. You should have seen him back in the day, when he used to rule the—"

Thankfully, Suzanne's phone rang with the song, "He Ain't Heavy, He's My Brother." Roman knew it was her ring tone for Alec, because her brother had called her cell repeatedly the first couple of days he'd worked with her, when she'd still been too mad at him to pick up. "You should talk to your brother."

"Alec can wait."

Roman appreciated that she wanted to be there for him no matter what. But if her family had heard about the fire in her apartment building, they were probably worried sick. He should already have contacted them to let them know she was safe with him, but he'd been too wrapped up in making love to her to remember how the hell to do his job.

"He might have heard about the fire."

Her face clouded over. "I'll be quick," she promised as she grabbed her phone and headed toward the glass sliding doors that led to his outdoor patio space.

As far as Roman was concerned, his father watched her walk away with far too much lecherous appreciation. "Good-looking girl you've got there. I hope you're tapping that fine ass."

Roman had his father by the shoulders before he realized what he was doing. "Don't ever speak like that about Suzanne again."

When his father winced, Roman made himself un-curl his hands from his shoulders.

"You've forgotten the rules, haven't you, Roman?" His dad lifted and lowered his shoulders a couple of times as if to make sure no serious damage had been done. "Never trust a good looking woman."

"I said not to talk about her again," Roman warned.

His father might be blood, but Suzanne had come to mean something deep and real to Roman. If he had to choose between his dark past and the promise of a brighter future, there would be no contest.

"All I'm saying is that you've got to be careful with a fancy woman like her. I can tell by the way she moves that she comes from money, comes from something better than us. Look what happened with me and your ma. She swore she didn't care about slumming it with me, but she didn't mean it. She ripped my heart out of my chest and this one will do the same to you if you let her."

"Enough," Roman said in a low voice. The last thing he wanted was to hear reminders of how far out of his league Suzanne was. He already knew it, had known it before he'd started to fall for her.

"I know you don't want to hear it," his father insisted, "but I love you, son. Too much to let you walk down the same road I did."

"How much do you need this time?" Done with the chitchat, Roman reached for his wallet. The sooner they concluded their business, the sooner his dad would leave. Hopefully before Suzanne got off the phone.

"A thousand bucks." His father scowled. "The refs must have rigged last night's match. But I'll win for sure tonight."

"Here." Roman added a couple hundred to the total, hoping it would buy him some time before the next paternal visit.

His father pocketed the money, but didn't turn to

go. Instead, he had that calculating look in his eyes that said he wanted more than some temporary cash to tide him over. "Sure you don't want to get back in the ring?"

"Nope."

After Roman had left Eddie's dad, Darrell, on a stretcher, bleeding so bad from one eye socket that they hadn't been able to save his eye—all so their dads could make a few bucks betting on their match— Roman had never stepped back into the ring again. Though he still made money with his fists when he needed them to protect a client, he only used brute force when he absolutely had to. Being a bodyguard was about being smart enough to outmaneuver the incoming threat. As far as he was concerned, if it got physical he hadn't done his job.

"Back in the day, the crowds were huge if you were fighting." His father loved to talk about what he considered to be the glory days. "There's never been anyone like you in the ring, Roman."

"I didn't know you used to box professionally." Suzanne walked back into the kitchen and put her phone on the counter.

Roman hadn't heard the patio door slide open. Damn it, why couldn't Alec have kept her on the phone longer? "I didn't."

"He could have, though. He was the best amateur

boxer in the city." His father was beaming at Suzanne. "If we could only get him back into the ring, I'd bet my last dollar on my son. He always won, no matter what it took. Even if he had to fight dirty," he added with a laugh that said he didn't give a crap how bad it had been for the other guys in the ring, as long as his son won.

Suzanne frowned as she looked back at Roman. "I can't see you fighting dirty."

"Oh yeah," his father got in before Roman could get him the hell out the door. "Anything to make sure his pop went home with more than he came in with. Best son a guy could ever have." He patted the wad of money in his back pocket. "Still is. Always there to help me out when Lady Luck is being fickle."

Roman could see Suzanne's wheels turning. He'd known all along that if he let her get this close—if he got out of control enough to take her to his bed—he was going to have to tell her the full truth about why he didn't deserve her. But he'd hoped to have the rest of tonight, at least, before she saw him for the scum that he was.

"It's been a long day, Pop. Time to go."

His father looked like he wanted to stay and get to know Suzanne better—and the half-full bottle of red wine on the counter was likely calling his name too. Fortunately, he was more interested in betting the money burning a hole in his pocket.

Moving toward Suzanne, Tommy took her hand and kissed the back of it. "There's nothing like a beautiful woman to make an old man's steps a little lighter." After he let her go, he nodded at Roman. "Thanks for the loan, son."

Roman didn't get riled up anymore about all the "loans" he'd given his father during the past fifteen years. His dad was just one more person to watch out for. Roman would never be able to save him from his gambling addiction—or the skanky women he fell in with—but he couldn't abandon him either.

The door had barely closed behind his father when Suzanne said, "He bet on your boxing matches?"

It was time for Roman to come clean.

Still, it was hard to change the patterns of over a decade—of diverting people from probing too deeply. "It's ancient history."

"History matters. Especially when it comes to family. If anyone knows that, I do." She put her arms around his waist. "Did you like boxing?"

"It didn't matter if I liked it."

"What happened if you lost?"

Her questions were too incisive. Too close to the parts of himself that he hated having to examine. "I didn't."

"Everyone loses at least once."

"We wouldn't have had the money to pay the rent if I had."

Her eyes widened with increased dismay. "He would bet that much?"

"He trained me to be a sure thing." He wouldn't tell her how painful that training had been. Especially right after his mom left and his dad was so angry. Roman had been the perfect person on whom to vent his fury. "So yeah, the bets got bigger every time." It had been a vicious cycle that Roman couldn't figure out how to escape for far too long.

When she went silent, he tried to change the subject before she could ask any more questions. "What did Alec say? Did he know about the fire? Is he on his way back to the city?"

"Ian was alerted by his building manager and he called me and Alec. Looks like Ian left a message for me a half hour ago." But they'd been too wrapped up in each other to hear it ring. "I told Alec I'm fine and that I'm staying with you, so they have nothing to worry about and shouldn't rush back from the lake tonight. But we can figure out all that tomorrow once they get here, bright and early. Right now I want to know—how badly would you get hurt in your fights when you were a teenager?"

So much for wishing the call with her brother would distract her. Roman had never let anyone get this close, had never planned to tell anyone what he'd kept hidden in his soul. But Suzanne already knew enough and cared enough—hell, she even thought she *loved* him—that there was no use trying to divert her again.

"Some nights were worse than others," he admitted in a low voice. "My injuries were never anything I couldn't heal from. But some of the guys I fought..." He swallowed hard, putting his hand on his neck and rubbing it as the dark memories flooded back. "They didn't always walk out of the ring in one piece."

"*Roman.*" Her voice wasn't pitying. Not judging, either. Understanding. "He shouldn't have done that. Shouldn't have used his own son that way."

Her empathy touched him deep down in a place where he'd never let anyone else go. The realization of how much he needed to unburden himself to someone who understood made his words extra rough as he worked to compensate for that need. Pushing out of her arms, he walked like a robot over to the couch they'd only just made love on and sank down on it.

"Eddie's dad, Darrell, was the last guy I fought."

Refusing to let him push her away, Suzanne came over to the couch and curled up on his lap, putting her arms around him while he spoke. She was a lifeline he hadn't wanted to need, but did. Needed more than anything else in the world.

"We went to school together. He was a nice guy. Bigger than I was, but slower. I knew his dad had problems with drugs, that there were people he owed money to, knew his father needed the money maybe even worse than my dad did. But my training—to always win no matter what—wouldn't quit. Even when I knew I should hold back, I didn't. I didn't know how. Didn't have that kind of control. Hadn't been trained for it." He'd been trained to destroy. He swallowed hard, stroking her hair as he spoke. "His eye started bleeding. Bad enough that he should have gone to the hospital. But they didn't have the money. And his father was mad enough at his loss that he took a few swings at him and made things even worse."

Roman remembered wanting to jump between them, but if anyone knew how messed up father-son relationships could be, he did. So he'd stayed out of it. Just collected his winnings and got the hell out of there.

"Darrell didn't come to school for a while. When I found out why—that he'd lost his eye and that an infection from leaving it untreated too long had nearly killed him—I left my dad's house. I didn't have any-where to go, and when Jerry from the pizza shop figured it out, he let me sleep in his back office. I never fought again. But since I needed money for a place of my own, I did the only thing I figured I'd be any good at. I became a bodyguard." When he finally emerged from his dark memories and looked down at her face, he saw tears swimming in her eyes. "Now you see why you shouldn't be with me, why you shouldn't give a damn about me."

But the horror he expected to see on her face never materialized. Instead, she gently—lovingly—caressed his jaw. "You've told me so much, but you haven't told me the whole story. Have you?"

"You mean about the other guys I hurt in the ring?"

"I'm sure they hurt you too," she pointed out. "But that's not what I'm talking about. I saw how much Eddie loves you, and that you love him too. You've always been there for him, haven't you? You wished you could step in to help Darrell, but you were just a kid. Once you were on your feet, once you could make a difference in his life, you did, didn't you?"

"Trying to help someone I had a hand in destroying doesn't make me a hero. Sending Darrell to career training classes, buying him and his wife a house, paying for the most expensive private school in town—none of that makes up for what I did. He won't ever get his eye back. And it won't make up for all the other people who got hurt because I wasn't tough enough to stand up to my father."

"It wasn't that you weren't tough enough, Roman. You thought your father had your best interests at heart. You thought he was taking care of you. You thought you could trust him." She looked fiercely protective. "It's not what you did as a kid who was failed by his father that defines you, it's the fact that you refused to continue making those mistakes as an adult. And I'm not the only one who sees how great you are. Jerry saw it, even back when you were still fighting. All the kids who worship you there see it. Eddie sees it. My brothers see it. At least they did, until they flipped out about us kissing." Her lips lifted at the corners. "You're going to have to face it, Roman— you're a good man. A good man I love."

"If I were actually good, I would have kept my hands off you." But even as he said it, he was running his hands over her, needing her softness. Her heat. Her love. "If I were truly good, I would have dreamed about you from a distance, would have remembered that you're too good for me."

"On the contrary," she countered in her smart and sexy voice, "you're too good a man to leave a girl hanging like that. All that unquenched need, all those unrequited emotions, were already making me crazy. Who knows what would have happened to my company if you hadn't finally put your hands on me? I might never have been able to focus on getting my work done again. Although," she added as she leaned in so that her breasts rubbed against his chest, "I might never want to work quite so many hours again, now that I know how much fun taking time off with you can be."

He didn't know if he was ready to concede to being full of shiny goodness yet, even though she had made some good points about his being a kid who had done the best he could in a shitty situation. But he wouldn't apologize for taking her away from her bruising work schedule.

"You work too hard, Suzanne. I've been worried about you burning out, hitting a wall. Everyone in your family is worried too."

"I know my dad is, but only because he told me so at the lake. But I thought my brothers were just on me because of the random calls and server attacks."

The reminder of the threat against her—which now included an apartment fire they needed to get to the bottom of—made his gut twist. "You said it yourself out on the dock last night. You've tried so hard to be everything to everyone. And I've personally seen that extend beyond your family to your employees, your investors, your customers, the charities you do pro bono work for. You're extraordinary. The most extraordinary woman I've ever known. You're brilliant, beautiful, loving, and capable of conquering anything you set your mind to. But no one can do it all. Not even you." He ran a hand over her cheek. "I know I'm pretty messed up from my childhood, but I don't think I'm the only one."

"No," she said with a hollow-sounding laugh. "You're definitely not." She sighed. "I decided a long time ago that surviving my crazy childhood wasn't enough. I wanted to thrive. I wanted to conquer the world. It didn't matter how many hours I worked, how little sleep I got, whether I forgot to eat or shower. All that mattered was making the mark on the world my mother never had, because she was never strong enough to step outside the box of being anything more than my father's muse."

When a shiver went through her from talking about her mother, she nestled in closer to him looking for comfort. The same comfort she'd given him when he was telling her his story.

"And it was okay to burn my candle at both ends, because I didn't have anything else that mattered more to me. Didn't have anyone to cuddle up with on the couch, or cook dinner with, or make love with in the middle of the afternoon." She shifted to look him in the eye. "Now I do. I want you, Roman, messy childhood and all."

He wanted all those things too. He'd been fighting loving her. But now he realized he'd been fighting for all the wrong reasons. Yes, he still wanted the best for her, but despite his past mistakes, no one would ever love her more. No one would ever treat her better.

And no one would ever love her the way he did. Deeply. Truly.

Forever.

"I want you too."

Her eyes went wide with surprise, and she seemed to be holding her breath.

"I love you." He'd never thought he'd say those words to anyone. Never thought he'd feel them all the way deep down in the center of his being. But he did. All because of Suzanne. "I still don't believe I'll ever be good enough for you, but I'll never stop trying. I'll never stop trying to make you happy. I'll never stop wanting to hear your laughter. I'll never stop wanting to make you gasp with pleasure. And I'll never stop needing to protect you—even though I'm going to be doing it as your boyfriend from now on, because I'm officially resigning as your bodyg—"

Her mouth was on his before he could finish his sentence. So much love poured from her to him that he could have sworn her kiss was healing the wounds he'd just confessed from his childhood. He kissed her back with the same devotion, the same sweet purpose.

"I love you," he said again in the tiny spaces between kisses. "I love you so much."

"I already knew you loved me," she said, her wide smile filled with the kind of happiness he wanted to always see. "But now that you've resigned your position as my bodyguard, I also know you *understand* me."

"You were right when you said you didn't need a bodyguard. But you do need to let the people who love you help you. Even the strongest people need backup, Suzanne."

"Even you?"

He brushed his cheek against hers as he admitted the truth. One that would have scared the crap out of him before he'd fallen in love with her. "Even me."

"You've got me now. Which means you also get my whole family." Before he could point out yet again that her brothers currently wanted to have him drawn and quartered, she added, "The boys will come around. I know they will. Even if it takes some of them longer than others. As you know, we Sullivans can be a stubborn bunch. Especially me. You're right that I need to stop trying to do everything myself. I've been so adamant about being the strong woman my mother wasn't, I'm probably going to need some practice letting other people take the wheel sometimes. Just like I'm going to try to be better about admitting when I'm wrong." He could see how hard it was for her to say, "I'm done sticking my head in the sand, Roman, and acting like whatever is going on is nothing more than a nuisance. I do need help dealing with whoever is trying to hurt me and my company."

"I'll do everything I can to help. So will your brothers. Your dad. Your cousins. Your friends. Your employees. Your investors." Which was why, though he wanted nothing more than to make love to her again, he couldn't ignore the fact that she had already lost too many hours of sleep this week. "You've had a heck of a week. One I've made more exhausting because I can't get enough of you." He stood, lifting her into his arms as he did so. "You need to rest now."

"I can rest later." She gave him the bright, wicked smile he'd never get enough of. "Tonight, the only thing I need is you."

CHAPTER TWENTY-EIGHT

Suzanne could get used to being carried up the stairs like this. And she could *definitely* get used to having her clothes stripped off by the most gorgeous man on the planet. Once she was naked, she started to head back toward the bed, but he pulled her toward the bathroom instead.

"I want you in the shower." He laughed roughly as he palmed her breasts, her hips, ducking his head to scrape his teeth over her shoulder. "I want you everywhere. But I've had this shower fantasy all week—"

"Yes, please."

Shower fantasy was all she needed to hear. Okay, so she hadn't even needed to hear that, as she grabbed his hand and dragged him the rest of the way toward the marble and glass enclosure.

It seemed to her that getting into the shower together was more than just a fantasy they needed to fulfill. They needed a clean start, needed to wash away anything hurtful they had said or done to each other before *I love you*, back when they were both working so hard to keep themselves safe from the harm they'd believed deep, passionate love would do.

As soon as they were inside the bathroom, he reached for her again. But she was too focused on unbuttoning and unzipping his jeans to let him pull her against him. And when the faded denim dropped from his narrow hips to the floor, she couldn't possibly resist the instinctive pull to do the same.

The plush cotton bathmat was soft beneath her knees as she marveled over his erection. She didn't waste any time putting her hands and mouth on him.

"Suzanne." He groaned her name, his large hands tangling in her hair as she kissed the long, thick length of his arousal.

She'd never get enough of hearing her name rumble from his chest. Every part of her sizzled from knowing how much she was pleasing him with the wet licks of her tongue over his hard flesh. Not to mention how much she loved making him lose even more of his hard-won control.

She now understood why he worked so hard at it all the time—to take back the control his father had never let him have as a kid in the ring. But Roman didn't have to be like that with her.

There was nothing he could do, nothing he could say, no way he could cut loose that would frighten her away. Especially when she wanted to cut loose with him in exactly the same ways. Suzanne was finally ready to give play to the deep passions, and the wildness, that she'd always kept caged up.

Still, she wasn't surprised when he drew back from her mouth so that he could pull her back to her feet and inside the steamy shower. Tonight, they needed their lovemaking to connect them as deeply as possible, arms and legs twined around each other, hearts beating together.

"If I'd known what you could do with that smart mouth..." He crushed her lips beneath his at the same time that he backed her up against the white marble, using one of his strong arms to pin both of her hands above her head.

"You knew," she gasped the words out against his lips. "That was why you tried so hard to keep your distance, to stay in control. Because you knew that if we ever touched, if we ever kissed, we'd never be able to go back to the way we were before."

Hot water rained down on them from multiple shower heads. It was so sexy being in the shower with Roman. Intense. Wonderful. Every dream she'd ever had come true as he stared into her eyes with so much passion, so much desire, so much love.

"Never," he vowed as he bent to nip at her lower lip. "I never want to go back to a life without you."

His raw, heartfelt words were almost better than

sex. Lord knew they had the same effect on her, making her body ache for his, making her heart swell with love. She'd felt desire before, but when love combined with the wanting?

It was more than she'd ever imagined it was possible to feel.

Safe, unthreatening romances were all she'd believed she could have. But though Roman made her feel perfectly safe, and he would never let anyone or anything harm her, being with him—*loving* him— meant taking huge risks with her heart. The same risks he was taking for her.

She wouldn't let him down. He'd been left to fly in the wind by his family, but he had her now. And her brothers and cousins and aunts and—

The brush of his fingers along the inside of her thigh had her thoughts scattering.

"Lost you there for a minute, didn't I?"

"No, you'll never lose me. I was just thinking about how I'd do anything for you."

"I'd do anything for you too," he said as his wandering fingers rose higher, closer to her sex with every passing second. "But now it's time for you to shut off that brilliant brain."

Before she could take her next breath, his mouth was over hers, and he was sliding his fingers into her. She was so wet, so ready, so desperate for him that she arched wildly into his touch. The dark hair on his chest scratched the tips of her breasts in the most wonderful way and when he pressed his erection against her belly, she moaned into his mouth.

She was hungry for release, hungry to feel the stretch of his thick shaft inside her, hungry to wrap herself all around him and know that he was hers.

Hers.

Joy combined with heat to send pleasure crashing through her as he rubbed, swirled, thrust his fingers against her, into her, so that she was barely coming down from one release before she climbed toward another.

Abruptly, he shut off the water and lifted her into his arms. They were both soaking wet when he tumbled them onto his bed. She could barely wait for him to get protection, and the second he had it on, she wrapped her arms, her legs, around him, and took him inside.

Every time they made love, it felt bigger, sweeter than before. And so right that she couldn't fathom how she'd lived thirty-one years without Roman in her life. She'd been happy, but she hadn't been whole.

Now she was.

As though he could sense the weight of her thoughts, he stilled over her and gazed down into her eyes. Even in the throes of passion, he was so honorable, so protective. Roman was already the best boy-friend, the most incredible lover, she could ever ask for. And one day, she knew he would be the best father in the world too.

"I love you." She never wanted to keep her feelings from him again. "I love every side of you. Past, present, and future. Dark and light. Sweet and rough. Even," she added in a teasing voice, "the domineering side that wants to protect me at all costs. I thought I was happy before, but since I fell for you...I finally know what real happiness is. *You.*"

The kiss he gave her was so full of love that she didn't need him to say anything in response. Not when she already knew everything he was thinking, everything he was feeling.

And yet, when he did draw back to speak, she realized how much he needed to tell her what was in his heart. He'd spent his whole life holding everything inside—she never wanted him to feel that way with her.

"I didn't believe anyone could love me with all my darkness, my scars, my mistakes. Especially not a woman who could have anyone. But I still couldn't stop falling for you, couldn't keep from loving you more every day, every hour, every second."

His body echoed his words as he wrapped his hands around her hips and thrust hard, sending pleasure exploding through her as he gave them what they both needed. Wild, reckless, desperate, wondrous lovemaking that sent their bodies—and hearts—soaring.

CHAPTER TWENTY-NINE

Suzanne was already up and sitting at Roman's kitchen island behind her computer by the time the door buzzer went off at six thirty the next morning.

"We're here for Suzanne," Alec Sullivan growled from the sidewalk below. "Let us in."

All out of clean clothes from the bag she'd packed for Smith and Valentina's wedding, she'd chosen to put on one of Roman's long-sleeved shirts. She'd wrapped one of his belts twice around her waist and rolled the sleeves up to her elbows, transforming his shirt into something that looked like a dress. A dress he was already dying to strip off. Knowing she was wearing only a pair of his boxer briefs beneath his shirt didn't make it any easier to keep his hands off her.

But if Roman was ever going to have a prayer of convincing her family to accept him as Suzanne's boyfriend—rather than the bodyguard who had overstepped his bounds—he knew better than to be caught pawing at her in his kitchen.

He moved away from the coffee machine, where

he'd been brewing them some much-needed caffeine. But instead of answering his doorbell, he put his arms around Suzanne from behind, pressing a kiss to the top of her head. "So even if your brothers try to boot me all the way to hell to keep me from you, I'm not going anywhere."

He'd said the same words to her at her father's lake house. But that was when he'd still been trying to convince himself that saying *I'm not going anywhere* was only about his job to keep her safe. The truth was that he'd always meant it on a much deeper level. He'd already been in love with her, whether he'd been ready to admit it to himself or not.

Suzanne spun around on the stool to stand up in the circle of his arms. "Trust me, they won't be booting you anywhere." She slid her hands into his and threaded their fingers together. "Not once they realize you're exactly the man they've been wanting for me all along."

He wasn't nearly as certain that her brothers were going to accept him that easily, but since Alec, Harry, and Drake were waiting downstairs, he lifted their joined hands to his lips and pressed a kiss to the back of each one. The buzzer went off a good half-dozen times in rapid succession, with threatening sounds coming from Alec.

"Although," she said with a little quirk of her lips,

"letting them in before my brother busts a vein would probably be a good first step."

He reluctantly let her go to hit the button that unlocked the thick metal door downstairs. "Come on up."

After opening the door to his loft, Suzanne moved beside him to take his hand again. Though he knew the sight of their linked hands would be enough to rile Alec as soon as he walked inside, Roman didn't pull away. Instead, he drew her closer.

She was smiling up at him when her family got out of the elevator, not looking at all worried about the fury heading their way. Her three brothers, her father, and Rosa were all there, along with her friend Calvin, the mayor from Summer Lake. Every one of them had come to support Suzanne.

As expected, Alec immediately snarled upon seeing Suzanne's hand in Roman's. And when he realized she was wearing his shirt as a dress, he looked close to apoplectic, given that it obviously wasn't the sort of thing a woman did with a friend. Only with a lover.

Releasing Roman's hand, Suzanne drew Alec in for a hug before he could throw any punches, and somehow managed to keep a hold on him while she hugged everyone else too. She might have told Roman she wasn't worried about how things were going to go down this morning, but she clearly wasn't taking any chances on fists flying either.

As soon as the group hug broke apart, she went straight back into Roman's arms. Alec slammed the loft door behind him in fury, but before he could speak, Roman needed them all to understand what he wished he'd been brave enough to own up to at the lake, that night on the dock.

"I love Suzanne."

He made sure to look each of them in the eye. Alec, Harry, Drake, Rosa, Calvin. And especially Suzanne's father, who had left his home in the Adirondacks to come back to the city that haunted him to help his daughter.

William Sullivan hadn't been a great father. But Suzanne had helped her father see that he didn't need to let his past mistakes define his future anymore. She'd shown Roman the very same thing.

"There's nothing I wouldn't do for her," he told the group. "Nothing I wouldn't give. No battle I wouldn't fight."

He hadn't planned it, but didn't think twice before doing what felt right, what he needed to do, what he knew she needed too. Roman kissed Suzanne. In front of everyone.

Her cheeks were flushed, her eyes bright when he finally lifted his lips from hers. She smiled at him, a smile so full of joy and love that it turned his heart inside out.

"I feel the exact same way about Roman," she told her family and friends as she leaned deeper into the crook of his arm. "We've got a lot of work to do if we're going to figure out who's behind the server attacks, the phone calls, and the fire. So if any of you have something to say, I'd appreciate it if you'd say it now. To both of us."

Alec didn't waste any time stepping into the fray, getting directly in Roman's face. "You lying son of a bitch. You admitted you weren't capable of changing your stripes. You promised us you would end things so that Suzanne could find someone good. Someone who could treat her the way she deserves. And now you have the nerve to stand here and tell us you *lied?*"

Roman couldn't blame Alec for coming at him like this. Roman had been so mixed up at Smith and Valentina's wedding—deeply conflicted not only about what he wanted and what he thought he was worthy of having, but *who* he was worthy of being as well.

"I wasn't only lying to you guys, I was lying to myself. Lying about my feelings for Suzanne because I was scared out of my mind about them. I'm not proud of my past. There are a lot of people I've treated poorly." Not only the guys he'd pummeled in the ring, but also the women whose hearts he'd stomped on without a second thought. "But your sister will never be one of them. She thinks I'm worthy of her and I'm damn well going to do everything I possibly can to prove to her—to all of you—that I am. You used to trust me, Alec. If you can ever trust me again, trust that I won't hurt her."

Suzanne reached out to put a hand on her brother's arm. "I know everything," she said softly. "I know about Roman's childhood. I know about how he's behaved with the women he's dated. He hasn't kept anything from me—and I haven't kept anything from him. I know you're worried that he's going to break my heart, but can't you see that the only thing that would truly break my heart is not being with him?"

A play of emotions crashed across Alec's face. "Goddamn it." He dragged Suzanne out of Roman's arms and into his. "I thought you'd stop being such a pain in the ass once you grew up."

"Are you kidding?" She laughed, though tears were streaming down her face. "Little sisters *never* stop antagonizing their big brothers." Drawing back, she looked around at everyone else. "Does anyone else have an issue with my new boyfriend?"

Roman had spent his entire career protecting people, only to lose his heart to a woman who would never stop protecting him. Life, he was starting to realize, was funny that way. No matter how hard you tried to stay on the course you thought was the right one, sometimes it took a few wrong turns to make you realize you were finally in the place you were meant to be.

In his case, that meant falling head over heels in love with a woman so incredible that he'd never stop being awestruck that she was his.

Drake and Rosa smiled as they shook their heads. "For the record," Drake said, "I've never had any real issues with the two of you being together."

"Same here," Harry agreed. "History matters, but as I tell my students all day long, the whole point of learning from our screw-ups is so we can do things better the next time around." He shot Roman a serious look. "Just to be clear, that doesn't mean I'm giving you license to screw up with my sister."

"Of course we're going to screw up," Suzanne interjected. "Because we're human." She turned back to Roman. "But we're also going to love each other enough to get past our mistakes with each other, aren't we?"

God, he loved this woman. "We are."

When Suzanne looked to Calvin next, Roman understood that as one of her closest friends from childhood—and an honorary Sullivan, from what Roman had seen during the wedding—Calvin's opinion clearly mattered to her.

"Finding someone to love, and having them love you back, that's a big deal. Pretty much the biggest deal there is. Especially if you're both committed to doing whatever it takes to keep that love alive." Grief seemed to flash through the other man's eyes for a split second before he smiled at them. "I'm happy for you, Suz, Roman."

Which left Suzanne's father still to weigh in. Roman knew how much was riding on his approval, and he prayed they'd get it.

"If I had been a better father," William finally said in a voice that resonated with emotion, "your brothers wouldn't have had to step in to watch over you when I wasn't there to do it. But I'm glad they did, because you've had three protectors instead of just one. And now," her father said as he met Roman's gaze and held it, "I'm even more thankful that you have another man who would give his life for you."

Roman had accepted a long time ago that he'd never be able to respect his own father, but as Suzanne threw herself into William's arms, he was glad she didn't have to do the same. He knew now that her father wasn't going to quit working to win back her trust and her love, no matter how humbling or difficult that might be for him.

While Alec still didn't look thrilled about how things had gone down, he didn't look like he was going to hire a hit man to take Roman out, either. Then again, he hadn't yet heard the final piece of news.

"I'm not working as Suzanne's bodyguard anymore."

Harry frowned, clearly confused. "I know you weren't going to let us pay you and were planning to find someone else to protect Suzanne, but surely now that we've hashed everything out—"

"She doesn't need a bodyguard." He nearly laughed out loud at the triumphant look she gave everyone. "She's already told you this, but now I'm going to reinforce it. Suzanne does a damned fine job of watching over herself. Just the way all of you do. The issues she's having at work—with her phone and the servers, with the fire—aren't because she's careless or weak in any way. She doesn't need some guy with big muscles to trail after her twenty-four seven. She needs to nail this sucker to the wall and then make it clear to anyone else who tries to come after her that she won't stand for it. And neither will the people she loves. I'm no longer on the job, but I'm still going to be standing beside her, just like all of you."

William, his arm around Suzanne, pressed a kiss to her forehead. Then, he looked at his sons, at Rosa and Calvin, and Roman. Though he might not have acted like the head of the family for far too long, it was obvious to all of them that he was finally ready to take on the role that should have been his all along. "Let's get started."

Suzanne's smile was a mile wide as she led the group over to the dining room table, where she'd already set up the computers and tablets she'd had with her in her wedding bags. "We need to go through three months of phone logs and server records and cross reference the information to see if anything strange comes up. For the DDoS attacks, I've pulled IP traces to find the origin of each broadcast packet for the CPU storm—"

Harry held up a hand. "In English, please."

"Sorry. What I'm saying is we need to find out where the attacks came from that sent all this garbage to overflow my corporate and personal computers, denying service for legitimate work. So for both the phone and the server logs, if each of you could note the cities and countries for each line item, I'm hoping we'll be able to put together a pattern that will give me some clues as to who might be behind this."

Everyone took a seat behind a screen and Drake let out a low whistle. "There's a hell of a lot of line items here."

"No kidding," Alec said. "This is why I went into planes instead of computers."

"Now you guys see why I didn't want to spend any time going through these logs before now," Suzanne told the group. "It's literally the most mind-numbing work in the world."

"Work we're happy to do," Rosa said, obviously already one of the family even though there wasn't a ring on her finger yet.

Suzanne said that once you fell in love with a Sullivan, the entire extended family would be behind you. But it went both ways—Roman and Rosa were both completely behind the Sullivans now too.

"Thank you." Suzanne looked beyond grateful. "As soon as I call the fire chief to check in this morning, I'll be right there with you combing through the logs. With everyone pitching in, hopefully we'll see some sort of pattern before our brains leak out of our ears."

Her phone jumped on the counter next to Roman and he recognized the number that flashed on the screen as the one the fire chief had given them yesterday. "It's the fire chief." He handed her the phone.

"This is Suzanne Sullivan. Do you have news?" She listened to his response. "Okay, we'll be right there."

She hung up then looked at Roman. "He'd like us to come to the apartment to take a look at something the investigator found."

CHAPTER THIRTY

"Good morning, Suzanne. Roman." Wayne, the fire chief, shook their hands in the lobby of her apartment building. "This is Lee Mitchell, one of our top fire investigators."

"It's nice to meet you both," Lee said. "Why don't we head up to your apartment and I'll show you what I found?"

Suzanne was a strong woman, but she was still glad that Roman kept his hand on the small of her back as they headed for the elevator. She could have faced all of this on her own—but she didn't have to be a one-woman battleship anymore. She had Roman beside her now. And, she thought with a smile, she had her family and friends too. They'd been there all along, waiting for her to open the door and let them in. At long last, she finally understood that needing other people didn't make her weak.

Roman's eyebrows rose in question when he noticed her smile. She answered him with a quick kiss, one that instantly brought a smile to *his* face.

When the elevator doors opened on her floor and her heart began to pound hard and fast, Roman took her hand before she even had a chance to reach for his. Whatever it was they found out today, they'd deal with it as a team.

Lee stopped just inside her front door in front of a hole in the wall where her home automation system used to be. "We were able to trace the start of the fire in your apartment to this wall. From what we've been able to ascertain so far, someone did an update to your home automation system, reinstalled it, and then one of the new parts got too hot and melted down. This is turn caused the electrical wires behind the unit to heat up and start smoking and sparking." He handed her a plastic bag with the unit inside. Previously bright white plastic, the device was now covered in soot and half melted.

"CP Systems. One of these home automation systems is also in the apartment next door." Fury rang out in Roman's voice.

But Suzanne was beyond furious at this point. She was stinging with betrayal.

"There's a CP Systems unit in every apartment in the building," the fire chief confirmed.

Suzanne refused to let her hands shake. "I know this is evidence, but could I please take this with me? I'll return the device as soon as I've shown it to someone."

"Who would that be?" Lee asked.

"Craig Boylan, one of the founders of CP Systems."

Lee looked to Wayne in question. When the chief nodded, Lee said, "Okay, but I'd like to be there with you when you show it to him."

"That's fine. Roman and I will meet you in the lobby of their headquarters in a few minutes." She handed the investigator the device, proud of how steady her hands were.

On the way down to Roman's car, Suzanne called her father's cell. "What did you find out, honey?" he asked. "I'll put you on speaker so you can tell us all."

"The fire started behind my home automation unit." It took some effort to keep her voice steady, but she managed it. "Evidently there was an update done to it while I was at the wedding that caused the wiring behind it to smoke and spark. We're going right now to talk to the founder of the company that makes the unit, but I was hoping you and the rest of the group might be able to tell me first—are the Philippines showing up on any of the server logs?"

"Yes." She recognized Calvin's voice. "None of the early logs show activity from the Philippines, but this week that's where everything originated."

"Thanks, guys. That information helps a great deal. I'll call you again as soon as we're done with our next meeting."

"Everyone in the security business used to set up their servers in the Philippines," Suzanne explained to Roman, "but over the years, CP Systems undercut everyone by so much that we all had to leave the country to find other places to host our servers." Despite the security work Suzanne did for a living, she had always believed that most people were fundamentally good. It was a big part of why she did what she did, in fact: She didn't want all the good people to be hurt by the few bad ones out there. But learning that her friend had targeted her...that was a low blow. "With so few companies there now, there's a really high chance it was them. I trusted Craig. I can't believe he would do something like this to me."

A muscle was jumping in Roman's jaw. "When I had him up against the wall, I looked into his eyes. I trusted him too when he said he wasn't after you."

She'd always thought she was a good reader of people, and she believed Roman was too. How could they have both been so wrong about Craig?

Peeling her clenched fingers from her phone, she found his number and dialed. "Craig, this is Suzanne Sullivan. We need to talk. I'm on my way over right now, and I'm going to need security passes for myself, Roman Huson, and Lee Mitchell." She slid the phone back into her bag. "He's going to have everything ready for us immediately."

"Surely he's got to know his game is up. So why would he cooperate?" Roman looked as confused as she felt as he pulled into the underground parking lot beneath the CP Systems building. "Unless he thinks you'll be willing to make some sort of deal with him. But he's got to know that you would never make a dirty deal with anyone."

Despite the ridiculously stressful morning they were having, sweet emotion burst through Suzanne's chest at how well he understood her. "I love you."

Roman parked, turned off the ignition, then pulled her close and kissed her breathless. When he finally let her go, her heart was pounding for reasons that had nothing whatsoever to do with the fire in her apartment.

"If that's your way of saying you love me too, I'll take it."

He stroked her cheek with one callused fingertip. "Ready to kick some ass?"

This time she was the one kissing him in lieu of a verbal reply, practically crawling onto his lap in the tight quarters of the car.

"If that's your way of saying yes," he said when they finally came up for air, "I'll take it."

"Thank you for making me forget to be mad, forget to be scared. I'm more than ready to kick ass now."

Lee was waiting for them when they walked into the lobby. If he could tell that they'd been making out in the garage, he didn't give any sign of it. The receptionist on the ground floor looked more than a little alarmed as she handed Roman his temporary security pass. After Suzanne and Lee were also given passes, a CP Systems security guard escorted them to Craig's office on the top floor.

Craig's office door was already open when Suzanne stormed in. "I thought we were friends." She was barely aware of Roman closing the door behind them.

"We are." Craig had his hands out as if to take hers, but she wouldn't let him touch her. She was sorry she ever had. "What's going on, Suzanne? Why are you so upset? Roman said you've been having some problems at work, but he didn't say what they were."

After all the years that she and Craig had been in the business together, shouldn't she have seen the darkness inside of him before now? "Don't try to act like you don't know about the endless phone calls. About the denial-of-service attacks."

Craig looked from her to Roman. "So that's why you were here earlier this week? Because you thought I was behind a big broadcast storm to max out your servers?"

"I said you couldn't be behind it all," Suzanne said before Roman could reply. "I swore that you were a good guy."

"I am," Craig said, hands up in the air now. "I wouldn't do that to you, Suzanne. Wouldn't do that to your company. I may not be as squeaky clean as you, but you know I have my limits. How could you possibly think I would stoop to something like that?"

As if on cue, Lee laid the half-melted CP Systems home automation device on Craig's desk. Craig's eyebrows lifted beneath the hair falling over his forehead. "What the hell…?"

"Roman and I left town for my cousin's wedding a couple of days ago and when we returned there were fire trucks in front of my apartment. Lee is the fire investigator who discovered that the fire started inside of this unit. One of your devices, which has obviously been tampered with."

Craig swallowed hard as he reached for the plastic bag.

"Wait." Lee handed a set of gloves to Craig. "Put these on first."

Suzanne noted that Craig's hands shook slightly as he donned the gloves. He took the unit from the bag and turned it over to look at the wires and chips that ran it.

"This chip was never supposed to be used." His teeth clenched as he looked back at Suzanne. "I don't know what the hell is going on here, but you'd better believe I'm going to find out."

Roman had already reached for Suzanne's hand and was holding it tightly by the time she said, "Either you're really good at acting surprised all the time—"

"Or I didn't have anything to do with this." Being innocent of the charges they'd come in with wasn't making Craig look any happier, however. He picked up his cell and dialed. "Dennis, it's Craig. Did you install a new chip in one of our home automation systems a couple of days ago at—" Suzanne gave him the address, which he repeated into the phone. "Who assigned the job to you?" Craig's face paled. "Got it."

He disconnected, then stared at the phone's screen for a long moment before dialing again. "Patrick, I need you to come to my office. No, this can't wait for your meeting to end. Get your ass in here now." Craig put the phone down, his hands shaking more than ever. "Suzanne, if anything had happened to you in a fire..." He looked anguished. "I want you to know I'm sorry. I didn't know about any of this, but I'm so sorry—"

Patrick burst through the door, nearly slamming into Roman. "You again. What the hell are you—" He belatedly realized Suzanne was standing beside Roman. "Suzanne? What's going on?"

"I'll tell you exactly what's going on, Patrick. My phones and corporate servers have been under attack for months. And then, yesterday, my apartment almost went up in flames because of an update done to this device while I was away at a family wedding."

Something that looked a heck of a lot like fear flashed in Patrick's eyes before he shuttered his gaze. "Our units have undergone strict testing and they are guaranteed to be fire safe."

"They're fire safe *with the approved chip*." Craig advanced on his partner, his Irish accent becoming more pronounced with his growing agitation. "This new chip installed in Suzanne's unit is unauthorized for use. You know damn well that I rejected it in early rounds of testing on the grounds that I never intended CP Systems to spy on its customers when that's what we're supposed to be protecting them from. Which is why we never took the chip far enough into testing to find out that it is also a fire hazard."

While Craig was speaking, Roman slid his hand from Suzanne's and shifted position so that her body was shielded by his. Lee, meanwhile, had backed into the corner of the office, as far from everyone as possible.

Danger crackled in the air as Craig advanced on Patrick. "You could have *killed* her."

"And listen to you cry over your lost love? I sure as hell wouldn't have signed up for that." At Craig's surprised expression, Patrick sneered. "You think I don't know that you were banging Suzanne?"

Roman was halfway across the room to make Patrick pay for saying that when Suzanne jumped in front of him. Though she spoke to Roman only with her eyes—*I know, he's pissing me off too*—she knew he would understand her. He always did. *But we need to let him talk, need to find out what he was involved in. And I'm strong enough to withstand anything he has to say.*

She watched as the man she loved warred with himself over his natural instinct to protect her in any way he could, before nodding his agreement that he'd let this scene play out a little while longer. If Patrick was stupid enough to lay a hand on her, however, she wouldn't hold Roman back again.

"Watch your mouth," Craig warned his partner.

"You should have watched *your* mouth," Patrick fumed. "If you hadn't gotten so cozy with her beneath the sheets, she wouldn't have found out that we were working on the same new software. As soon as she found out we were also in the game, she ramped up production and beat us to the punch by a flipping mile. You lost us hundreds of millions of dollars in future revenue, and for what? She might have thought you were fun for a couple of nights, but she was never going to stay with you. Girls like her look innocent, when all they really want is to do dirty things with guys like *that*." He jerked his thumb in Roman's direction.

Before either Craig or Roman could get their hands around Patrick's neck, Suzanne moved in front of him. Yet again, she was glad she'd learned how to be so quick, growing up in a house with three brothers.

"I always knew CP Systems was trying to build a similar program, Patrick. Creating affordable digital security software is a no-brainer." She made sure to emphasize the *no brain* part. Though she connected with Craig on a technical level, she'd never been able to find a point of connection with his sales-focused co-founder. But that didn't mean she'd thought Patrick was capable of going after her the way it now seemed he had. "I didn't speed up my game after talking with Craig. I just went at the same speed I always do." She bared her teeth at him in a smile that wasn't a smile. "Fast. Sullivan Security is going to beat you to the market fair and square. Even with all the distractions you kept sending my way."

Patrick's pupils had grown so large that his irises barely showed. "I don't know what the hell you're talking about. I didn't send any distractions."

"Funny," she said, even though it wasn't. "The phone and server logs my family and friends have been poring over point to a different story."

"Those logs can't prove a damn thing."

"I know you're not the most technical person in the

world," she deliberately taunted, "but I've spent the last three decades eating, breathing, and sleeping so much technology that I could paint the *Mona Lisa* out of those logs if I wanted to. Which means that even with no more evidence than that, I can prove CP Systems has sabotaged me and my company."

"Bullshit." But there was unmistakable fear in his eyes as he began to move away from her.

"It's true, Patrick." Suzanne had never seen Craig look so angry. Or so disappointed. "Suzanne is that good. Worlds better than you or I will ever be. And Dennis already told me you had him install the unauthorized chip in her unit—one that I'm sure he thought was no different than any other install he's done this year. As soon as you heard that she was away, you must have thought that was your chance to get in there and do the deed undetected, didn't you, you son of a bitch?"

Before Craig could throw the punch he was clearly itching to launch, Patrick spun and leaped for the door. He was quick enough that Suzanne had barely started after him when she realized he wasn't standing there anymore.

Because Roman already had him on the ground in a wrestling hold that looked—and sounded—not only painful, but unbreakable.

Lee finally moved out of the corner. "I've sent a

message to the chief and he's calling the police. They'll be here shortly."

"I truly am sorry about this," Craig said to Suzanne. "You have my word that I'll make sure Patrick is brought to justice, no matter the impact on my company."

"I do want justice," she agreed, "but I'd like to work to find a way to make sure none of your shareholders, employees, or customers have to pay for your partner's bad decisions."

At the same time, the truth was that she didn't exactly hate hearing Patrick's groans as Roman dug his kneecap even harder into the other man's lower back. Though she'd never been a fan of things like ultimate fighting, she had to admit it was pretty darn hot to see how easily Roman held the other man flat, as if he weighed almost nothing instead of two hundred pounds.

Patrick wasn't right about much, but he'd been spot-on about one thing—she *did* want to do dirty things with Roman. What woman wouldn't? And not just because they'd finally caught the bad guy.

Roman loved and trusted her enough to know that she could protect and defend herself. And she loved and trusted him enough to let him protect and defend her—just the way she'd protect and defend him against anything or anyone who might try to hurt him in the future.

CHAPTER THIRTY-ONE

So this is what it's like to have a big family.

Roman didn't bother to hold back his grin as Suzanne and Alec verbally sparred over a recent movie. "The layered messages about humanity were what made it great," Suzanne insisted, while Alec countered, "There weren't any layered messages, just nonstop action. *That's* why it was great."

Roman's dining room table was covered with platters of pizza and pasta from Jerry's restaurant. Every seat was full as Suzanne's family mowed through lunch with everyone talking over one another. Her phone had been ringing like crazy for the past half hour, but not with junk calls. One by one, each of her cousins, aunts, and uncles who had heard about the apartment fire were checking in to make sure she was okay.

She'd barely eaten one slice of pizza when she put her food down yet again to take a call from her Aunt Mary, a lovely woman in her seventies whom Roman had met at the wedding. Suzanne had told him that Mary had raised her eight kids by herself in San Francisco after her husband passed away in his early forties, which frankly blew his mind. The Sullivans were a force of nature. He couldn't believe he was lucky enough to be in any part of their circle, let alone in the heart of it with Suzanne.

"I should have set up a family conference call to explain things to everyone at once," Suzanne joked once she put her phone down.

"If you wouldn't mind explaining it to us again," Harry said, "I'm sure we'd all appreciate it. I was so relieved you weren't hurt today that I didn't catch much of your original explanation."

"Let me shove this last bite into my mouth first." Suzanne's cheeks puffed out like a chipmunk's as she inhaled the pizza Jerry had renamed after Roman. "Best pizza ever." She grinned at Roman. "You should get an award for creating that combination." The kiss she gave him was the best reward he could have asked for.

Alec half-snarled, "Time to get to the explanations, Suz."

Out of respect for his friend, Roman held back his grin that time. Drake, Rosa, and Calvin, on the other hand, didn't bother. Nor did Suzanne hold back her eye roll at her brother's irritation.

"In a nutshell," she said, "one of the co-founders of CP Systems was upset about my progress on the new digital security product I've been working on for a while now. Even though they were nowhere near close to being able to launch it, he was hoping that if he could distract me enough with phone and server attacks, I would lose momentum. But when that didn't work, and he realized I was away at the wedding, he decided to take things to the next level by switching out a chip in my home automation system." She made a face. "The new chip would have controlled not only my temperature levels, lights, and Internet, it would also have been able to tap into my phone and any computers I connected to my home Wi-Fi. His partner, Craig, shut down production on the new chip last year because of privacy issues, but it turns out Patrick kept a secret stash just in case."

"The scumbag was trying to steal her code." Though Roman had long ago vowed not to use his fists unless absolutely necessary, he couldn't help but wish the guy had put up a fight rather than going down so quickly. Smashing the guy's pretty face would have been extremely satisfying.

"Could he really have done that?" Rosa asked.

"Not the whole thing, although he probably could have accessed enough messages sent between me and my development team to figure out our methodology. But the chip burned up before he could access anything at all."

"Thank God you weren't home," William said, going pale at the thought of his daughter trapped in a fire.

"Everything's okay, Dad. No one got hurt, and happily, there won't be any more junk calls or server attacks." She looked at everyone sitting at the dining table. "Thank you. Not only for being here today, but for *always* being here for me. Even when I tried to push you guys away, you never left me. You never gave up on me." She turned to Roman. "Especially you."

"When you love someone," he said softly, "you stay. No matter what."

And as everyone got up to give both Suzanne and Roman hugs, he finally understood: *This is what it's like to have a loving family.*

* * *

Two hours later, Suzanne closed the door behind Alec and locked it with firm purpose. "I thought he'd never leave." She walked into the kitchen, where Roman was loading the dishwasher. It turned out that big, close-knit families were not only great—they were also really messy. "He was afraid that the minute you and I were finally alone, I was going to jump you." She kicked the dishwasher shut, then reached for the buttons on Roman's shirt, deftly slipping them free one by one. "He was right."

Roman didn't waste any time on removing Suzanne's clothes as he headed straight for her mouth.

She tasted sweet and spicy and so delicious he couldn't wait to make love to her again. And again and again and again.

Of course, that was right when both her phone *and* her computer buzzed with incoming calls.

Lifting her into his arms, he headed for the stairs. She'd already fielded enough calls and meetings for one day. Soon enough there would be more, and she would continue to thrive working with technology. But for the rest of the day—and the night—Roman was determined to give Suzanne the break she so desperately needed.

Fortunately, his bed wasn't far away...and he was more than happy to keep her from work by any means necessary.

Only pausing long enough to strip away their clothes, Roman soon had Suzanne lying naked and warm and breathtakingly beautiful beneath him. "You went too easy on that scumbag today." He ran his hands from her hips, up over her waist and breasts, until he was cupping her face. "It's one of the millions of reasons I love you."

"Millions?" She turned to press a kiss to his palm before teasing, "And here I thought there couldn't be more than a dozen."

"I already loved you a dozen different ways by the time we left the gallery that first night your brothers introduced us. By the time you kicked me out of your apartment that night, we were up into the hundreds."

"*Wow.*" She bit her lip, and he had to bend down to lick the wet spot left behind when her teeth lifted away. "That was the first thing I thought when I saw you for the first time. And then I wondered how my brothers could have hidden you from me for so long."

"Alec would have hidden me forever if he hadn't been so worried about you."

"I'll never admit it to my brother, but I'm so glad he went behind my back and hired you." She laughed softly at herself. "A part of me is even thankful that Patrick lost a screw. Because if he hadn't, I might never have found you."

"Yes, you would. And I would have found you. Because I was meant to fall for you." Roman let all his walls drop, removed every last barrier he used to have around his heart. "I was meant to love you, Suzanne."

"I was meant to love you too." Her eyes were full of unconditional love as she whispered, "Now and forever."

Her lips were soft and warm as they met in the middle for a sweet kiss. One that quickly turned sinful as their tongues slipped together and she wrapped her arms and legs around him. He loved hearing her whimper of pleasure as they sank deeper into the kiss and he ran his hands back down over her curves, then followed the heated trail with his mouth. Once, twice, three times, he let himself feast on the slippery flesh between her thighs, before quickly putting on protection and climbing back up over her so that the full length of her naked skin was pressed all along his.

Suzanne gasped as he filled her, her gasp turning to a moan as he rocked against her faster, harder, deeper, until her release crashed through them both and became his too.

"I love you," he whispered against her lips. He would never grow tired of saying it, would never get enough of loving her. And he would never stop being thankful that he'd signed on to protect Suzanne Sullivan.

She hadn't needed a bodyguard. But she had needed love.

His love.

Forever.

EPILOGUE

Alec Sullivan barely held himself back as Suzanne gave Roman a seriously inappropriate thank-you kiss for the ruby earrings he'd given her to celebrate the huge success of her new digital security product.

"You're holding up like a champ," Calvin noted in a low voice beside him.

Alec reached for his bottle of beer, before realizing he'd already emptied it. "Just wait until *your* sister starts dating. You're going to be a freaking mess."

Calvin didn't argue with him as he looked over at Jordan, his ten-year-old sister he'd raised practically from birth. "Hopefully we're at least a decade away from that."

Alec decided the kindest thing would be to let that one go. Calvin would surely be put through the wringer of watching his sister fall in love and get her heart broken soon enough.

He turned to gaze out at Summer Lake through the Inn's large parlor window. His father was here, along with Drake and Rosa and Harry. They'd grown up coming to the lake, so plenty of locals had turned out too. Christie was supposed to be celebrating with them, but half the time she was running around supervising her staff. Denise and Olive from the knitting store were there, along with his father's business partners, Henry and Jean. Alec loved the fast pace of the city, but there was no question that Summer Lake was a great community. His father had been lucky to land here.

"You guys are pairing off so fast lately," Calvin said. "I was half expecting you or Harry to show up today with someone on your arm."

"There's no chance of that happening with me," Alec said with a firm shake of his head. "Although Harry's always been a quiet one, so he could surprise us one of these days. Or," Alec added with a grin, "maybe you'll be the next one to lose your mind over someone."

"I don't think so."

Alec didn't know the full story of what had happened between Calvin and Sarah, Calvin's high school sweetheart. Back when they were teenagers, everyone thought the two of them were going to be together forever. But that hadn't happened. Sarah had left Summer Lake in the dust, and Alec always had the sense that Calvin had never quite gotten over her.

Alec was happy Drake and Suzanne had found their

happily-ever-afters. But Calvin's brutal lost-love story was yet another reminder that no matter how good Alec's siblings had it now, the rest of them should stay the hell away from love.

Grabbing two beers from a passing waiter, Alec handed one to his friend. "Here's to being mayor of a hell of a great town with a new group of pretty tourists to choose from each week. What more could a guy need?"

As Calvin knocked his bottle against Alec's and drank, he pretended not to notice his friend's heart didn't seem to be in it. And if his own heart wasn't either, well, that was too damned bad.

Because Alec Sullivan was never going to fall in love.

* * * * *

**For news on upcoming books, sign up for Bella
Andre's New Release Newsletter:
BellaAndre.com/Newsletter**

ABOUT THE AUTHOR

Having sold more than 5 million books, Bella Andre's novels have been #1 bestsellers around the world and have appeared on the *New York Times* and *USA Today* bestseller lists 32 times. She has been the #1 Ranked Author on a top 10 list that included Nora Roberts, JK Rowling, James Patterson and Steven King, and Publishers Weekly named Oak Press (the publishing company she created to publish her own books) the Fastest-Growing Independent Publisher in the US. After signing a groundbreaking 7-figure print-only deal with Harlequin MIRA, Bella's "The Sullivans" series has been released in paperback in the US, Canada, and Australia.

Known for "sensual, empowered stories enveloped in heady romance" (Publishers Weekly), her books have been Cosmopolitan Magazine "Red Hot Reads" twice and have been translated into ten languages. Winner of the Award of Excellence, The Washington Post called her "One of the top writers in America" and she has been featured by Entertainment Weekly, NPR, USA Today, Forbes, The Wall Street Journal, and TIME Magazine. A graduate of Stanford University, she has given keynote speeches at publishing conferences from Copenhagen to

Berlin to San Francisco, including a standing-room-only keynote at Book Expo America in New York City.

Bella also writes the New York Times bestselling "Four Weddings and a Fiasco" series as Lucy Kevin. Her sweet contemporary romances also include the USA Today bestselling Walker Island series written as Lucy Kevin.

If not behind her computer, you can find her reading her favorite authors, hiking, swimming or laughing. Married with two children, Bella splits her time between the Northern California wine country and a 100 year old log cabin in the Adirondacks.

For a complete listing of books, as well as excerpts and contests, and to connect with Bella:

Sign up for Bella's newsletter:
BellaAndre.com/Newsletter

Visit Bella's website at:
www.BellaAndre.com

Follow Bella on Twitter at:
twitter.com/bellaandre

Join Bella on Facebook at:
facebook.com/bellaandrefans

Follow Bella on Instagram:
instagram.com/bellaandrebooks

Made in the USA
Lexington, KY
29 November 2016